inside**the**out**side**

KENNY !

THANK YOU SO MUCH

FOR YOUR SUPPORT AND

FOR BEING SUCH AN AMAZING

SPPORT. AND THE BEST !

Matt

12/13/11

insidetheoutside

a novel

martinlastrapes

ISBN: 978-0-615-44029-3

Cover Artwork: Colin Frangicetto
Book Design: Authorsupport.com

Printed in the United States of America
First Edition

CANNIBAL
PRESS

For Chanel

If we reserve ethical conduct for those whom we feel close to, the danger is that we will neglect our responsibilities toward those outside this circle.

-The Dalai Lama

I am the living bread which came down from heaven: if any man eat of this bread, he shall live for ever: and the bread that I will give is my flesh, which I will give for the life of the world.

-John 6:51

prologue

During the course of her life, at various points, both in her youth and as an adult, Timber Marlow was, what *you* might call, a murderer. But she wasn't a murderer so far as I'm concerned. For certain, she killed—and, so that there is no confusion, she was a killer of men. The word "murder," however, has sinister connotations and Timber Marlow was not sinister. Nor was she cold, callous or without conscience. And she was by no means a sociopath. She was simply a girl who's view of the world—by which I mean her perception of right and wrong—was skewed by the circumstances of her upbringing. Timber Marlow was raised as a cannibal.

I won't lie to you—once you learn the details of some of Timber's bloodier deeds, you may very well find it difficult, if not impossible, to sympathize with her. I hope, however, you would feel differently if you knew Timber Marlow was born and raised in a cult, growing up on a remote combine deep in the San Bernardino Mountains. I'll tell you about the strange rituals she was raised to believe were normal, of the men and women she saw killed in the name of righteousness.

Perhaps it would help if you knew Timber was raped before the age of fifteen as a punishment for breaking the rules of the cult and that the seed planted inside her young womb would give her a daughter. I'll tell you about the courage it took for her to run away with only her little girl in her belly, entering the mainstream society most of us take for granted.

If you're ready to learn more about Timber Marlow, the story of who she was and why she did the things she did, then I encourage you to read on. As for me, my role here is to be something of a balancer, to tell you the whole story, to tell you the truth. I can't force you to understand the truth, but I can ask you to listen. I can't tell you that Timber did not kill, but I can tell you why. And if you wonder why I know so much about Timber Marlow, while you know so little, well that—and so much more—will be revealed in the pages that follow.

part**one**

The Divinity of Feminine
Reproach

chapter**one**

The Main Dwelling

Timber Marlow began her life as a cannibal within an anonymous cult called the Divinity of Feminine Reproach. The Divinity existed in a remote combine, deep in the San Bernardino Mountains. The practice of cannibalism within this combine was just sophisticated enough that, save for Luna Marlow, no member of the Divinity ever had to participate in the dismembering or butchering of a human carcass. Timber could be counted amongst those who lived a life free of butchery—that is, up until her fourteenth year. That was the year Timber carved the flesh of Idea Marlow, a man eleven years her senior.

The Divinity balanced around two or three hundred members at a time—sometimes more, sometimes less—all huddled together on a patch of land no bigger than a couple of acres, if that. Members of the Divinity, for the most part, were born on the combine and died on the combine, without ever knowing anything else about the world around them. Because it has since burned to the ground, leaving no trace that it ever existed at all, I can only guess, based on the stories Timber told me, as well as my own research, where the Divinity was actually located.

My best estimate places it somewhere east of the Cajon Pass, where so many travelers drive through on their way to Las Vegas. Somewhere south of Lake Arrowhead, but north of Silverwood Lake, where the Divinity could benefit from the creeks and rivers that branched off. Someplace so small and so remote that no map-maker ever endeavored to give it a name. Someplace where a single dirt road stretched out through the trees and around the boulders, winding about until it connected to an asphalt road which hadn't enjoyed the benefit of state money for a very long time; that road would get you to Highway 173, through Rim of the World and eventually onto Interstate 15, where you were free to enter the Outside. The world of paved roads and bright lights, brick and concrete, deviance and shame.

That world, where it concerned the Divinity and its members, was little more than an afterthought. It was a fairytale world, one that every Divinity member grew up knowing to stay clear from— not that they had much choice in the matter. Daddy Marlow, the leader of the Divinity, saw to it that nobody left without his permission. And, with the exception of Daddy Marlow's Boys, his permission was rarely granted.

The laws Daddy Marlow enforced predated Timber, as well as most every other living member of the Divinity. Being the leader of the Divinity brought with it many perks and benefits; chief among them, Daddy Marlow was the sole resident of the Main Dwelling, which was a small house in the center of the combine. Surrounding the Main Dwelling was a series of smaller dwellings, some of which were nothing more than four walls and a roof, a door to walk in and a window to look out. No dwelling housed any less than three Divinity members at a time, though the average number was likely around five or six.

Each dwelling, with the exception of the Main Dwelling, had been built from the ground up under the watch of Daddy Marlow.

Before he took over as leader, Divinity members crammed into the Main Dwelling, spilling out of the bedroom, sleeping on the floor and in the hallway, across the couch and most anywhere else they could fit; those members not able to find a place within the Main Dwelling slept outside in tents and sleeping bags, under the stars, amongst the elements.

There were many Daddy Marlows in the Divinity's history, each dying off, whether by nature's will or a Sustenance Sacrifice, and passing on their power to the next in line. When the last of the Daddy Marlows took over the reins of the Divinity—and, for the sake of clarity, this was the only Daddy Marlow that Timber ever knew—he made it clear that the Main Dwelling was for him and him only. Of course, he was only too happy to welcome the company of any number of Divinity women who would share his bed for days or weeks at time.

Very often the time Daddy Marlow spent with these women resulted in their becoming pregnant, which always pleased him. Through his efforts, and the efforts of every fertile man on the combine, the Divinity kept a steady population. As many as ten or fifteen younglings were born every month. Not all of them survived, but those who did grew into a life of devotion and loyalty, wanting nothing more than to preserve and maintain the order of the Divinity.

When a Divinity woman was made pregnant, she rarely knew who the father was; when the youngling was born, it was immediately carried away into the Nursery Dwelling, where it would be cared for until placed under the care of a Dwelling Mother. By not letting mothers know who their own younglings were, it allowed them to love all younglings as their own, which was the way Daddy Marlow wanted it.

Younglings grew up together not knowing anything of siblings or kin. With the exception of Daddy Marlow's Boys, blood relations were not acknowledged in the Divinity. Everybody grew up and was simply one part of the greater whole. Of course, by not keeping track of who was blood and who was not, this increased the possibility of a brother and sister discovering the joys of sex together; whatever genetic repercussions awaited such a dubious pairing didn't concern the Divinity as, by and large, they were oblivious to such things.

One day, not long before her fourteenth year, Timber heard an unfamiliar moaning coming from Daddy Marlow's bedroom in the Main Dwelling. She had gone into the Main Dwelling to hide from her best friend, Jupiter Marlow, who was leaning up against a tree outside, eyes closed, counting down from ten. While it was generally frowned upon for just anybody to mingle in the Main Dwelling, younglings were generally welcome to linger about, so long as it wasn't in the middle of the night, during the Hours of Recuperation. While Timber crouched beside the front window, arms wrapped around her knees watching Jupiter run around outside, her ears pricked to the aforementioned moaning.

It sounded to Timber as if one of the women was in danger, so she hurried through the Main Dwelling, following the moans as they became louder and louder. When she approached the bedroom, she could hear banging on the walls. Always the bravest of the younglings, Timber didn't hesitate in pushing the door open; what she found was Daddy Marlow lying on top of Charlotte Marlow, each of them naked but for the sweat that slicked their skin. Daddy Marlow was pushing himself against Charlotte, inspiring a moan with every thrust, banging the wooden frame of the bed against the wall. Daddy Marlow's long hair stuck to his back and ribs, falling down across his body and sticking to Charlotte's arms and fingers as she clawed his shoulders. Charlotte's legs wrapped around his waist like they were wrestling, but there was no sign of struggle; what they were doing, Timber came to understand, they meant to do.

It was Charlotte who caught Timber's eyes, before patting Daddy Marlow on the back to stop. Turning his head, his long hair shifting along his back, Daddy Marlow smiled at Timber. "Come on in, youngling," he said. "It's okay." Timber walked into the warm room, past the half-opened window, taking a seat on the bed where Daddy Marlow motioned for her to sit. He straightened up on his knees, between Charlotte's thighs, sitting on the balls of his feet. He let her look at where he entered Charlotte, in the place Timber had believed was only meant for pissing. Smiling at Timber, he encouraged her to watch, to learn, to understand that one day she would do this with him. Charlotte took Timber's hand, smiling, unable to refrain from the moans that Daddy Marlow pushed out of her; with her other hand, she ran her fingers over the smooth skin of her bald head.

Through the half-opened window, the sound of the Marlow Bell could be heard ringing in the distance. "Go on now," Daddy Marlow said. "It's time for Daily Lessons." Timber scooted off the bed and ran out, her bare feet sticking to the wooden floor with every step, out the front door of the Main Dwelling, all the way to the Learning Tree.

chapter**two**

The Learning Tree

Daily Lessons took place once a day, underneath the Learning Tree, which was a large pine tree adjacent to the Main Dwelling. So large was the trunk of the Learning Tree, it would take three younglings to hug it, fingertip to fingertip. The Learning Tree's large roots, which pushed up from the ground like giant fingers working their knuckles from the grave, served as a seat for those younglings lucky enough to get there first. A blanket was spread at the base of the tree's large trunk, upon which the Lesson Giver sat, surrounded by younglings. There was a rotation of about ten women who, on any given day, served as Lesson Giver.

Not every youngling attended Daily Lessons. Infants who couldn't yet speak or walk could gain nothing useful by attending; young boys just beginning to grow into their physical strength were more likely to be assigned to some form of manual labor; and young girls approaching childbearing age were usually assigned to work in the Nursery Dwelling, assuming they weren't already pregnant. Even still, female younglings represented the majority in attendance for Daily Lessons. Before she became the talk of the Divinity by becoming its first member—youngling or adult—to be assigned to the Sustenance Dwelling with Luna Marlow, Timber regularly attended Daily Lessons.

The lessons offered during Daily Lessons ranged from practical to mythical; as for the history of the mountains they lived in, those details went unlearned, mostly out of ignorance, as much as anything else. Younglings never learned, for instance, that the reason they had such limited encounters with any wildlife was because much of it had been killed off, run off and/or just plain scared off by man. They didn't know that before the earliest of pioneers moved through those mountains—possibly some of the same pioneers who would eventually establish the Divinity—grizzly bears were abundant; thanks to those same pioneers, there's not one grizzly bear left anywhere in California. Black bears, on the other hand, can still be found. Of course, no Divinity member that came into contact with a black bear would have known that they weren't native to the San Bernardino Mountains; they were exported in from Yosemite National park in 1934, for the benefit of tourists. Younglings also wouldn't have been taught that the most dangerous creature they were likely to run into was the western rattlesnake; neither would they know that it would sooner slither off than pick a fight with a human. The lessons that *were* given to younglings ranged from how to immobilize a broken femur to the inherent evil of man and how it manifests itself in the form of hair.

More than anything else, Daily Lessons provided younglings with an opportunity to socialize in an organized setting and, consequently, this was how Timber's friendship with Pepsi Marlow came to be. Pepsi was slightly older than Timber, about halfway through her fifteenth year. While Pepsi was Timber's favorite girl amongst the younglings, it was Jupiter Marlow, a boy, who was Timber's *best* friend. Jupiter had recently entered his sixteenth year and, while he still attended Daily Lessons, it was only a matter of time before Daddy Marlow's Boys would pluck him up and put him to work with the other men. Between the three of them—Timber, Jupiter and Pepsi—a kinship was formed, bonded over little more than age and proximity. They always sat together during Daily Lessons, giggling at quiet jokes and rolling their eyes at the Lesson Giver when she wasn't looking, especially when they found themselves sitting through a lesson they had already heard many times before—like, for instance, the story of the Learning Tree and how it came to be.

When the Founders adopted their land in the mountains, the terrain around them was bare, like a desert who'd only just discovered water; some green here and there, bushes and grass, some plant life, but not a tree in sight, just hill upon hill, rolling out as far as the eye could see, smooth as it pleased, not a single branch growing from the soil. By the sight of it all, it was clear to the Founders that something needed to be done. Relying upon the guidance of the Creator, the Founders deciphered a spot on the ground where they dug a hole and planted a handful of seeds, one for each of the founding pioneers, all of which were individually blessed before putting them in the soil. Once the seeds were planted, the Founders began the construction of the Main Dwelling. As the foundation of the Main Dwelling was laid out, the seeds began to open inside the earth, sprouting their roots; and as the skeleton of the Main Dwelling was erected, the tree pushed its way through the ground; and as the walls of the Main Dwelling were sealed in, the tree grew out its branches; and when the roof was set on the Main Dwelling, the tree sprouted its pine needles and was fully formed.

Soon thereafter, without a single seed being planted, another tree began to sprout from the ground—and another and another, until pine, cedar and fir alike inhabited the Founder's adopted land. "So, what started as one tree, in the middle of a barren mountain range," the Lesson Giver would say, "became the miracle forest that surrounds us today." Because the Founders agreed that their deed should not go untold, they promised each other that their story would be passed down through every generation, forever and ever, and that it would always be told underneath the tree from which its legend began.

While the Learning Tree had thousands of branches, reaching out with their infinite supply of pine needles, it was one branch in particular that always captured the attention of the younglings. It grew out of the tree much lower than the other branches and was horizontal, growing perpendicular to the trunk. It was just low enough that any youngling with the appropriate motivation could scale the tree and hang from it; and strong enough to support the weight of ten younglings, before giving even the slightest bend. The elders in the Divinity didn't understand what was so fun about hanging from a branch; they seemingly couldn't remember what it was like to be a youngling, capable of being entertained by the simplest things. Of course, because the Learning Tree was held as sacred, hanging from its branches was strictly forbidden. This, of course, only made Timber and Jupiter want to hang from that peculiar branch all the more.

chapter**three**

Daddy Marlow's Boys

The intrigue that would ultimately seal the fate of Timber Marlow began when, still in her fourteenth year, she awoke in the middle of the night to find Daddy Marlow's Boys passing by the window of her small dwelling. Daddy Marlow's Boys were a group of three brothers, triplets in fact, all of them fully grown and not one of them separated in age by more than a few moments. They held the distinction of growing up with Daddy Marlow claiming them as his own progeny, an honor that no other member of the Divinity, living or dead, could claim. Daddy Marlow's Boys were easily the three biggest and strongest men in the Divinity, which, genetically speaking, served to validate their blood relation to Daddy Marlow himself, as he too was a physically impressive man.

Despite their similar builds, there was in fact no way of actually knowing if Daddy Marlow's Boys belonged to Daddy Marlow at all. There was a policy within the Divinity that stated: "No woman shall be the mother to only those younglings born of her womb; she who roams the Divinity shall be a mother to all." This was true, even for those women who never had younglings of their own. As for the men, no man in the Divinity acted as father to any youngling, for that was the job of Daddy Marlow. Because of the Divinity's policy, Timber never knew who her parents were. She never knew which of them made her strong like a boy or if they'd have been proud of her for what she would one day do to Daddy Marlow.

Daddy Marlow was, regardless of the seed in question, the father figure to all the boys and girls of the Divinity. For any man to be so bold as to bestow an act that should so much as hint at paternal guidance towards any youngling in the Divinity would be seen as highly disrespectful. And, make no mistake, Daddy Marlow was not a man to be disrespected. Of course, this highly simplified version of parenthood (one father and many mothers) made Daddy Marlow's Boys quite the exception. Daddy Marlow, in general, heeded the same rules that he enforced, which is to say, all of the younglings were his, regardless of whose seed they grew from.

During their first decade, when it was clear from an early age that the triplet boys were the most genetically gifted of all the younglings in the Divinity, Daddy Marlow took them under his wing. After conducting highly secretive rituals somewhere deep in the surrounding forest (the processes for which Daddy Marlow made clear could not be shared with the general brethren of the Divinity, because, "Your minds and consciousnesses, collectively and individually, are not, and may never be, evolved to such a degree that you could comprehend the processes for which my work is done.") he came to the divine conclusion that the three physically superior boys were entirely and indisputably his own.

Individually, Daddy Marlow's Boys were known as One, Two and Three Marlow. Whatever their names were before the Naming Ritual, nobody remembered, on account of Daddy Marlow's edict that everybody was to forget. As triplets, Daddy Marlow's Boys were identical, except for the scars on the backs of their bald heads, which reflected their names. The scars weren't anything more than vertical slashes—tallies, really—which Daddy Marlow personally inscribed with the hot end of a metal rod, heated over a bonfire in the middle of the night during the Naming Ritual. Timber wasn't alive when the Naming Ritual took place, but elder members of the Divinity had told her that the Boys' screams were like nothing they had ever heard.

Each boy, starting with One Marlow, was held belly down in the dirt by the other two, while Daddy Marlow meticulously inscribed the slashes. Three Marlow had it worse than his two brothers, because not only did his fear have time to build while he watched the ritual take place twice before his own, but he also, by virtue of his name, had to suffer through the searing of three slashes in the back of his young skull. When the ritual was over and the large audience caught their collective breath, Daddy Marlow stood with the triplets as they shuffled their feet over the small craters of dirt where their tears had fallen. "These three boys," Daddy Marlow said, "*my* boys, tonight, before you all, earned their stripes and proved their worth. No one, other than my own blood, could withstand such a test." He hugged all three boys at once, kissing the tops of their bald heads. "And they will, here and now, forever and always, be known to you and all as Daddy Marlow's Boys."

And so they were.

As teenagers, Daddy Marlow's Boys resembled fully developed men, all of them standing well beyond six-feet tall, each with physiques as strong as they were defined; by their sixteenth year, they were already shaving the dark tufts of hair that grew from their forearms and backs. While they were many things to Daddy Marlow, they were mostly his enforcers. When grunt work had to be done, Daddy Marlow gave the order and his boys took care of it. If a member of the Divinity was to be the center of a Sustenance Sacrifice, it was Daddy Marlow's Boys who fetched them; if said member was reluctant to participate in his or her impending death, Daddy Marlow's Boys applied brute force in liberal doses as a means of influencing their cooperation. If a collection of Divinity members was called upon to tend to the crops or build a dwelling, it was Daddy Marlow's Boys who acted as foremen.

Daddy Marlow's Boys were fiercely loyal to Daddy Marlow, in part because they took pride in being his perceived progeny, but also because, while other members existed within the rigid laws of the Divinity, Daddy Marlow's Boys were free to do most anything they pleased. Sometimes their freedom manifested itself in random beatings of other members, but mostly they used their freedom to engage in sexual conquests with the many different women in the Divinity—willing or otherwise.

While you wouldn't find a fence in or around the Divinity's compound, Daddy Marlow had very strict rules about who came in and who went out. Nobody was allowed to leave the compound without the consent of Daddy Marlow. He scarcely received requests however and on the rare occasion somebody *did* ask for permission to leave, the answer was usually no, followed a few days later by a random beating from Daddy Marlow's Boys. The beatings were always attributed to some rule that had been broken, but it was mostly understood why the punishment had actually occurred.

If some member of the Divinity were bold enough to leave the premises without permission, their best chance was to stay away; even still, Daddy Marlow's Boys were like well trained hound dogs, more than capable of hunting down any stray members, bringing them back bloodied and bruised—and, in all likelihood, destined to a Sustenance Sacrifice. So rare was it that anybody tried to flee the Divinity, Daddy Marlow allowed for certain members, other than his boys, to guard the vague borders of the compound; both for keeping members in, as well as monitoring visitors from the Outside.

Along with their other freedoms, Daddy Marlow's Boys were free to pass through the borders of the Divinity's compound, always in their rusty orange pickup truck. The license plates on their truck changed often. Daddy Marlow's Boys had a collection of license plates, at least two or three for every state, which they kept in the Garage Dwelling; this dwelling served as a hangout where Daddy Marlow's Boys could relax, when not patrolling the Divinity. They would sit around and play cards by candlelight or make repairs to their truck, gathering grease beneath their nails and cuts on their knuckles. More times than not, it was the Garage Dwelling, reeking of oil and sweat, where Daddy Marlow's Boys brought their sexual conquests, laying them down on the oil- and blood-stained concrete floor.

Daddy Marlow's Boys' obese orange truck was displaying Texas plates the night that Timber Marlow snuck from her dwelling in the middle of the night. While not the smallest dwelling, Timber's was one of the smaller ones on the combine; she shared the dwelling with Charlotte Marlow, her Dwelling Mother, and two other younglings—Syracuse and Oakland Marlow. Dwelling Mothers were in charge of looking after the younglings under their roof, making sure they attended Daily Lessons, received two Sustenance Portions a day and, most importantly, participated in the Cleansing Ritual every five to seven days. There was no such thing as a Dwelling Father; men in the Divinity shared dwellings with each other, but never with women or younglings.

Timber's dwelling had one bed, which was large enough for Charlotte and two younglings at a time. Being the oldest of the younglings, Timber spent her nights sleeping on the floor, so Syracuse and Oakland could dream their innocent dreams in the comforting proximity of Charlotte. Timber could scarcely sleep through the night and often spent her evenings lying in her sleeping bag, staring out the window, marveling at the moon and the stars.

It was on one very normal night, with Charlotte, Syracuse and Oakland asleep in their bed, and Timber staring out into the ebony sky, that Daddy Marlow's Boys passed by her window, unwittingly capturing her attention and setting into motion the first of many imperceptible steps that would ultimately seal the fate of most everybody living in the Divinity at the time, as well as a few individuals living in the Outside—Ginger Falls and Billy D. Luscious, among them.

A twitch of adolescent curiosity was what got Timber out of her sleeping bag, shuffling on her knees to the window, resting her chin on its sill; her nose pressed to the lowest pane, her warm breath fogging the glass, she watched the strapping triplets walking across the moonlit dirt, shoulder to shoulder, in complete lockstep with one another. Timber was enamored with Daddy Marlow's Boys, the way they strutted around the Divinity, commanding respect wherever they went, holding court over most every Divinity ritual and, of course, being the acknowledged progeny of Daddy Marlow himself.

And so it should surprise no one reading this narrative that upon seeing Daddy Marlow's mythical triplets pass by her window in the middle of the night, practically gliding, like three brilliant statues brought to life for the sole purpose of fascinating her imagination, Timber quietly left her dwelling and, while keeping a discreet distance, followed Daddy Marlow's Boys all the way to their rusty orange pickup truck.

Having left her sneakers behind, she walked barefoot through the dirt and the pebbles and the weeds, the cool midnight air chilling her bald head, her eyes transfixed on Daddy Marlow's Boys. Their blue jeans were dark enough to be absorbed by the ebony sky, leaving their white T-shirts and pale skin to carry through the night like ghosts.

For every twig that broke beneath her heel, or dry leaf that crackled under her toes, Timber held her breath in anticipation of Daddy Marlow's Boys turning their heads, spotting her on their trail and subjecting her to whatever the requisite punishment would be. Though they never did turn their heads to find Timber following them, she continued to duck behind bushes and trashcans, gutted cars and dwellings, all in an effort to remain invisible. Timber stood around the corner of one dwelling, careful not to pass in front of the window in case there were any curious eyes looking out. Peaking around the corner, she watched Daddy Marlow's Boys get into their obese pickup truck and drive down the single dirt road that led out of the Divinity.

The still night shook against the rumble of the engine and soon the rusty orange truck was kicking up dust as it disappeared in the distance. The bright red of its rear lights, glowing through the darkness, were all but gone when a hand came to rest on Timber's shoulder.

chapter four

The Almost-Assassination
of Daddy Marlow

"What're you doing out here?"

Timber didn't answer. She simply stared straight ahead, hoping to disappear into the night. The hand resting on her shoulder began to pull, attempting to turn her around; she tensed her body against the unwelcome fingers, her heart dropping to her belly, engulfing her in the most tangible fear of her young life. Her mind raced, trying to imagine which of all the possible punishments within the Divinity might be hers, for she was certain that whoever was standing behind her would report her to Daddy Marlow. When finally she gave in to the hand's pull and turned her body around, she came face to face with Jupiter Marlow.

Relieved and angry, Timber punched Jupiter in the chest, sending him to the dirt.

"Goddamn you, Jupiter!" Timber said, in a hushed yell. "Why're you sneaking up on me like that?"

"Gee whiz, Timber, I said your name at least three times before I grabbed you."

"What're you doing out here, anyway?"

"I was looking to take a piss," he said. "Then I wanted to hang from the Learning Tree. What are *you* doing out here?"

"Just out, is all."

Jupiter and Timber Marlow were separated by about two years in age and had first met, as most younglings did, under the Learning Tree. Their first and most lasting bond was the bottomless well of bravery they each possessed. This became apparent on the day that Jupiter came to Daily Lessons and revealed a tarantula in his palm. While all of the younglings under the Learning Tree screamed and panicked, only Timber remained, curious about the eight-legged creature. Even when the Lesson Giver stood up in disgust, leaving to get help, Timber sat with Jupiter, playing with the tarantula until Daddy Marlow's Boys showed up.

It was Three Marlow, the meanest of the triplets, who snatched the tarantula from Jupiter's hand, gripping it with such force that Timber was sure he had killed the furry arachnid on impact; Three Marlow clinched his fist hard around the tarantula, causing a thick green ooze to leak down his wrist. Three Marlow briefly opened his hand, displaying the mangled, furry blob that was once a living creature, silently making his point to the two younglings.

As he chucked the dead tarantula aside, One and Two Marlow grabbed Timber and Jupiter by the arms, dragging them to the Main Dwelling, with the Lesson Giver right behind them. Perched on his sofa, holding a metallic mug of hot pine needle tea, Daddy Marlow listened to the Lesson Giver as she told him what the two younglings had done.

"Younglings," he said, "your youth is a handicap, like a bird with a broken wing. Over and over, you will fall to the earth with every attempt of flight—not because you're unwilling, but unable. One day your youth will be behind you and you will be able to fly, carrying your load, making the Divinity proud. However, this does not mean you shall go unpunished for your deeds. You, boy," Daddy Marlow said, pointing to Jupiter, "what are you called?"

"Jupiter Marlow."

"And you, girl?"

"Timber Marlow."

"Jupiter and Timber," Daddy Marlow said, "you are my younglings and therefore you are blessed with my love. Jupiter, you shall be subjected to eight lashings of the Marlow whip, one for every leg of your foul deed. And you, Timber, shall be set in isolation in one of the Prison Dwellings, where you will go without drink or sustenance for the next three days. Boys," he said, turning his attention to his triplet sons, "my word is spoken. Make it so."

Jupiter bore the scars from his eight lashings for the rest of his life, each of them looking like a scabby serpent slithering across his back. As for Timber, after the first day of her isolation, she suffered from such thirst and hunger that she could hardly sleep, spending most of her time standing on her tip-toes, just barely able to reach her eyes over the window sill, anything to keep her mind occupied. The Prison Dwelling stank of piss and shit, which, when the time came, Timber added to, squatting in the cleanest corner she could find.

When Timber's three days were complete, Charlotte Marlow stood at the door of the Prison Dwelling, waiting to greet her. She wanted to get her a Sustenance Portion right away, but Timber, before she did anything else, wanted to go back to the scene of the crime. There she found the dead tarantula, dusty from the passing days, still lying where Three Marlow had thrown it, covered with ants. Using a sharp rock, Timber broke the earth, digging a hole as deep as a man's fist and, as gently as she might her own child, set the tarantula into it, covering it with its final dirt.

Timber and Jupiter bonded over their joint punishments and spent most every minute of every day together afterwards. For the rest of her life, Timber would never love a boy as much as she did Jupiter. They were like brother and sister, the best of friends, secret lovers that knew nothing of the intimacy of the flesh and cared not to learn. Their companionship filled them with a satisfaction that defied words, not that they ever tried to name it. They were just happy to be in it—whatever it was. And so, it could hardly be thought a coincidence that the second most influential event of their lives would, like the great tarantula incident, be one that they shared together.

Timber and Jupiter, both of them barefoot and neither too scared to walk under the moon, made their way to the Learning Tree. On the way there they decided they would have a hanging contest, which consisted of each climbing up the trunk, grabbing the large horizontal branch and shimmying along it, until they were both dangling at its center; whoever could hang the longest would win.

What made their game interesting wasn't the physical endurance necessary to hang from that peculiar branch, but rather the mental challenge. As soon as they hung themselves from the branch, they would be face to face with the bedroom window of Daddy Marlow. No doubt, to get caught hanging from the tree was bad enough, but the punishment that would come from being caught by Daddy Marlow in the middle of the night, when they should have been deep into the Hours of Recuperation, would have been monumental. With neither one of them wanting to concede to being any less brave than the other, Timber and Jupiter hung from that large branch, their fingers gripping the bark, their weight putting a burning strain on their shoulders.

A stirring came from Daddy Marlow's bedroom and Jupiter Marlow immediately dropped from the branch and ran into the surrounding forest which, at night, was an effective hiding place. Despite the stirring, Timber continued to hang from the branch, staring straight into Daddy Marlow's window; like a ghost, he passed before her eyes, his skin white, his chest and belly thick with hair. Timber ignored the pang of fear that blossomed in her belly and continued hanging on the branch. Even though Daddy Marlow was no longer in front of the window, Timber detected another stirring in the bedroom. Squinting her eyes, she was just able to make out the shape of a girl sitting on the edge of the bed. If it were not so dark out, Timber might've been convinced that the girl was staring right back at her. But she knew it was too dark for anybody to see her—a fact that had escaped Jupiter.

Timber finally decided to drop from the branch when the back-door of the Main Dwelling opened up and Daddy Marlow strolled out. Joining Jupiter in the dark safety of the forest, she squatted down as quietly as she could, keeping her breathing to an absolute minimum. Daddy Marlow was naked, but for a bed sheet wrapped around his waist. He held his metallic mug in one hand, bringing it to his lips while he rubbed his hairy belly. It was then that Timber saw Idea Marlow come out from the darkness with a knife meant for killing Daddy Marlow.

For the rest of her life, Timber would wonder why she didn't let Idea do what he meant to do. She could tell by the look in Daddy Marlow's eyes that he was lost in some other world and never heard Idea come up behind him. When she saw Idea raise the knife over his head, she knew what he meant to do with it and, acting solely on instinct, ran out from the trees, yelling for Daddy Marlow to look out. Both Daddy Marlow and Idea were surprised to see Timber, staring at her like she was on fire.

As she ran towards them, Daddy Marlow appeared to think she was charging for him, but Timber ran right past him and buried her shoulder in Idea's belly, knocking the knife from his hand, as they each went to the dirt. Idea pushed Timber off of him and got to his feet, but by then Daddy Marlow had figured out what Idea meant to do, so he grabbed him by the front of his neck and pushed his head into the wall of the Main Dwelling, knocking him unconscious.

While Daddy Marlow gathered himself, Timber looked in through the window and, standing on the other side, completely naked, was Pepsi Marlow. Pepsi and Timber locked eyes for just a moment, before she looked down to see Idea lying in the dirt, his body resting awkwardly against the Main Dwelling. Daddy Marlow rapped his knuckles against the window, shooing Pepsi away.

"Youngling," he said to Timber, "you should know better than to be wandering about at night. Bad things are always waiting to happen. I might be awfully disappointed in you, if you hadn't just saved my life."

He rested his hands on his hips and it was only then that Timber realized Daddy Marlow had lost his sheet during the struggle, leaving him completely naked; a statuesque figure, all muscles and hair, his long locks hanging across his shoulders.

"You, youngling, are a paragon of strength and bravery," he said, "and I'll see to it that you're properly rewarded."

Daddy Marlow pulled Timber into his chest, embracing her in a hug, his naked penis pressing into her chest. Her head was facing the window and she saw Pepsi sitting on the floor, her back against the bed, crying into her knees. Timber knew exactly what Pepsi was crying about and, in the days that followed, she couldn't help but wish she had let Idea do exactly what he had intended to do.

chapter**five**

The Love Affair of Idea
and Pepsi Marlow

Idea Marlow was well into his twenty-fifth year the night he tried to kill Daddy Marlow. Like most any young man, Idea was incomplete. A hole the size of a woman existed inside of him and it meant to be filled. Of course, that hole generally gets filled with all of the wrong things—namely, sex. Being only human, and nothing more, Idea wasn't immune to that part of the human condition that dictated his body be shared with another. However, within the Divinity, relationships were frowned upon; in fact, they were all but forbidden. For this reason, Idea grew up without seeing what a relationship looked like between two adults who loved and cared for each other, which meant he had no better chance of filling that hole inside of him than he did of growing a pair of wings and flying to the moon.

Having no other compass to guide him, Idea Marlow filled his hole by fucking. He fucked as many women as would lay down with him—and a few more than that. His fucking conquests ranged from thirty-three-year-old Gertrude Marlow and twelve-year-old Chimney Marlow, and many more in between. Once he even fucked his buddy Tripper Marlow, just to see if fucking a man was anywhere near as fun as fucking a woman. While the answer, so far as Idea was concerned, was a resounding no, Tripper would regularly invite Idea out into the woods in the hopes that he might decide to mount him one more time. But, for all of his fucking, never once did Idea ever feel like he had managed to fill his own hole—that is, of course, until he met Pepsi Marlow.

Pepsi wouldn't tell Timber why she couldn't stop smiling, at least not while Jupiter was there. But Timber kept asking all the same. The two girls, and their male buddy, were walking through the combine, heading nowhere in particular upon completing Daily Lessons. Despite herself, Pepsi kept giggling under her breath.

"What's going on with you?" Timber asked.

"Nothing," Pepsi replied, smirking. "I swear it."

"You swear on your spot in Better Days?" Jupiter asked.

"Oh, hush up," Pepsi said.

Jupiter huffed, but this didn't bother Pepsi any, nor did it convince her to divulge the source of her good spirits. So the three of them kept walking, past the Sustenance Dwelling, where Luna was inside, hard at work, carving up the day's Daily Portions; past the Nursery Dwelling, where Carpet Marlow was watching over all the Divinity's newest members; past Hickory Marlow, who was sitting through the Cleansing Ritual; and past Daddy Marlow's Boys who, in their stoic silence, were almost scarier than those all-too-familiar moments when they stood by Daddy Marlow's side, covered in blood, overseeing a Sustenance Sacrifice.

As they walked, Pepsi cupped her hands around Timber's ear and whispered that she would tell *her* why she was so giggly, but not Jupiter.

"Jupiter," Timber said, "I have to talk to Pepsi alone."

"What about?"

"It doesn't concern *you*," Pepsi said.

"Just something between us," Timber said.

"Will you tell me what you talked about?"

"She certainly will not!" Pepsi said.

"I wasn't talking to *you*," Jupiter said.

"That wouldn't be fair, Jupiter," Timber said.

"I don't care about what she has to say anyway," he said.

"Good," Pepsi said, "because I ain't telling you."

"Go on, Jupiter," Timber said. "I'll catch up with you."

No sooner had Jupiter walked away, did Pepsi grab Timber by the arm and begin running toward the trees, into the forest, giggling as they pushed leaves from their faces and ducked branches, leaping over tall roots and plucking pine needles with their fingertips. They didn't stop until the Divinity was just barely visible in the distance. They sat down beside a large fir tree, out of breath, but still giggling. With great effort, Pepsi managed to compose herself.

"I have feelings for a man," Pepsi said.

"Really?"

"Oh, yes," she said, clutching her hands to her heart. "My chest beats so fast when I'm around him. And my stomach, oh, my stomach wraps itself into knots when he touches me."

Pepsi laughed out loud, burying her face in her hands.

"Who is it?" Timber asked.

"If I tell you, you can't tell anybody."

"Of course."

"Okay," Pepsi said, taking a deep breath. "Idea Marlow."

"*Idea Marlow!*"

"Hush," Pepsi said. "Not so loud."

"Do you want to make a youngling with him?"

"I think so," Pepsi said. "I bleed now, you know."

Timber didn't yet know what this meant.

"I wonder if he's made younglings before," Timber said.

"Probably," Pepsi said. "He's very good at it."

"You've done it with him?"

"Not yet."

"How do you know he's good at it?"

"Because I want him to be, I guess," Pepsi said with a shrug, causing them both to burst out laughing.

Timber couldn't relate to any of Pepsi's feelings. She had never had feelings for a man before. She assumed it was because of her age and figured when she was older those feelings would just appear, naturally, like the hair that had begun to grow beneath her arms. She also assumed that, when she was older, she would no longer house her intense, unspoken urge to touch Pepsi between her legs.

Pepsi Marlow was ten years Idea's junior, which means they lived in the Divinity together for just as long without ever exchanging a word or knowing the other existed at all. However strange that might sound, it wasn't out of the ordinary for a youngling to grow up all but invisible in the eyes of the elder men of the Divinity. The only elders who really spent time with the younglings were the women; the men were busy tending to those chores about the Divinity that called for extra testosterone. Realistically, Idea had no reason to even notice Pepsi before she reached childbearing age.

Timber never did know when Pepsi and Idea actually met. It never occurred to her to ask. But as soon as Pepsi told her about her affinity for Idea, Timber made it her business to know as much as she could about their love affair. Not that she knew they were in love—at least not then. Around the Divinity, nobody used the word love when it came to how men and women felt about each other. But looking back on that time, remembering the way Idea and Pepsi looked at each other, the way they held hands for seconds at a time when they thought no one was looking, Timber was confident that they were indeed in love.

One afternoon, Pepsi and Idea walked into the forest together, looking over their shoulders, making sure they hadn't been seen. They hadn't looked well enough to notice that Timber had decided to follow them. From a safe distance, Timber followed the young lovers, watching as they held hands, their fingers intertwined, swinging their arms in rhythm with their buoyant steps. Idea and Pepsi were approaching Marlow Stream, a shallow body of water that traveled year round, even in the middle of winter, when the air was cold and snow gathered on the leaves. But, on this day, it was summertime; the heat was dry and heavy, making for a perfect setting to cool off in the water.

Careful not to be discovered, Timber hid behind the thickest tree she could find. She watched Idea and Pepsi as they stood beside Marlow Stream, removing their clothes; Idea quickly tugged his jeans down and removed his T-shirt, tossing them aside, while Pepsi lifted her dress over her head, setting it neatly on top of Idea's pile of clothes. They stepped into the stream, walking out toward the center where the water moved past their thighs. Crouching down, Idea and Pepsi submerged themselves in the stream, leaving only their bald heads poking out. Without warning, Idea put his hand on top of Pepsi's head and pushed her under. Jumping up from the water, Pepsi looked incredulous, while Idea laughed. Leaping towards him, Pepsi returned the favor, though it took all of her weight to dunk him. This game turned quickly into a splashing match, each of them pushing as much water as they could into the other's face, laughing all the while.

When the splashing subsided and the laughter stopped, Idea and Pepsi fell into an embrace; he bent forward to meet her lips, while she locked her fingers around his neck, her arms stretched like a monkey hanging from a tree. Their naked bodies shivered as they held each other, the river moving gently through their legs. Breaking the embrace, Idea took Pepsi by the hand, leading her to the shore, helping her over the rocks that lined the edge. Timber marveled at his erection, wagging stiffly with each step. Idea spread his jeans out on the ground, inviting Pepsi to sit down on them, which she did; he rolled up his shirt and laid it on the ground, a pillow for her head. Timber watched Pepsi open her legs, her knees pointing to the sky, her wet feet planted in the dirt, mud forming between her toes. Ever so gently, Idea mounted her.

What Timber noticed more than the unbridled fashion in which Idea bounced on top of Pepsi—elbows planted, toes searching for traction—was the large, brown birthmark on his right butt cheek; it had the appearance of a crude hand print, slapped on by a disfigured child, fingers webbed and crooked. The handprint seemed to be pushing Idea into Pepsi, harder and harder, stopping only when he released a primal howl. Pepsi wrapped her legs around Idea's waist, hooking her feet, caressing his bald head with her fingertips. Her eyes were closed and she was smiling the smile of pure happiness. Timber didn't yet understand that she had gotten a firsthand glimpse at love and what it looked like to be made.

chaptersix

The Sustenance Dwelling

The day after Timber foiled Idea's assassination attempt, she and Charlotte Marlow picked up the first of their two daily Sustenance Portions and took them back to their dwelling. When they had finished their meals, Charlotte sat back in her rocking chair, while Timber sat on the floor, between her legs, letting her arms hang over Charlotte's knees like a scarecrow. This had been their routine for as long as Timber could remember, as Charlotte had been her Dwelling Mother since she was an infant.

Before Daddy Marlow came knocking on their door, Timber and Charlotte sat in silence, relaxing, enjoying the softness of the morning's first rays. Timber broke the silence with a burp, which left the hot taste of flesh mingling on her tongue, inspiring a fit of laughter between she and Charlotte. The two of them were so oblivious with laughter that they hadn't noticed Daddy Marlow pass before their window.

Upon hearing him knock, Timber opened the door and was surprised to see Daddy Marlow on the other side, hands on hips, his long, long hair giving way to a slight breeze. His beard, peppered with grays and whites, hung low and thick, past his neck, resting against his chest. His white T-shirt was draped over his shoulder, leaving his rippling muscles exposed for Timber's curious eyes to take in. Without a word or salutation, Daddy Marlow entered the dwelling

"Good morning, Daddy Marlow," Charlotte said.

"Good morning to you, dear," he said. "And how are *you*, young Timber?"

"Good."

"I've come here because I have some glorious news for you," he said. "On this morning, before my brethren woke, I entered the forest to converse with the leaves. In their silence, our Creator's voice may be heard, but only if you know how to listen. In His words, He told me that you, Timber, have shown yourself to be an extraordinary youngling with a bountiful future. He told me it was necessary to reward you, so that you may begin the journey that will someday lead you to a position of great responsibility both here in the Divinity and, someday, in Better Days."

"Oh my, Daddy Marlow," Charlotte said. "How wonderful!"

"Wonderful, indeed," he said. "Timber, how many years do you have?"

"Fourteen."

"And, with only fourteen years, you are strong like a boy, are you not?"

Timber shrugged.

"In His very own words, the Creator told me of your strength and bravery. Such rare traits in a youngling. I asked Him what it is you are meant to do and He told me that you are destined to take charge of the Sustenance Dwelling."

Charlotte squealed with excitement.

"In order that I may please my Majesty the Creator, tomorrow morning, Timber, you will begin work in the Sustenance Dwelling as apprentice to Luna Marlow. And one day, on the day that Luna stands no more, you will take her place."

The Sustenance Dwelling was where all the food was stored and prepared, from the homegrown vegetables to the dead human bodies. Inside was a kitchen with a heavy wooden table at its center, stained with red, where corpses were laid down for carving; sawdust covered the floor for the purpose of soaking up any spilled blood. There was also a large freezer where all the butchered flesh was stored until it was time for Sustenance Portions.

Before Daddy Marlow took over the duties as Divinity leader, the process by which Divinity members ate was much more primitive. After any given Sustenance Sacrifice, flesh was butchered on the spot, using knives and sharp rocks. There was often not enough meat to go around, so those who weren't aggressive enough lost out until the next sacrifice. Left to other means, hungry Divinity members fed on edible shrubbery or easily-hunted critters. And if a fire couldn't be immediately started in order to cook the flesh, it was eaten raw, still warm and wet from the kill.

A few years after Daddy Marlow took over the Divinity, he facilitated the construction of the Sustenance Dwelling. "We must treat our sustenance as we would the purity of our younglings," he preached. When it was done, the Sustenance Dwelling was second only to the Main Dwelling, both in size and stature. Upon its completion, Luna Marlow was put in charge of the Sustenance Dwelling. And, until the day Daddy Marlow placed Timber under her wing, Luna had always run the Sustenance Dwelling by herself.

Timber met Luna for the first time the following morning while the sky was still black and every other youngling was asleep. Through a cool morning breeze, Charlotte walked Timber to the Sustenance Dwelling and knocked on the door. When there was no answer, she knocked again, harder. When again there was no answer, she knocked a third time, harder still. Before she could knock a fourth time, the door swung open and there stood Luna Marlow in her white rubber apron, clearly irritated. In her hand was a heavy cleaver, its blade slick with blood. Timber watched the blood slowly stream down to the tip of the blade, bloating into pearls of red, before dropping to the ground.

"Good morning," Charlotte said.

Luna turned and walked back inside without saying a word, leaving the door open behind her. Charlotte and Timber followed her, moving through a short hallway, past a tall pantry, before entering the kitchen with the heavy wooden table. There was fresh blood on the table, but no body in sight. Wiping the blood from the cleaver against her rubber apron, Luna took hold of the leather strap that hung from the table and began sharpening the blade. Her arms were strong and her skin clung tight against her muscles, a map of thick veins pushing out along her forearms and the tops of her hands.

"I've brought you Timber," Charlotte said.

"Leave," Luna said.

"Pardon?"

"Now."

"But we arrived by wish of the Creator."

"The youngling stays."

Even as she spoke, Luna continued scraping her cleaver against the leather strap. Charlotte crouched down, meeting Timber at eye level. "Remember, work hard and do what you're told," she said, stroking her thumb across Timber's cheek. "The Creator will be watching over you."

After Charlotte left, Luna addressed Timber.

"You ever hold one of these?" she asked, lifting the cleaver in front of her face.

"No."

Without warning, Luna placed the cleaver in Timber's hands, catching her off guard. It was heavier than she realized and, despite her best effort to keep it in her grip, the cleaver fell at her feet, clanking off the concrete floor.

"Why do you think you're here?" Luna asked, picking up the cleaver.

Timber shrugged.

"Follow me, youngling," Luna said, laying her cleaver on the heavy wooden table. "May as well get some use out of you."

Luna walked past Timber to the large metal door of the freezer.

"Listen up," Luna said. "I got more fingers on one hand than there's folks who know what's behind this door."

Timber nodded.

"No matter what you see," she said, "can't no questions be asked. What we do in here is privileged. Daddy Marlow put me in this dwelling himself, because he knew I was strong. *Here,*" she said, pointing to her bicep, then, pressing her finger to her temple, "and *here.* Now I don't know you from nothing. Didn't know you existed in the world at all until Daddy Marlow told me he was sending you my way. I may not agree with him, but I trust him. If you're here, it's only because he thinks you can handle it, thinks you're strong. So, how about it? You strong?"

Timber nodded.

"All right," Luna said. "Step back."

Luna gripped the long metal handle of the freezer, pulling it towards and opening the door. A wall of condensed air, thick as fog, pushed out of the freezer, like a winter's sigh, disappearing almost as quickly as it had escaped. Standing before the doorway, Timber looked into the freezer, which was large and deep, long enough to fit two automobiles bumper to bumper. Hanging from the ceiling on hooks were husks of flesh, grainy and red, marbled with fat. Lying on the floor, directly in front of her, was a full-grown man, completely naked. His pale skin was a faint shade of gray, death's shadow cast upon him. His arms rested at his side, palms up, and his feet pivoted away from each other at the heels like a V with toes.

Luna placed a brick in front of the door to keep it from closing behind them. Stepping inside, Timber took a long, hard look at the dead man. His head was still attached and, what was more odd, he had a full head of hair. As soon as she recognized the oddity, words formed in her head and, before she could think to censor herself, the question formed on her lips, tumbling out as if of its own volition.

"Why does he have hair?"

Luna looked at Timber for only a second, before slapping her face with the flat of her hand, dropping her to the cold floor, beside the dead man.

"What did I tell you, youngling?"

Luna took Timber by the wrist and pulled her up to her feet. She was crying, despite her best efforts to keep the tears at bay. She refused to whimper, however— refused to sob. If the tears were going to fall, they would do so silently.

"No questions," Luna said.

Timber nodded.

Luna moved to the dead man's head, crouching down and hooking her hands under his armpits.

"Grab his legs," she said.

Timber did as she was told, crouching down like Luna did, taking hold of the dead man's ankles. At the touch of his cold, waxy skin, she recoiled, dropping his legs.

"Damn it all, youngling!" Luna said. "If you can't do the simplest task, why in the hell are you here?"

Timber crouched back down, again grabbing the dead man's ankles.

"You're going to have to take him by his thighs," Luna said, "under your arms."

Timber stepped between his legs, dangerously close to his tuft of pubic hair; she scooped her arms under his thighs, feeling the tickle of his leg hairs on her wrists. Luna counted down from three and they stood up, lifting the dead man from the cold concrete. Rejecting every instinct that told her to let go, run away and never look back, Timber held tight to the dead man, helping to carry him out of the freezer to the heavy wooden table. Luna went back to the freezer door and moved the brick out of the way, letting it close.

"You see that, youngling?" she said. "This door doesn't stay open by itself. So, if you're not careful, it can close up with you inside that freezer. There ain't no way to open it from the inside, so you be sure not to get yourself stuck, because it's airtight. You know what that means?"

Timber shook her head, no.

"Means you'll run out of air if I ain't here to let you out," she said. "You know what happens when you run out of air?"

Timber nodded.

"I bet you do," Luna said. "So don't go getting yourself trapped in my freezer. The last thing I need is to find a dead youngling in there."

Luna picked up her cleaver and caressed the dead man's thigh, before lifting the blade over her head—holding it there, she looked over at Timber, whose face was white as a ghost. Luna set the cleaver down on the wooden table and said, "Go wait outside. You ain't ready for this yet." Timber did as she was told, exiting the Sustenance Dwelling and sitting down in the dirt, her back against the wall. She pulled her knees to her chest and stared out at the trees, watching the sun slowly rise behind them, pushing its light through the leaves.

She had lived there all her life and yet, that morning, she felt like she had entered a whole other world, one that made her long for the time before she knew it existed. Her cheek still throbbed as she touched it with her fingertips. It didn't hurt as bad as she expected it would, but she cried anyway, letting her tears fall freely until Luna came out and told her it was time to get back to work.

Outside, behind the Sustenance Dwelling, were Luna's barbecue pits, which she used to cook the flesh. She had enough pits to handle the day's supply of flesh, but decided to build another, letting Timber do the grunt work. Leaning against the wall, staying cool in the shade, Luna barked instructions.

With a rusty shovel, Timber dug a hole large enough to step in knee deep, before lining the bottom with rocks and chopped lumber. Stepping away from the wall, Luna grabbed a handful of oily rags from a large metal barrel, throwing them into the hole. "We get these rags from the Garage Dwelling," Luna said. "Whenever I need more, that's where I'll send you." Luna patted her pockets, cursing when she didn't find what she was looking for. "C'mon," she said, leading Timber back inside, where she opened a drawer and retrieved a box of matches.

Standing over the pit, Luna demonstrated for Timber how to light a match, before blowing it out. Handing her the box, she let Timber try. Her first attempt snapped the wooden matchstick in half. Adjusting her pressure, she tried again to no avail. After Luna offered another demonstration, Timber tried once more, this time igniting the tiny match head; so startled was she by her success, Timber dropped the match and the flame extinguished before it touched the ground. Luna retrieved a fresh match from the box, lit it with ease and gingerly set it on top of the oily rags in the pit, engulfing the lumber in flames.

"Them rocks will soak up the heat," Luna said, "keeping the pit good and hot."

While the fire was blazing, Luna took Timber back inside and showed her how to wrap the flesh. In a large bucket, Luna kept sheets of burlap soaking in water. Pulling a sheet from the bucket, she laid it flat on the heavy wooden table, placing three large pieces of the dead man on top. Along with the dead man's pieces, she placed a couple of carrots and an ear of corn, wrapping it all up and folding the burlap under itself to keep it secure, before taking it outside.

"Now," Luna said, "get the shovel ready. Once I drop the meat in that pit, you start filling it as fast as you can. It's gonna put the fire out, but that's what we want." Luna dropped the wrapped flesh into the fiery pit and Timber immediately began shoveling the dirt back in. Luna took a long tree branch and stuck it on top of the filled pit, marking it. Buried in the pit, the rocks would stay hot for days if need be, cooking the meat for just as long, but Luna would only wait a few hours before having Timber dig it up.

Once the flesh was cooked, Luna showed Timber how to cut it up. After they took a short break to eat some of the freshly prepared meat and vegetables, Luna sent Timber to the Marlow Bell, where she was to tell Jefferson Marlow it was time for the distribution of Sustenance Portions. Twice a day, the Divinity formed a long line in front of the Sustenance Dwelling and, one by one, each member collected his or her portion of food. It was a simple process, one Timber had gone through her entire life, never knowing how much work went into it all. Daddy Marlow's Boys were always first in line, even if they arrived after everyone else, collecting their portions as well as the portion to be delivered to Daddy Marlow.

At the end of the day, when the sun had set and both of the day's Sustenance Portions had been completed, Luna excused Timber from the Sustenance Dwelling. Timber's back was sore and the muscles in her arms and shoulders burned as she walked to her dwelling where Charlotte was waiting for her. Timber lay down on the floor, flat on her belly, letting Charlotte rub her back, until she fell asleep. And when she awoke, it would be time to start the whole process again.

chapter**seven**

The Sacrifice of Idea Marlow

When it was time for Daily Lessons, the Marlow Bell rang once. When it was time for Sustenance Portions, the Marlow Bell rang twice. And when it was time for a Sustenance Sacrifice, the Marlow Bell rang three times. On the third toll a current of excitement would course through the Divinity, as its members gathered in Marlow Square, which was a large space of dirt and grass adjacent to the Main Dwelling.

Any secret fears Divinity members held towards the Sustenance Sacrifice were rarely voiced—in fact, the Sustenance Sacrifice was scarcely talked about at all. And when it *was* talked about, it was revered—genuinely or otherwise—as a sacred and honorable ritual, which sent one of their own into the Next World. The Next World, as it was believed in the Divinity, was a post-mortal waiting room where souls—past, present and future—congregated in anticipation of Better Days.

Any Divinity member being prepped for a Sustenance Sacrifice was held in isolation in the Sacrifice Dwelling, a small structure with a roof, four walls and a door, but nothing else—most notably, no window for eyes to look out or light to go in. This is where Idea Marlow had been since the night he meant to kill Daddy Marlow. To make sure Idea—or anybody else being primed for a Sustenance Sacrifice—didn't try to escape, Daddy Marlow made sure that at least one of his boys was always keeping guard of the Sacrifice Dwelling. Of course, it wasn't exactly clear why the Sacrifice Dwelling needed to be guarded if, in fact, being sacrificed in the Divinity was so sacred and honorable. But, as it were, nobody in the Divinity ever asked these sorts of questions; it was well understood that Daddy Marlow was smarter and more powerful than everyone else and therefore he would worry about the details, so his people didn't have to.

Timber was working in the Sustenance Dwelling, sweeping up clumps of red sawdust from the floor on the day of Idea Marlow's Sustenance Sacrifice. When the Marlow Bell struck once, she assumed it was time for Daily Lessons. When the Marlow Bell struck twice, she knew it wasn't time for Sustenance Portions. And when the Marlow Bell struck a third time, her stomach dropped.

"Well, youngling," Luna said, "I suppose we ought to get out there."

Timber and Luna walked out to Marlow Square, where a crowd had already gathered. Moving with the crowd, Timber walked slowly, staying close to Luna, until, from the corner of her eye, she saw Pepsi Marlow leaning against the doorway of her dwelling, arms crossed, tears running down her face. When she saw Timber walking by, Pepsi spat at her feet. There was no way for Timber to know that Pepsi would be dead within the week, but if she had she would have gone out of her way to reconcile with her friend. The last thing Timber ever wanted was for Pepsi to leave this world thinking that she had done her wrong.

While Idea and Pepsi had attempted to keep their affair secret, it's likely that others, besides Timber, knew about it. In fact, it's not all that hard for me to believe that the reason Daddy Marlow chose to have sex with Pepsi at all, amongst all the other women in the Divinity, was to impress his will on both her and Idea. He probably wanted to make a point that, when it came to the women of the Divinity, nobody was off limits to him. It was his way of claiming his territory, like a dog pissing on a tree.

The chatter, which had buzzed nonstop since the Marlow Bell struck its third toll, came to a sudden halt when, from out of the distance, Idea Marlow could be seen being dragged barefoot to Marlow Square, his head concealed by a burlap sack, his wrists fastened behind his back. One and Two Marlow were flanked on either side of him, their arms looped through his, pulling him along. Three Marlow walked behind them, carrying a large shovel.

The crowd of Marlows formed a large, congested circle around the Sustenance Cradle, which sat right in the middle of Marlow Square. The Sustenance Cradle was a bed of lumber that had the appearance of a crude coffee table with four stubby legs, none of them quite equal in length. There were three leather straps, each of them weathered and cracked, built into the Sustenance Cradle—one to hold down the legs and two to hold down the arms. Beside the table, a few feet away, was a small pile of wood beneath a charred, metal grill.

The circle of Marlows opened up, allowing space for Daddy Marlow's Boys to pass through with Idea. Releasing his wrists, One and Two Marlow lifted Idea off the ground, laying him onto the Sustenance Cradle. Struggling as much as he could, Idea was easily overpowered as One Marlow held him down and Two Marlow fastened the straps—first around his ankles and then around his forearms; his head, still cloaked in burlap, hung back over the edge. The final piece of the Sustenance Cradle was a piece of wood, with a half circle cut out of it, carved to fit over the neck; Two Marlow set this final piece in place, isolating Idea's head from the rest of his body. While this was going on, Three Marlow lit the woodpile, igniting a flame beneath the charred grill, and laying down the shovel so its spade rested on top of the flaming grill.

The front door of the Main Dwelling opened and every head in the crowd turned to watch Daddy Marlow stroll out, ax in hand, moving leisurely as if he were about to take an afternoon walk—nothing at all like he was about to kill a man. The crowd of Marlows opened up once again, letting Daddy Marlow into the circle, where he took his place at the Sustenance Cradle.

"What a glorious day this is!" he said, his words like lightning, exploding the air around them into a giant clap of thunder. "Men, mothers and younglings, welcome. As the Creator tells us, to truly live, one needs only the fruit of the land, the warmth of the sun and the sustenance of the flesh. Today we again will be blessed with the sustenance of one of our own, a man who has graciously chosen to give himself to all of us so that our bellies shall be quantified, our strength solidified and our spirits fortified. We should all be so lucky as to give ourselves up to the Greater Good. But, one day, the blessing of our Creator permitting, we will all be sacrificed into Better Days."

Daddy Marlow paused, allowing for the crowd to cheer and applaud, fists pumping in the air, hands clapping shoulders.

"Today, we will be celebrating the glorious departure of a very generous and giving man. Always sacrificing his time and efforts to aid whatever cause was in need of tending. Whether it was lending an extra hand in the tilling of crops or offering his services in repair of one of our dwellings, his presence was always available. So, when three nights prior to this day, he came to me, embraced me in a hug and said he wanted to give himself up to a Sustenance Sacrifice, I can tell you all that I wasn't in the least surprised. I asked him if he was sure, if he was truly ready, as Better Days is still a day that has yet to be determined. None of us, you see—not even myself—can ever know the day it will come. But what I do know is that when your earthly body is extinguished, your soul is released into the sky, settling in the Next World, where it will wait patiently to be joined by all the rest of us in Better Days. Your soul may lay in wait for days, months, years or generations. Because the wait may be so long, it behooves all of us to spend as much of that time waiting here on earth, where we can still enjoy the company of our family, the taste of flesh on our tongues and the laughter of younglings in our hearts. I needed to know if this man was really and truly prepared to sacrifice all of his blessings here on earth in exchange for giving sustenance to all the rest of us. When I asked him this, he looked me square in the eye and said, 'Daddy Marlow, nothing here on earth could bring me as much joy as I would receive from giving myself up to the Divinity.'"

Daddy Marlow paused for effect.

"Now," he said, "let the Sustenance Sacrifice begin!"

The crowd of Marlows erupted into cheers and applause. Standing no less than fifteen feet from the Sustenance Cradle, Timber marveled at the view, as she had never been in such intimate proximity to a Sustenance Sacrifice. Because the word had quickly spread in the passing days that Timber worked in the Sustenance Dwelling and, perhaps more relevantly, because she stood in the company of Luna Marlow, nobody elbowed or nudged her back.

"Evil is in all of us," Daddy Marlow said. "Every day it feeds on our flesh and our spirits. When death arrives for any of us, it also means the evil within us will lose its sanctuary. Evil does not like this. Despite the joy any of us would feel at the moment of our redemption, evil will kick and scream, because, unlike us, it does not have an afterlife. For evil, there are no Better Days. But evil has no physical body of its own. It feels through ours, hears through ours and sees through ours. As I speak now, the evil within this great and generous man can hear me. It knows that soon its parasitic ways will be over. The tangled dance that takes place between the soul of he and the evil within will end, relinquishing its occupancy in his human shell. So, in just a moment, when I look into his eyes, I will be looking into the eyes of evil. And when I speak into his ears, I will be speaking into the ears of evil. And when he screams and struggles, it will not be he, but the evil within him."

Daddy Marlow stepped over to Idea and, looking down on him, spoke directly to his burlap-covered face.

"Before this moment, your fear was blind. Now I give it eyes and it sees me."

With that, Daddy Marlow snatched the burlap sack from Idea's head, revealing his bruised and tired face to the Divinity crowd. The terror that radiated from him was tangible, like you could scoop it up with your hands and squeeze it through your fingers. Daddy Marlow stepped over to the side of Idea's head, giving himself the perfect angle to bring his ax down. Closing his eyes, Daddy Marlow tilted his face to Heaven and mouthed a silent prayer—it was then that Idea began to scream.

With the shadow of death upon him, adrenaline coursed through Idea's body, giving him more strength than he had ever previously had, which served only to produce the most horrible shriek you would ever want to hear. Still screaming, he began jerking his body, hard and desperate, pulling his wrists and ankles against the leather restraints; the straps, however, wouldn't give, leaving only his pelvis to thrust up, pushing his body into a perfect arc. Daddy Marlow opened his eyes, took a step back and gathered his strength, before bringing the ax down with all his might—only, it landed on the wrong side of the wooden divider.

In Daddy Marlow's tenure as Divinity leader, which I can reasonably estimate was somewhere in the area of twenty years at the time of Idea Marlow's sacrifice, he had performed anywhere from one to three Sustenance Sacrifices a month. When he wasn't sacrificing one of his followers, Daddy Marlow spent a good deal of time chopping down trees, splitting fire wood and most any other exercise that involved the swing of his ax. He was an expert with his tool, honing his abilities over time, understanding just how to marry precision with strength. It wasn't unusual to find him entertaining younglings with feats of strength and accuracy by splitting a piece of lumber right down the middle, while gripping his ax in only one hand. Or throwing it, end over end, twenty feet away, sticking it into a tree trunk. So, when Daddy Marlow brought his ax down on Idea and, rather than chopping off his head, stuck the blade firmly in Idea's left arm and a portion of his chest, Timber understood immediately that this was not an accident.

"Now, now," Daddy Marlow said, addressing the crowd, "please don't fatigue yourselves with concern. While my blade did move astray, the screams you are hearing from this human shell in no way reflect any pain or discomfort. Remember, this was a blow to the evil within it and it is from there that these calls of agony are born."

Three Marlow briefly struggled to retrieve the ax, as it had gone completely through Idea's arm and into the Sustenance Cradle. When the ax was finally pulled free, the gathering of Marlows saw that Idea's arm had been severed from his body, through the upper part of his bicep; as his body thrust up in agony, again creating its familiar arc, his severed arm lay motionless atop the wood of the Sustenance Cradle.

Blood squirted from where his arm had been chopped, shooting straight and hard, transforming into a dark, crimson mud as it fell to the earth. Three Marlow handed the ax over to Daddy Marlow, who again lifted it over his head and, with a minimum of effort, swung it down through Idea's neck, severing his head and silencing his screams. Three Marlow lifted the shovel from the fire and pressed the hot metal spade against Idea's bloody neck, causing an audible sizzle as it cauterized the large wound; he did the same to Idea's stump of an arm.

When the Sustenance Sacrifice was complete, Daddy Marlow was soaked in Idea's blood, his long hair clinging to his back and arms in thick, red clumps. All that was left to do was for Daddy Marlow's Boys to unfasten Idea's lifeless body from the Sustenance Cradle and deliver him to the Sustenance Dwelling.

What remained of Idea Marlow lay on the heavy wooden table in the Sustenance Dwelling, completely naked, waiting for Timber and Luna. His body, unlike the first dead man Timber saw, was completely hairless, from his shorn arms and his smooth legs to his naked torso and his barren crotch. His penis, Timber noticed, looked much different in its flaccid state; the uncircumcised foreskin, which was noticeably darker than the rest of his body, stretched across his limp shaft into a puckered opening, an eyeless socket. His severed arm had been laid across his chest and, as for his severed head, it was nowhere in sight.

When Luna picked up her cleaver to begin her work, Timber started for the backdoor where she would wait outside, as usual.

"Not today, youngling," Luna said, stopping her. "You're going to help me cut this boy."

Luna handed Timber a rubber apron to wear, along with a pair of rubber gloves.

"When your hands get tough like mine," she said, displaying her hard and calloused palm, "you won't need to wear those."

With very swift and precise motions, Luna opened a long slit along the side of Idea's thighs and another along the side of his ribcage.

"We've got to let him dry out," she said, as Idea's blood spilled from the fresh cuts, across the wooden table and onto the floor.

Timber gagged, disgusted by the sight of Idea pouring out of himself, while Luna walked around the table, making bloody foot-prints in the sawdust. With Timber's help, she turned Idea over onto his belly, inadvertently putting on display that strange birthmark on his butt, the sight of it leaving Timber with a sharp pang of guilt.

"I'll start you off with something easy," Luna said. "Watch."

Luna took her cleaver in one hand and Idea's ankle in the other; she lifted the cleaver above her head, pausing a moment to measure her aim, and brought it down hard against the back of his knee. The skin split open, exposing muscle and bone. Luna brought the cleaver down again in the same place, just as hard, sounding a loud crack as the blade met the bone. With her hand still on Idea's ankle, Luna began twisting it, left and right. "You want to try and work that bone off as much as you can," she said. Another couple of strikes with the cleaver, along with the continued twisting of the ankle, and

Idea's leg was completely severed at the knee. Luna tossed the leg onto the metal counter against the wall.

"All right," she said, handing Timber the cleaver. "Your turn."

Timber felt her gag reflex flaring up and fought it off as hard as she could. She held the cleaver with both hands and brought it over her head, pausing to measure her aim—as well as consider what she was about to do—before bringing it down as hard she could on Idea's other leg. Missing his knee completely, Timber stuck the cleaver into the meat of his thigh, splitting the skin and exposing the yellow layer of fat beneath. Timber left the cleaver where it stuck and brought her hands to her mouth, apologizing to Luna through her rubber gloves.

"Try again," Luna said, removing the cleaver.

Timber again brought the cleaver over her head, measured her aim, and brought it down hard—this time, nailing her target.

"There you go," Luna said, smiling. "Right in the sweet spot. Do it again." Timber did do it again, feeling the blade hit the bone. Luna took hold of Idea's ankle and began twisting it for Timber, while she continued to bring the blade down, until the leg was successfully severed at the knee. Soon enough, after they repeated this process all about his body, Idea had been severed into several pieces, at which point Luna taught Timber how to remove the skin.

She started with Idea's thigh and, using the point of her cleaver, slit long ways up the back. Working her fingers into the slit, she pulled back on it in hard bursts, tearing it away from the fat and muscle. With the skin removed, she used the cleaver to shave off the thick layer of fat, wavy and yellow like a bloated cob of corn, tossing it into a large bucket beside the heavy wooden table. Every night, Timber learned, Daddy Marlow's Boy's collected the fat and delivered it to Scissor Marlow, who spent her days rendering it into tallow, which she used to make soap and candles.

With the fat removed, Luna carved off a small piece of flesh, popping it in her mouth. Cutting off another small piece, she handed it to Timber. "Go on," she said. Timber put it in her mouth and was immediately disgusted by its soft, chewy texture. With Luna watching on, she tried desperately to chew it up and swallow it down, but as soon as she did, it came right back up, along with everything else she ate that day. Anticipating the wrath of Luna, Timber was surprised to hear her laughing.

"I can't say the same thing didn't happen to me my first time," Luna said. "You'll get used to it, though. It's important to get used to the taste of meat fresh off the bone. Should the day come when we can't cook it, you'll still need to eat. While others may choose to starve, we can fill our bellies."

Luna took Idea's thigh, which was now just a red husk of meat, still attached to the femur, and wrapped it along with a few slices of squash, three carrots and two ears of corn in a wet sheet of burlap. They did this with all of Idea's severed parts, before taking them out back and placing them in the fire pits.

In the days that followed Idea's Sustenance Sacrifice, Pepsi Marlow took on the appearance of a ghost, pale and gaunt, appearing only occasionally in the window of her dwelling. Timber knew she hadn't eaten, as she had not seen her collect any food during the distribution of Sustenance Portions. While Pepsi hadn't spoken to Timber, she was convinced it was more than grief that stole her appetite. I think it's fair to assume that Pepsi didn't want to eat her dead lover. There's no doubt that, without proper sustenance, Pepsi would have eventually died of hunger. But, no more than a week after her lover's death, Pepsi Marlow was found in her dwelling, dead on the floor, her neck deeply severed beneath the jaw, a bloody piece of glass in her hand.

chaptereight

The Legend of Sissy Marlow

Sissy Marlow was the closest thing the Divinity had to a saint. While she wasn't prayed to or worshipped, her story was remembered fondly and passed along the lips of those who knew her and those who wished they had. Her story was taught during Daily Lessons, discussed over Sustenance Portions and—with regard to those who believed they really and truly knew her—whispered about deep in the forest, beneath the leaves. And though she was only a child, no more than seven or eight years old when she was killed, she was the conduit by which Daddy Marlow attained his position as leader of the Divinity.

Daddy Marlow was not born in the Divinity. He wasn't even raised in the Divinity. He was an Outsider. The first time he stepped foot on that anonymous compound, he was about thirty years old. He arrived on the bed of a rusty orange pickup truck with his head completely shaved and a young girl on his lap. The child, too, was bald, but her baldness was different. Whilst she shaved neither her head nor her eyebrows, there wasn't a hair to be seen.

When the orange pickup truck parked, the anonymous man who would become Daddy Marlow stepped out, holding the bald child in his arms. He was led to the Main Dwelling by the driver of the truck, a man by the name of Vegas Marlow; as they passed through a quickly developing crowd of curious Divinity members, the anonymous man and the child in his arms were gawked at like aliens from a far away planet. Vegas knocked on the front door and Daddy Marlow—the one who preceded the current Daddy Marlow—answered. Seeing the bald child at his doorstep, he smiled.

He was expecting her.

One of the first lessons taught to every youngling during Daily Lessons was that of the inherent evilness of hair. It was such an important principle in the foundation of the Divinity, going right to the core of their beliefs, that Daddy Marlow would often take it upon himself to preach the word. "We are, by our very nature, evil," he would say. "It is simply the way the Creator made us. But why would he instill us with evil? What sense does that make? The answer is simple. He makes us evil, so that we may know what it is to be good. We know what we are, by knowing what we are not. Evil is natural. But to be good, that is the work we must make of our lives. That is what makes us divine. And hair is the excrement of evil. It is a constant reminder of our original flaw. So a smooth, hairless body represents the ultimate in purity and goodness. This is why the Purity Ritual is perhaps the most important duty we engage in, until the Creator calls us up to Better Days."

The Purity Ritual was the process by which heads and bodies were shaved and it was conducted on every Divinity member, without fail, at least once a week. This shaving chore was seen as menial, filthy work—akin to cleaning the shit from someone else's ass. For this reason, it was a chore left to the women, most of whom took to it with pride, if for no other reason than to not show disrespect to the principles of their faith and, more importantly, to Daddy Marlow himself.

Daddy Marlow was the only person in the Divinity who freely grew hair. It was long and thick, reaching far down, past the small of his back, hanging like a cape, swaying with the slightest movement or kick of wind. It was a testament of his love towards the Divinity and its members. "As your leader," Daddy Marlow preached, "it is I who must bare the burden of evil for all of you, so that you don't have to. That I can live my days under the weight of your collective evil, without crumbling like a brittle bone, is a testament to my strength and a validation in the prophecy of the Creator, who, in his divine wisdom, chose me to lead you."

In the early days of the Divinity, members sat in the Purity Chair during the Purity Ritual. The Purity Chair was actually a stool, carved from the trunk of a tree and crafted by the hands of Bunyan Marlow, a man who was sacrificed and eaten, long before Timber was born. There was nothing terribly impressive about the Purity Chair in and of itself; even to the untrained eye, it was clear that Bunyan Marlow probably didn't know much of anything about building beyond chopping wood and hammering nails. However, he did do one thing right: he built a sturdy stool that served the purposes of the Divinity for a very, very long time.

While the Purity Chair was important, it wasn't the physical stature of the chair itself that validated its importance, nor was it the surprising durability it displayed—quite simply, it was the reverence that the Divinity placed on it, which, as mass reverence will do, created the illusion of importance. Over the years, from one generation to the next, this perception of importance was passed along, making the reality stronger and stronger. By the time Timber and her generation came along, the Purity Chair, and its place among Divinity lore, was set in stone—literally.

A stone carver, by the name of Jacob Marlow, had devoted a significant amount of time etching the story of the Purity Chair and the importance of the Purity Ritual into a slab of stone the size of a large pancake; like Bunyan Marlow before him, Jacob Marlow had been sacrificed and eaten. The sacrifice of Jacob Marlow was the first that Timber could remember watching. The idea of being killed by Daddy Marlow seemed to make Jacob Marlow proud. There was no kicking or screaming with him. He barely even flinched when Daddy Marlow brought his ax down. In her memory of Jacob Marlow's sacrifice, Timber could swear that, just before his head rolled, she actually saw him smile.

When the previous Daddy Marlow learned of the young Outsider girl who could not grow hair, he demanded an immediate audience in her presence. "If such a child exists," he told Vegas Marlow, his right hand man, "then she is surely the Chosen One." Vegas made regular trips to the Outside on behalf of Daddy Marlow for various reasons, such as picking up supplies or dumping garbage. Vegas was entirely obedient to Daddy Marlow and would never do anything to cross him—that is, until he befriended the future Daddy Marlow.

Befriending Outsiders was so fiercely against Divinity rules, that it wasn't even acknowledged with words; it was simply understood, the same way one understands not to lie down in fire. Despite his fierce loyalty, Vegas allowed himself his secret Outsider friend—a butcher in San Bernardino. The butcher was a large man, all brawn and muscles. Vegas enjoyed conversing with the butcher, finding himself satisfied by the empty simplicity of it, a task free of ritual or discipline. Vegas and the butcher spent time together at a downtown bar, where Vegas enjoyed his first sip of beer. On the night that his inhibitions were first jarred loose by alcohol, Vegas told the butcher about the Divinity.

He told him about how they were a blessed group of people, not at all like the Outsiders, and that one day, they would live forever in

Better Days. He told him about the women and their obedience and how they could have sex with any of them, whenever they pleased. The butcher liked the sound of the Divinity and wanted to see it for himself, but Vegas told him that it wouldn't be possible, not without the approval of Daddy Marlow.

Vegas continued his friendship with the butcher and soon, no longer needing the lubricating presence of alcohol, he opened up more and more, telling his friend about the inherent evilness of hair and how those in the Divinity shaved it off. The butcher told Vegas that he had a child, a little girl, and she too was completely bald. He explained to Vegas that for her entire life she had never been able to grow hair of her own.

Vegas was overwhelmed by the notion that such a child was possible. This girl would have to be the most pure and good person ever born, for she would have no evil inside of her at all. When the butcher told Vegas about how difficult her life had been, feeling isolated in a world where she was forever surrounded by cruel children and an intolerant society, Vegas knew she was the Chosen One.

Had Vegas been a more worldly man, had he not spent his entire life void of education and information, he might have understood that there was nothing particularly special about the little girl who couldn't grow hair. Had Vegas had the ability or desire to read, he might have learned that this girl was not divine at all—at least not in the way the Divinity believed her to be. She simply had an autoimmune disease called Alopecia Areata Totalis, a disorder that caused her body to mistakenly treat her hair follicles as foreign tissue, consequently stopping hair growth. Had Vegas known such a disease existed, had he even a clue that the little girl with no hair was afflicted with it, he might not have agreed to bring the butcher and his daughter up to meet Daddy Marlow. But because he did, both his life and the future of the Divinity would be changed forever.

The butcher and his divine daughter, Outsiders both of them, were baptized into the Divinity in the waters of Marlow Stream. And during the naming ritual—a version that bore no resemblance to the tortuous incarnation used to name Daddy Marlow's Boys—Daddy Marlow christened the newest members of the Divinity. "For you," he said, holding the butcher's head in his hand over the water, "I shall christen thee Lexicon Marlow." Then, taking the little girl in his hands and holding her above the water, Daddy Marlow said, "And you, youngling, you shall be christened Sissy Marlow."

Lexicon Marlow was immediately put to work in the compound, while Sissy Marlow became the shadow of Daddy Marlow. He took her everywhere with him, holding her hand, sometimes carrying her on his shoulders. She was glad for the attention, not just of Daddy Marlow, but of everyone in the Divinity—especially the younglings. Having spent so much of her life as an outcast, Sissy Marlow had suddenly been placed in a world where everyone looked just like her; not only did they look like her, but they appreciated her. "And one day," Daddy Marlow preached, Sissy by his side, "she will lead us all into Better Days, for she is the Chosen One."

Now here's where things get fuzzy: If you could ask her yourself, Timber would freely admit that she has no way of knowing what happened next. She has spent more than a few sleepless nights, lying in bed, trying to piece everything together, trying to make sense out of it all. But the reality is, for all the many stories she *can* vouch for regarding the Divinity, what follows is a narrative completely of her imagination. As best as she can make sense of it, the story of Sissy Marlow probably proceeded as follows.

Vegas Marlow, while still important to the Divinity, was no longer Daddy Marlow's sole confidante. He was made to share the attention of Daddy Marlow with Sissy—and he didn't appreciate that. With his feelings hurt, Vegas leaned on his friend, the former butcher, Lexicon Marlow. Lexicon embraced the ear of his friend, taking in his woes, validating his bruised ego. Lexicon was delicate with Vegas, letting weeks and months go by, just listening and consoling, letting him know he was right to feel hurt, that he had done nothing to deserve such pain. And then, one day, when Lexicon sensed that Vegas Marlow was ripe, he made a very simple proposition.

"Let's kill him."

Vegas was jarred by the suggestion, just as Lexicon expected; he walked away, cursing Lexicon for letting such an idea cross his lips. But it was too late. The seed was planted and it grew in Vegas's mind, setting its roots deep in his subconscious, pushing out branches and sprouting leaves, until one day he went to Lexicon, almost in a trance, and asked what they needed to do.

Lexicon had observed how immediately the Divinity accepted Sissy Marlow as the Chosen One and, while it was never spoken aloud, he knew that he, himself, was held in quiet esteem for being her father; Lexicon regarded this as social capital, a collective goodwill that, when the time came, he could cash in on. "They'll accept me as leader," he told Vegas, "because my seed spawned the Chosen One." Lexicon told him that, in time, he would convince the Divinity that Vegas should be the new Daddy Marlow.

Vegas, emboldened by delusions of grandeur, snuck into the Main Dwelling with Lexicon, while Daddy Marlow and Sissy slept. Lexicon, with the help of Vegas, snatched Daddy Marlow from his bed, tying him up and leaving him in the corner. Vegas then took Sissy Marlow, muffling her screams with his hand, and escaped into the forest. Upon his return, Sissy Marlow would never be seen again.

The next day, Vegas and Lexicon dragged Daddy Marlow into Marlow Square. They told everyone that he had betrayed them, that he had become greedy and, in an act of deviance and weakness, had sacrificed Sissy Marlow, devouring her into his belly. With the help of Lexicon Marlow, and with the blessing of the Divinity, Daddy Marlow was sacrificed—and all, including Lexicon, feasted on his flesh. Just as he anticipated they would, the Divinity embraced Lexicon as their new leader. "Within my loins," he told his new followers, "exists the residue of the Chosen One. I created her once and, with your loyalty and praise, I shall create her again." His first order of business, as the new Daddy Marlow, was the Sacrifice of Vegas Marlow.

When Daddy Marlow took over as leader of the Divinity, his follower's existence could be accurately described as primitive. While the Main Dwelling had already been built, the standards for which it was maintained were not very high. As it was, the Main Dwelling was the only actual house constructed within the boundaries of the compound. Daddy Marlow wanted the Main Dwelling to be more than the place where he slept. He wanted to instill it with a sense of nobility. His vision was to mold the Divinity into a kingdom where he was the king and the Main Dwelling his castle.

Not thinking just of himself, Lexicon, the former butcher, became the first Daddy Marlow to organize a collective effort to build the first set of small dwellings. Within the first six months of his reign, three dwellings were built; within the year, there were eight. For years after that, eight was more than enough, as there were less than fifty Divinity members on the compound. The added shelter, however, raised the survival rate in the Divinity. No longer were members living the lives of primitive mountain people; they were living longer, healthier lives, which increased the population of the Divinity. This increase in population size would necessitate the construction of even more dwellings.

This growing population also meant that Daddy Marlow would have to sublimate the Divinity's sustenance, so he began planting crops. Nothing more advanced than certain vegetables and herbs to begin with. He also planted a series of fruit trees. His farming efforts, all of which started out as modestly as one man could afford, grew over the years. In time, Daddy Marlow taught his followers how to maintain the crops year round and they, in turn, passed down their knowledge to others. Soon enough, Daddy Marlow would never have to touch his fingers to the soil again.

Under the guidance of Daddy Marlow, the Divinity had become efficient and prosperous. For the first time in their existence, they had reliable water resources; a water well, which Daddy Marlow helped build with his own hands, as well as a simple system of catching rain off of dwelling roofs. And, as soon as technology and resources permitted, the Main Dwelling surged with solar power, causing Divinity members to sit beneath its windows at night, marveling at the light. In the wake of all this prosperity, Daddy Marlow accumulated the trust and loyalty of his followers, insuring the Divinity would always have an endless source of reliable foot soldiers to keep things in order.

But to his mind, the best thing Daddy Marlow ever gave the Divinity was the Sustenance Dwelling. When construction of the Sustenance Dwelling was complete, Daddy Marlow surprised his followers with the presence of a woman who, before the moment they laid eyes on her, had never existed before. And in the waters of Marlow Stream, she would be christened Luna Marlow.

chapter**nine**

Sustenance Chips

Timber and Luna had spent much of the morning and afternoon cooking flesh in the fire pits, cutting it up into reasonable servings and preparing for the distribution of Sustenance Portions. In the early hours, before the sun was up, Timber would complete the first of the day's chores, which was to pass out the Sustenance Chips—they were actually just plastic poker chips. Each member of the Divinity received two Sustenance Chips per day, one for each distribution of Sustenance Portions. Every morning, Timber went from dwelling to dwelling, dropping off the appropriate number of chips in front of each door. When it was time to distribute Sustenance Portions, it was Timber's job to collect back the chips.

Timber had a good memory and, early on in her apprenticeship with Luna, she was keenly aware of City Marlow, a large boy in his seventeenth year, and his ploy to collect extra portions. Having already collected his two Sustenance Portions for the day, City arrived for his third. City no doubt assumed, due to the large number of Divinity members, that a young girl like Timber couldn't possibly keep track of everybody, but as soon as he showed up, Timber knew something wasn't right. Having no immediate proof of City's stolen Sustenance Chip, Timber gave him his portion, without speaking a word. When, on the next day, City again showed up three times to collect Sustenance Portions, Timber went to Luna.

"Listen," Luna told her, "I put you in charge of those chips, so the problem is yours to solve. I've got enough to do around here already. How many portions the boy gets is none of my concern."

Timber paid extra close attention the following day, focusing her sharp memory on everybody who collected portions. Before City showed up, once again, for his third portion of the day, Timber had recognized a young girl who had only collected one Sustenance Portion. Timber had never met the girl before, so the next day when she showed up for her Sustenance Portion, she introduced herself and learned the girl's name was Flower Marlow. Timber asked Flower which dwelling she lived in, so she could pay her a visit later that day.

Upon her visit, Timber and Flower sat outside on the dirt, leaning their backs against the front wall of the dwelling. Timber asked Flower why she had only collected one of her portions the previous couple of days and Flower hesitantly replied that she simply wasn't hungry. Timber had only to look into her eyes to know this was not the truth.

"I know someone's been stealing your Sustenance Chip," Timber said. "You don't have to tell me who, because I already know."

"You do?" Flower asked.

"Yes, I do. And I promise that tomorrow you'll have all of your chips. Okay?" "Okay."

Flower smiled and Timber patted her on her bald head, before excusing herself. She found City Marlow cutting firewood over a tree stump, along with three other boys about the same age. Without any consideration for the ax he held, Timber grabbed City by his shirt and threw him to the ground. Picking up the ax, Timber told the other boys that they had best leave her and City alone. In her periphery, she saw City move to get up, so she stomped her foot on his chest, knocking him back into the dirt. At the sight of her brute behavior, the other boys immediately left. Timber set her knee on City's chest, pinning him to the ground and, with one hard stroke, stuck the blade of the ax deep into the dirt, just barely missing his head. With her free hand, she gripped his neck, leaving just enough slack for him to gasp for air. Her hands and arms had become so strong from working in the Sustenance Dwelling, City found himself helpless against her grip.

"Now listen up, you," Timber told him, "I'm not as stupid as you think I am. Starting tomorrow, my little friend Flower is going to get all of her Sustenance Portions and, for the rest of the week, she's going to get one of yours as well."

City, whose face was turning purple, managed a slight nod. Timber stood up and City rolled into the fetal position, gulping in air and dirt. Timber kicked him in the gut before leaving him to himself, where he whimpered out his tears in private.

The story of what Timber did to City passed very quickly through the Divinity and when no immediate repercussions were taken against her, she knew they wouldn't come at all. In her own way, without confirming it with Luna, Timber realized that she had inherited an elite sort of status in the Divinity, the sort of status that was not usually given to girls. And, thanks to this elite status, Timber would soon kill her first man.

chapter**ten**

The Outsiders

Nobody outside of the Divinity was permitted to enter the compound without the expressed permission of Daddy Marlow. Even *with* Daddy Marlow's permission, nobody outside the Divinity was allowed to enter the compound without being personally escorted by Daddy Marlow's Boys. And nobody, without exception, was to enter the compound without first being blindfolded, to keep from surveying or memorizing the route from the Outside.

Despite all of the hurdles and protocol, many Outsiders still made regular visits to the Divinity. Most Outsiders, upon completion of their visit, went back into the Outside to conduct their ordinary lives as if nothing happened, sworn to a secrecy that they would almost certainly be unable to keep—but, occasionally, certain unlucky Outsiders would not remain alive long enough to make it out at all.

Beneath his impressive mane of hair and his brawny physique and the faith he preached and the rituals he enforced, Daddy Marlow was a businessman. And like so many other businessmen looking to make a dollar, Daddy Marlow never put principle before profit. While Outsiders and their way of life went against everything the Divinity believed in, they had money to spend and Daddy Marlow was more than happy to let them spend it in the Divinity. He didn't sell flesh to wannabe cannibals, though there were plenty of them willing to take their chances; nor did he sell any of the fruits or vegetables produced from the Divinity's crops. Daddy Marlow sold sex and, for the right price, every woman in the Divinity was available.

Billy D. Luscious, along with being an Outsider, was a reformed prostitute, a retired porn star and an entrepreneur of Internet erotica. He was also the Divinity's liaison to the Outside. And in due time, though neither of them yet knew it, he would become Timber Marlow's guardian angel. He had a striking sense of fashion, especially when he visited the Divinity, since nobody on the compound ever saw anything more than T-shirts, blue jeans and long flannel dresses. In contrast, Luscious wore bright clothes, often featuring yellows and reds. While he was wont to wear a more casual—albeit stylish—polyester tracksuit, on the day Timber first met him, he was wearing a yellow business suit, with stocking socks and matching alligator shoes.

When she saw him for the first time, he was blindfolded and riding in the back of the rusty orange pickup truck with two Outsider men who were also blindfolded. The truck drove along the dirt road into Marlow Square, past the Sustenance Cradle, parking in front of the Main Dwelling. Daddy Marlow stood in the doorway, smiling, his arms crossed. He walked up to the truck, helping Luscious get out and removing his blindfold. After a brief handshake, Daddy Marlow led Luscious in through the front door; the two Outsiders followed them in, with Daddy Marlow's Boys right behind them.

"Would you quit staring and get back in here," Luna said, smacking Timber on the back of her head.

"Who are they?"

"None of your business is who," Luna said. "Now come on, we got work to do."

Luna piled some freshly prepared flesh onto a large platter, with a couple of corncobs and roasted carrots.

"Take this down to the Main Dwelling," she said, "but don't go meddling about. Just take the food and come back. Got me?"

Timber held the platter with two hands and watched every one of her steps all the way to the Main Dwelling, avoiding rocks and fallen branches, barking at any careless youngling that crossed her path. When she arrived at the Main Dwelling, Three Marlow opened the door.

"Timber," Daddy Marlow said, "please enter."

Three Marlow took the platter from her and set it on the large, wooden trunk in front of the couch where Luscious sat with the two Outsiders. Daddy Marlow sat in his sofa chair, One and Two Marlow flanking him on either side.

"You've brought Sustenance Portions," Daddy Marlow said. "What a pleasant gesture. Gentlemen, please fill your bellies."

"I'm not hungry," Luscious said with a polite nod. "However, my friends are more than welcome to partake at their discretion."

The two Outsiders dug in, eating with their fingers, presumably unaware that they were engaging in cannibalism. One of the men, while still eating, took a long look at Timber, leading Luscious to say something to Daddy Marlow.

"Timber," he said, "come meet our guests."

"It's a pleasure to meet you, Miss Timber," Luscious said, standing from the couch and offering his hand. "My name is Luscious."

Timber looked to Daddy Marlow for approval, before shaking Luscious' hand.

"My, my," he said, "that's quite a grip you've got."

Timber was far too fascinated with Luscious's bejeweled fingers to reply. She had no concept of money and therefore couldn't appreciate how expensive Luscious' rings were or the diamond encrusted chain that hung from his neck or, for that matter, the platinum watch that adorned his wrist.

"She's one of my prize younglings," Daddy Marlow said.

"I don't doubt it," Luscious said.

Luscious looked to the Outsider on the end of the couch, who nodded back with a smile.

"Timber," Luscious said, "I'd like you to meet my friend, Richard."

Richard didn't say a word, but simply held his hand out. Timber recoiled from the feel of his moist and calloused palm.

"Timber," Daddy Marlow said, "you may go back to the Sustenance Dwelling now."

Timber did as she was told and was happy to get back to work. She was in the middle of wrapping a husk of flesh in burlap when Three Marlow turned up.

"What do you want?" Luna asked.

"I'm here for the youngling."

"What do you need with her?"

"Daddy Marlow has sent for her on behalf of an Outsider."

"No."

"On orders of Daddy Marlow, I'm to take her to the Outsider."

"Well that's too fucking bad, because she ain't going nowhere!"

"These are the orders of Daddy Marlow."

"She's a fucking *kid*, asshole!" Luna yelled. "So go tell whatever sick bastard is out there to pick someone else."

"He made his choice and Daddy Marlow has agreed to it," Three Marlow said. "Unless you're prepared to take this up with Daddy Marlow personally, the youngling will come with me."

With an almost audible breaking of her spirit, Luna turned to Timber, grabbing her shoulders and looking her square in the eye.

"Listen, youngling," she said, "You've got to go for a little bit."

"Where to?"

"Just listen to me."

Timber nodded.

"You're probably not gonna know what's going on," she said. "So when you get scared, remember that you're strong, just like me."

"We must go," Three Marlow said.

Taking Timber's hand, he led her out. Walking through Marlow Square, Timber gazed up at the vertical scars on the back of Three Marlow's head, which looked like three bloated worms burrowing beneath his skin. She wondered if they served as impediments to the Purity Ritual, hurdles for the razor as it cleared its path; she wondered also if any hair grew from those three slashes at all. Perhaps, she thought, burning the flesh destroyed any portal for evil to enter the world. They arrived at an out of the way dwelling, which was unoccupied.

"Do you understand what you're doing here?" Three Marlow asked.

Timber shook her head, no.

"You're here to please the Outsider."

"*Please* him?" she asked. "Why would I do that?"

"It's what Daddy Marlow wants."

"What do I do?"

Three Marlow looked at her, seemingly taken aback. As much as he was capable of it, Three Marlow seemed to actually feel sympathy for Timber in that moment, like maybe—just *maybe*—there might once have been a beating heart in that monster's chest. As quickly as his flash of sympathy came, it was gone.

"Go inside the dwelling and remove your clothes," he said. "The Outsider is waiting for you, so you must do whatever he asks of you."

"I don't understand."

"It's what Daddy Marlow wants."

Three Marlow let Timber into the dwelling, closing the door behind her. Richard was sitting on the bed against the back wall. Timber stood in front of the door, her hands behind her back, afraid to move. Richard patted his hand on the mattress, welcoming her to sit down beside him. Timber didn't move.

"It's all right, honey," he said. "I won't bite."

Timber stayed put.

"Your name's Timber, right?"

She nodded.

"Come on over, Timber. I'll be nice. I promise," he said. "We just met, remember? My name's Richard."

Timber stared at him and found herself fascinated by the hair he had all over his body. His scalp was covered and his beard was full; his forearms were thick with hair and from beneath his collar more hair pushed out. As she stared, Richard removed his shirt, exposing a round, soft belly that was also covered in hair.

Not knowing what else to do, Timber removed her clothes, pulling her T-shirt up over her head, kicking off her shoes, and pushing her jeans to the floor. There she stood, completely naked, shaved from head to toe. While her adolescent body was still years away from maturing into the womanly form it would ultimately take, she was still extraordinarily fit for a girl her age. The previous months she had spent in the Sustenance Dwelling had sculpted her fourteen-year-old frame into an impressive display of muscularity.

Richard put his hand between his legs and began massaging himself over his jeans, keeping his eyes on Timber. Again, he patted the mattress, silently inviting Timber to sit by him. Timber walked slowly across the dwelling, taking a seat on the bed, Richard's musky odor catching her off guard. With a grunt, he reached over and squeezed Timber's right breast, his calloused palm scraping her skin; with his free hand, he continued to massage himself over his jeans.

Richard hastily removed his pants, kicking them off the bed, proudly displaying his erect penis, which sprouted from a tangled bush of black hair. Timber was mortified at the sight of it and, as a matter of reflex, resisted Richard when he took hold of her hand. But he was stronger than she was and she couldn't stop him from putting her hand between his legs. When she didn't do anything with her hands, he took her fingers and manually wrapped them around his erection. Though Timber didn't know what she was meant to do with it, Richard was satisfied for the moment and continued to massage Timber's breasts.

She felt a cool wetness drizzle over her knuckles and, looking down, saw that it was coming from the tip of Richard's erection, like melted wax. She snatched her hand away, not knowing what had happened, thinking that, perhaps, she had hurt him somehow.

"Don't worry, honey," Richard said. "I'm not done yet."

Gently taking her shoulders, he tried to lay her down, but Timber resisted.

"Come on, sweetie," he said. "It's all right."

He pushed harder, but Timber continued to resist.

"Quit fucking around and lie the fuck down!"

Not liking the aggressive tone of his voice, Timber stood up from the bed and began collecting her clothes from the floor. Richard grabbed both of her arms from behind and threw her onto the bed, causing her to hit her head against the wall. The blow didn't knock her out, but it left her dazed. Richard climbed on top of her and, from where she lay, Timber could see a string of melted wax clinging from the tip of his erection to the meat of his thigh. Timber clawed at his face, dragging three of her fingernails across his cheek. When he recoiled backwards, she began furiously punching the thick flesh of his arms and chest. With the back of his hand, Richard smacked Timber across the cheek, quickly snuffing the fight out of her. For good measure, he punched her in the mouth, splitting her lip.

"Now, just relax, damn it," he said. "I'm not here to hurt you."

With all the eloquence of a jackhammer, Richard pushed himself inside of Timber, ending her fourteen years of virginity. He pumped away for about a minute and, just like that, it was all over. Without proper lubrication, Timber's virgin skin was rubbed raw and bleeding. Richard began putting his clothes back on, while Timber lay still on the bed, her legs open, the remnants of Richard's melted wax slowly drizzling out. After he was gone, Timber's body relaxed and she passed out.

Timber woke up on the heavy wooden table in the Sustenance Dwelling, with Luna gently cleaning the blood from her bruised face. The front door burst open and Charlotte Marlow ran to Timber's side.

"What happened?" Charlotte asked.

"This is how I found her."

"*Found* her? Where was she?"

"Daddy Marlow sent her off with an Outsider."

"But how did she end up like *this?*"

"The Outsider did it."

"What's to be done?"

"Nothing."

"What do you mean, *nothing?*"

"There's rules and protocol that are to be followed," Luna said. "You know that as well as I do. So, nothing is to be done. The youngling's wounds will heal soon enough, so I'd advise you to forget about this as soon as possible."

"That's not good enough."

"Listen," Luna said, "I know you care about this youngling and you're all broken up about what's happened, which is the only reason I haven't kicked you out yet. The reality is she got a taste of what it means to be a woman in this world. I'm sorry if that doesn't satisfy you, but that's how it is. Now, please excuse yourself."

Timber passed out again and when she awoke Daddy Marlow was in the Sustenance Dwelling. He and Luna were off to the side and she couldn't quite make out what they were saying. Luna was doing most of the talking, expressing her anger as much with her hands as her words. Daddy Marlow listened to her, nodding his head as she spoke. Finally, he rested his hand on her shoulder and spoke a few hushed words, which seemed to calm her down.

A week later, when Timber reported back to the Sustenance Dwelling, she discovered the naked body of Richard laying on the heavy wooden table, tied down with a length of frayed rope.

Standing beside him, with a big smile on her face, was Luna. The three scratches Timber had left on his cheek were scabbed over and healing. His skin was pale and Timber had assumed he was dead, until he stirred awake.

Luna handed Timber the cleaver.

"Do whatever you like," she said. "He's all yours."

Richard caught sight of the cleaver in Timber's hand and began to scream.

On the day Richard sexually assaulted her, he had inadvertently planted a dark seed in Timber's soul. And it was as if his screams served to water that dark seed, sprouting charcoal branches around Timber's heart, squeezing a primal rage through her veins. With this renewed rage merging with the shame that still boiled over in her belly, Timber lifted the cleaver over her head and brought it down on Richard's throat. Blood spurted out, wetting Timber and Luna, while Richard gagged on his bloody gasps. Timber brought the cleaver down again, silencing his gags. She brought the cleaver down three more times, before his head finally rolled off the heavy wooden table, landing with a wet thud on the floor.

"That's enough now," Luna said, caressing her back. "That's enough."

The sound of Luna's voice set Timber's heart free of the charcoal branches, which receded back into their dark, little seed. Climbing down from the table, Timber felt as though she were jarred from a trance. Suddenly overwhelmed with emotion, she wrapped her arms around Luna's waist and began to cry into her rubber apron. Luna held her tight, embracing a motherly instinct that was probably, on the whole, unfamiliar to her.

chapter**eleven**

The New Dwelling

I t had been over a year since Daddy Marlow assigned Timber to the Sustenance Dwelling and now, in her fifteenth year, Divinity members regarded her with a silent respect, the same as they would Luna or Daddy Marlow's Boys. Her muscles were rock solid; she could dig ten barbecue pits before the sun came up and she was capable of carving an entire body—head to toe—all by herself. Despite her evolution, Timber didn't feel all that different from the little girl she had been a year earlier, sitting beneath the Learning Tree for Daily Lessons.

Because the condition of the Main Dwelling had begun to suffer from time and the elements, it was about this time that Daddy Marlow decided it was time to build a bigger and better Main Dwelling. The New Dwelling, which would replace the Main Dwelling, would be an ambitious project, resulting in a two-story structure, which meant that, for the first time in its history, there would be a set of stairs in the Divinity. Construction like this meant manpower, which meant it was time for a few select youngling boys to make their rite of passage into manhood, joining the men who had been selected to work on the New Dwelling. Jupiter, who was in his seventeenth year, had long since stopped going to Daily Lessons, but this would be the first significant project he would have the opportunity to be a part of.

During the last year, Jupiter had experienced a growth spurt. As his teenaged frame rapidly filled out into a strong young man, Jupiter found that, compared to his peers, he could carry heavier loads of chopped wood, beat anyone in a foot race and, for anybody who cared to challenge him, hold his breath the longest under Marlow Stream. So far as Timber was concerned, this was why Jupiter seemed to be spending increasingly more time with Daddy Marlow's Boys; at that point all she could do was assume, since he wasn't willing to tell her much else about it.

On account of his growth spurt, Jupiter also experienced a charge in testosterone, as all young men do, which manifested itself into a voracious sex drive. Jupiter had a hard-on that scarcely seemed to go down and he was only too happy to show it to Timber one day. Of course, Timber knew Jupiter's display was neither an invitation nor a request; he was simply proud of his rock solid erection and wanted to share his pride with his best friend. Some of the other young men about the Divinity had befriended Jupiter and, among other things, taught him how to masturbate. Not only did this provide an avenue of relief, but it also gave him one more proud achievement to share with Timber.

Jupiter took Timber down to Marlow Stream one day where, in seclusion, he demonstrated his new skill. Dipping his hand in the water, he began stroking his erection and, in a decidedly unsexual way, Timber found herself fascinated. Within a minute or so, Jupiter opened his eyes and told Timber she needed to put her face right in front in order to get a good view. No sooner did Timber kneel down in front of him, did Jupiter release in her face. Timber jumped back, falling into a pile of dried leaves, while Jupiter burst into a laughing fit. With leaves stuck to her face, Timber got up and tackled Jupiter to the ground, punching him in the arm until he stopped laughing. It turned out that Tripper Marlow had played the same trick on Jupiter.

Timber had just finished helping Luna carve the Divinity's most recent sacrifice, when, upon removing her rubber apron, she noticed a blood stain in the crotch of her pants. Going over to Luna, she showed her the stain.

"I think I cut myself."

"That ain't no cut, youngling," Luna said. "That's just your monthly blood."

"Monthly blood?"

Luna looked at her, the corner of her mouth curling into a smile. "Ain't you never bled down there before?"

"No."

"Well, holy shit, youngling," Luna said. "You're a woman now!"

"I am?"

"Yes, ma'am," she said. "You're a youngling, no more. Once a month you can expect to bleed down there from now on."

Timber made a face, clearly disapproving.

"I'm gonna bleed like this *every* month, forever and ever?"

"Well, not always," Luna said. "If you get yourself knocked up with a youngling in your belly, you won't bleed until it comes out."

While Timber didn't necessarily enjoy the idea of bleeding once a month, she was still fascinated by it and wanted to share this new discovery with her best friend. Later that night, after they were each done working for the day, Timber took Jupiter out to the woods to show him where she was bleeding.

"What in the world did you sit on?!"

"Nothing," Timber laughed. "It's natural. It don't even hurt. I'm gonna bleed like this once a month now, forever."

"Is the same thing going to happen to me?"

"Probably, yes."

"Ah, hell!"

With the designated group of Divinity men working hard, the New Dwelling was making timely progress. Most of the first week was spent mixing concrete and laying down the foundation. Jupiter, for his part, was one of the mixers, as he wasn't yet experienced to do much else; but after a bit of begging, he was allowed to help build the shallow lumber frames that would hold the concrete until it solidified.

Midway through the second week of construction, the New Dwelling was beginning to take shape. Long pieces of lumber stood erect, forming the skeleton that offered a glimpse of how the New Dwelling would look. While the structure itself was turning out well, the effort to build it didn't come without incident. Even though the Divinity's men had the *ability* to build a dwelling, it happened with such infrequency that there was almost never time to properly hone their skills. And for this reason, accidents and mishaps occurred more often than not.

Hunter Marlow, who was somewhere in his twenty-third year, tripped over a piece of lumber and, on his way down, cracked his wrist on a rock, leaving him with a minor fracture. He was set right with a traction realigning and a simple splint. Luckily for Hunter, the bone didn't push through the skin, which not only would have resulted in a potentially fatal infection, but would have required the sort of surgery that the Divinity simply wasn't equipped to perform. Of course, as long as he had one good arm, Daddy Marlow's Boys made sure that Hunter continued to do his work.

Kern Marlow, a young man who had only just reached his seventeenth year, tripped over his own feet on his way up the staircase, tumbling back down. Despite the two large gashes that opened up on the back of his head, the most critical damage he sustained was a dislocated shoulder. Kern was carried from the construction site and laid out on the dirt, where a small crowd gathered around him. One Marlow took a long length of rope, tying a lasso around Kern's ribs and kneeling beside him. Two Marlow sat on the other side, taking hold of Kern's bad arm. In a well synchronized effort, One Marlow pulled the rope his way, while Two Marlow pulled Kern's arm the other way, leaving him screaming between them, his body sliding back and forth on the dirt, until his shoulder popped back into place.

About a month into it, in an effort to bring some added efficiency to the construction of the New Dwelling, Daddy Marlow recruited a man he called Copper Marlow to manage the finer details of the project. Before he showed up, nobody had ever seen Copper Marlow before; however, the Divinity's population was big enough that nobody thought much about seeing an unfamiliar face. Within a few days of his arrival, it was clear that he had an expert hand in the ways of construction and carpentry.

While the staircase was already proving to be the biggest novelty as far as the younglings were concerned—as evidenced by how often they were scolded for running up and down them while the men were busy working—it would be the New Dwelling's bathroom that would capture the imagination of the Divinity's elders. There were no bathrooms on the Divinity's compound, only outhouses. In its more primitive days, before Daddy Marlow's vision and leadership shifted the cultural paradigm, Divinity members pissed in the dirt and shit in the forest.

All of the outhouses in the Divinity had compost toilets and the toilet in the New Dwelling would be no different. Buckets were placed beneath the toilet seats to catch the shit and piss. Sawdust and dry grass were thrown on top of the waste every time somebody completed their business, absorbing any excess liquid and discouraging the presence of flies. Once the buckets were full, they were emptied out into a compost heap, where the contents were treated into fertilizer, which was then used for the Divinity's crops.

Within six weeks time, the New Dwelling had its floors built in on both the first and second levels. One night, Timber and Jupiter snuck into the not-yet-complete New Dwelling, tiptoeing up the staircase and laying side by side on the wooden floor. Staring up into the sky, all ebony and starlit, Jupiter asked Timber about sex.

"Do girls and girls ever have sex with each other?"

"I dunno," she said. "Why?"

"Just wondering, is all."

"How come?"

"I dunno," he said, "I just wondered why only the men and women have sex together."

"That's just the way it is," she said.

"Yeah, I guess."

They were quiet for a long while after that, until the rusty orange pickup truck roared to life, breaking the silence. Timber and Jupiter turned over in time to see Daddy Marlow's Boys driving off onto the main road, disappearing into the night.

"They take me with them sometimes," Jupiter said, "into the Outside."

"Since when?" Timber said, almost yelling.

"I'm really not supposed to be talking about it."

"What was it like?"

"Different," he said. "It's big. They have dwellings the size of mountains and the people don't do nothing. No tending crops or chopping down trees, no digging wells or cleaning outhouses. Nothing. At night, they got lights that float up in the air, so you can see even when it's dark. The women have long hair, like Daddy Marlow, and they eat animals for sustenance."

"You going back?"

"Probably so, yes."

"Take me with you."

"Timber, I can't."

"Please!"

"I swear, I can't."

"Please, Jupiter," she said. "I'll never ask you for anything else ever again."

"Fine," he said. "I'll see what I can do."

Soon enough, the New Dwelling was completely built. It was bigger, better and as close to modern civilization as anyone in the Divinity had ever seen. Copper Marlow, for his part, enjoyed about a week's worth of good living. He ate every day and wandered about the compound, smiling, making friends and having sex with a great number of the Divinity's women.

One morning, when Timber showed up for work in the Sustenance Dwelling, the naked body of Copper Marlow was laid out on the heavy wooden table. Copper's head, which was still intact, was cocked at an awkward angle and his neck was bruised.

"No matter how many times I see it," Luna said, "I can't help but feel a little bad for these bastards."

Without another word, Timber and Luna took to the task of butchering Copper Marlow and preparing him for the day's Sustenance Portions. While they worked on him, Timber shared with Luna what Jupiter had told her about the Outside.

"That all sounds about right," she said.

"You've seen it?"

"I was born in the Outside," Luna said. "Lived there my whole life until Daddy Marlow brought me here."

Timber's stunned silence made Luna chuckle.

"Listen, youngling, you've been working with me long enough

that I've actually come to like you, so I'm gonna share a few things. But if I ever found out you was telling folks my business, you'd find yourself on the wrong side of my blade. Got me?"

Timber nodded.

"That man who runs this roost, the one we call Daddy Marlow, ain't no daddy of mine," she said. "He's my brother. Now the way they raise you younglings up around here, you don't know from brothers and sisters, so I'll explain it to you real simple. Daddy Marlow and me had the same mother and father that raised us up in the Outside. The same blood that runs through my veins runs through his."

"You knew your mother?" Timber said. "The one who carried you in her belly?"

"Sure did," she said. "Strong woman. Worked on a farm with our daddy, milking cows and wrestling pigs. Mean fuckers, both of them. When we was old enough, me and Daddy Marlow left the farm and got jobs as butchers. We shared a home together, the three of us."

"Three of you?"

"Daddy Marlow had a little girl in the Outside," she said. "A real sweet child with no hair. Made her with some woman who didn't stick around long enough to learn the child's name. One day I come home and they're both gone. No explanation, no warning. Just gone. A few years passed and, out of the blue, he turns up looking like a hippie with hair past his shoulders. I asked him where the hell he'd been and he tells me he found his very own slice of Heaven up in the mountains. Said he wanted to share it with me. Said I had to give up everything. Said I had to trust him. Been here ever since."

"Did you like it in the Outside?"

"I liked it fine," Luna said. "But, things are simpler here. I like it that way."

"Did you used to be evil?"

Luna laughed.

"If there was anything evil about me," she said, "it had nothing to do with the world outside these mountains or the hair I used to keep on my head. All that mess is a bunch of hullabaloo and don't you forget I'm the one who told you so. Daddy Marlow, on the other hand, probably believes in it more than anybody. And while I love him for the blood we share, he's a crazy son of a bitch. I go along with it, though. Like I said, things are simpler here. And I like it that way."

Timber had a far away look in her eye, thinking about the world outside. Luna must have picked up on this, because the warning she gave Timber came seemingly out of nowhere.

"I know you're young and it's natural to become curious about the world around you," Luna said. "But don't let curiosity be your curse, youngling. If you're not careful, it'll get you into a heap of trouble you'll wish you never knew."

chapter**twelve**

The Sacrifice of City Marlow

In the weeks and months that followed Timber's roughing up of City, he was made to deal with a lot of teasing from the other Divinity Boys. City resented Timber for it and she knew it. If she hadn't had the security of working in the Sustenance Dwelling, City might have retaliated sooner. So, until he decided to strike back at Timber, the worst he was willing to do was give her an evil stare twice a day when he picked up his Sustenance Portions.

Timber became suspicious something was up on the day City didn't show up for his Sustenance Portions. At first, in the morning, she assumed he must have slept through the Marlow Bell or, perhaps, chose instead to get an early start working on the crops. But he also missed his second Sustenance Portion later in the day. As she and Luna cleaned up the Sustenance Dwelling for the night, Timber told her about City's peculiar absence.

"Well if he's missing, then be gone with him," Luna said. "One less mouth to feed is all that is."

"Where might he be?"

"Hell if I know," Luna said. "Maybe he got himself lost in the forest or something ignorant like that."

"You think he'd try to run away?"

"To the Outside? Let me tell you, there's not a man with two good legs who could walk all the way to the Outside."

"Could Daddy Marlow do it?"

"Not Daddy Marlow, not nobody," she said. "As plain as I can tell you, youngling, it simply cannot be done. Certainly not by an overgrown youngling like City Marlow. Even if he was dumb enough to try it, Daddy Marlow's Boys would catch him before he got too far. And, believe you me, once those boys get a hold of you, you'll be begging for a Sustenance Sacrifice."

That night as she was walking back to her dwelling, Timber heard a small pair of footsteps running behind her. She turned around to find young Flower Marlow chasing after her. Timber stopped walking, so Flower could catch up.

"Timber," she said, all out of breath, "I forgot to give you these."

Flower handed her two Sustenance Chips.

"Where'd these come from?"

"City gave them to me this morning. He said he wouldn't be needing them anymore. I wasn't hungry enough to use them and I meant to give them back earlier, but I plain forgot."

"Did City say why he wouldn't be needing them?"

"Nope."

"Well, thank you for bringing them to me."

"You're welcome!"

Flower ran off, back in the direction she came from, catching up with a group of younglings who were preparing to play tag.

Back in her dwelling, Syracuse and Oakland were already asleep, while Charlotte waited for Timber in her rocking chair. She was about six months pregnant with her third youngling and was rubbing her hands along her taut belly.

"How was your day?" Charlotte asked.

"Fine."

Timber kneeled in front of Charlotte, resting her ear on her pregnant belly.

"Has he kicked anymore?"

"Not for a few hours," she said. "I think he tuckered himself out in there."

Timber sat down between Charlotte's legs, letting her arms hang over her knees like a scarecrow. Charlotte rubbed down Timber's shoulders, as she did every night, until she was good and sleepy. When she could barely keep her head up, Timber crawled into her sleeping bag and passed out.

Timber awoke in the middle of the night to the sound of tapping on her window. Rubbing the sleep from her eyes, she looked over at Charlotte, who was sound asleep with Syracuse and Oakland. The tapping came again and Timber just managed to see a hand in front of the window drop from sight. Going over to the window, she peered out, but, in the black of night, Timber could hardly see anything. Figuring it was Jupiter, she opened the door, but saw nobody there. She stepped outside and looked around, but still saw nothing. Out in the darkness, amongst the trees, she heard a rustling.

"Who's there?" she whispered.

There was no reply, but the rustling continued.

"Jupiter, is that you?"

She heard a laugh.

"What are you doing out there?"

A small pebble sailed through the darkness, pinging off of her dwelling. Another sailed after it, hitting Timber in the arm.

"If I have to come out there and find you, you're gonna get it."

This was met by mischievous laughter, so Timber grabbed her

shoes from inside the dwelling, quickly put them on, and ran out into the darkness to find Jupiter. She listened closely, following every rustle and twitch. When it got silent, she stopped and waited. She heard footsteps and started walking towards the sound, as best she could. There was silence again, followed by a rock sailing past her head.

"Jupiter," she said, "that wasn't funny!"

"It wasn't supposed to be," said a hushed voice that most definitely didn't belong to Jupiter.

Before she could respond, City Marlow erupted from the darkness and tackled Timber to the ground. They struggled in the dirt and the leaves, rolling around, punching and clawing at each other. Breaking free from the struggle, Timber managed to get back to her feet, only for City to charge back into her; instead of falling to the ground, his momentum pushed her straight back into the trunk of a large pine tree. With Timber stunned, City threw a couple of wild punches, but, on account of the darkness, he couldn't aim his swings very well.

The first punch landed flush on the side of Timber's head, stinging her ear. The second punch, however, missed the mark completely and City inadvertently punched the tree trunk, breaking his hand. While City was bent over, wailing in pain, that dark seed began to sprout its charcoal branches around Timber's heart. Charging forward, she tackled City into the dirt and sat on his chest, punching him in the face as hard as she could. City managed to throw her off, but Timber, unrelenting, simply jumped back on, punching and clawing as that primal rage coursed though her blood.

City was reduced to holding his arms over his face in self-defense, no longer fighting back as Timber continued her assault. On the ground, beside City's head, Timber spotted the large rock he had thrown at her. Without hesitation, Timber picked up the rock and, feeling the charcoal branches squeezing her heart, brought it down on City's head, like a hammer, over and over, until his arms fell to the side and his skull was cracked open.

Out in the distance somewhere, Timber heard the rusty orange pickup truck roar to life, the sound of its primitive engine jarring her from her trance. She listened to the sound of the tires crunching over pebbles as it headed off onto that long, dirt road into the Outside. When the truck was gone and silence once again filled the air, Timber looked down at her hands, slick with blood, realizing what she had just done. Standing up from City's lifeless body, she walked from out of the trees, looking around to make sure nobody was wandering about.

Taking hold of City's ankles, Timber dragged him from the forest, back into the main grounds of the Divinity, his blood spilling in the dirt as they went. With all the strength she had, Timber pulled City through Marlow Square, past the Sustenance Cradle, moving quickly until she reached the Sustenance Dwelling. Dragging him inside, she pulled him through the short hallway, past the pantry and cupboards, until he was lying in sawdust beside the heavy wooden table. Leaving the lights off, she sat down next to City and contemplated what to do next.

She decided it would be best to drag him into the freezer and tell Luna what happened in the morning. She didn't know for sure if Luna would be mad at her or if she would get into trouble for killing City, but she couldn't imagine any other options. She gripped the large metal handle and opened the freezer door, the cold air stimulating her senses as it rolled out. She set a brick in front of the door to hold it open, then grabbed City's ankles and began pulling him in. Because it was still dark in the Sustenance Dwelling, Timber hadn't noticed City's body brushed against the brick that held the door open until it was too late and the freezer door had closed shut.

Timber sat in the back of the freezer, hugging her knees and trying to stay warm. She had already exhausted herself by screaming and kicking on the door, hoping against hope that it might open. But, just as Luna warned her on her first day in the Sustenance Dwelling, the freezer door didn't open from the inside. Timber was stuck. She wondered how long it would take her to die in there and if she would freeze to death or suffocate. She cried into the bend of her arm when she thought about dying alone in that freezer. She wondered if Luna would carve her body and stuff her pieces into the barbecue pits. She wondered if anybody would miss her, if Jupiter and Charlotte would ever know what happened.

And then she heard sounds coming from outside the freezer—then voices and footsteps. The freezer door opened and a flood of light poured in. As her eyes adjusted, she was able to make out the image of Three Marlow standing in the doorway, with a dead Outsider hanging limp over his shoulder.

"Boys," he said, staring at City, then Timber, "come take a look at this."

One Marlow and Two Marlow stepped beside him, each of them carrying dead Outsiders.

"Well," Three Marlow said, "you gonna come out?"

Timber gingerly stood up, her joints stiff from the cold, and walked out of the freezer.

"How long have you been in there?" Three Marlow asked.

"I dunno."

"What happened to him?"

"I killed him."

"Why?"

"He attacked me."

Daddy Marlow's Boys laid the three dead Outsiders in the freezer next to City Marlow, before stepping out and closing the door.

"Does Luna know about this?" Three Marlow asked.

"Not yet."

"Why were you hiding in the freezer?"

"I got trapped," Timber said. "It was an accident."

"Maybe we should stick you back in there," Three Marlow said. "Teach you a lesson."

"I didn't mean to kill him," Timber said, "but he attacked me."

"So, if I attack you now," Three Marlow said, "does that mean you will kill me?"

"What's going on in here?"

Timber and Daddy Marlow's Boys all turned to see Luna had arrived in the Sustenance Dwelling. She didn't look pleased to have it so crowded.

"We were making a delivery," Three Marlow said, "when we found your helper trapped in the freezer. Seems she took it upon herself to make a Sustenance Sacrifice."

"Timber, what are they talking about?"

"He's in the freezer," Three Marlow said. "You can look for yourself."

Luna walked past all of them and pulled open the freezer door, staring down at the four dead bodies.

"We delivered the Outsiders," Three Marlow said. "She killed that one herself."

Luna closed the freezer and looked at Timber.

"Is this true?"

Timber nodded.

"Good," she said. "Well done."

Timber and Daddy Marlow's Boys all looked at Luna, confused.

"He tried to run away," Luna said. "Timber told me so herself. I told her if Daddy Marlow's Boys didn't bring him back, then she should do it."

"If he tried to run away," Three Marlow said, "we would have caught him."

"Daddy Marlow will find it awfully interesting that a youngling girl had to do your job for you." She paused, looking at all three of them in the eyes. "Unless, of course, you don't think he needs to know about it."

Daddy Marlow's Boys were silent, with One and Two Marlow looking to their brother for a response.

"I don't see why he needs to be bothered," Three Marlow said.

"I agree," Luna said. "Now why don't you boys go on your way.

Timber and I have a lot of work to do."

Daddy Marlow's Boys turned around and left the Sustenance Dwelling, leaving Timber and Luna alone.

"You all right, youngling?"

"Yeah."

"Good," she said. "You can tell me all about what *really* happened later, after we get these bodies carved up."

chapter**thirteen**

Inside the Outside

I t was the middle of the day and, having finished all the prepa-
rations for the second distribution of Sustenance Portions,
Luna let Timber take a break. So she went to her dwelling, where
she found Charlotte relaxing in her rocking chair. Taking a seat on
the floor between her legs, Timber rested her head back against
her very large and very pregnant belly, her arms hanging over her
knees like a scarecrow. Oakland and Syracuse Marlow were out of
the dwelling, playing with a group of younglings, giving Timber
and Charlotte some rare alone time.

"Timber," Charlotte said, her voice like honey, "have you been
approached by any men?"

Timber said nothing.

"I mean, you know," Charlotte went on, "to try and make a
youngling?"

Timber remained silent, her eyes closed, hoping Charlotte
would assume she was asleep.

"I don't mean to embarrass you," she said. "It's just you're a woman now and I want to make sure you're prepared to begin your primary obligation to the Divinity."

Timber continued her silence.

"I had about as many years as you when I began having young-lings," Charlotte said. "Maybe a little younger, but I started bleeding when I was younger, too. It really is a joyful experience, Timber, truly wonderful."

More silence.

"I mean, it's not always the same," she said. "Some men are better at it than others. I couldn't tell you why, either. Sometimes it's the size of their thing, I guess. But, there's certainly been men who I've gone back to *many* times, simply because I enjoyed it. And if I made a youngling out of it, then it was all the better."

Timber shifted her weight, but stayed silent.

"If you're lucky," she said, "you'll do it with Daddy Marlow some-day. He really is the best. Of all the men, Daddy Marlow makes it the most wonderful."

Timber remained silent.

"*Timber*," Charlotte said, raising her voice, "would you please say *something?*"

Timber tilted her head back, the stubbles of her scalp scraping against Charlotte's belly, and said, "I've got to get back to the Suste-nance Dwelling."

"Not yet, you don't," Charlotte said. "I want to talk about this. Have you been approached by any men?"

"I don't think so."

"Have *you* approached any men?" she asked. "I find they like it when you do that."

"No."

"Perhaps you should consider it."

Timber didn't respond.

"It's because of that Outsider, isn't it?"

Timber shook her head, no, but it was too late. Charlotte was crying, her face in her hands, and Timber understood it was this she was getting at all along. Charlotte feared that Timber was on the cusp of womanhood, ready to open her legs at the first beckoning interest, only to have her untapped libido extinguished by the foul hand of an Outsider.

"Timber, I know he hurt you," she said through her tears, "but please believe me when I tell you it's not always like that. Maybe sometimes, but, that's only—"

Charlotte stopped speaking mid-sentence, her words replaced by an urgent moaning, which quickly turned into a guttural scream. A sudden wetness spread down Timber's neck and shoulders, running down her back. Turning around to face Charlotte, Timber saw her cupping the underside of her swollen belly with both hands. A small puddle had gathered on the floor, beneath the rocking chair.

With gritted teeth, Charlotte said, "I think this youngling's ready to make its way out of my belly."

"What do I do?"

"Go down to the Nursery Dwelling and get Carpet Marlow," she said. "Tell her I'm fixing to push one out."

Charlotte leaned over in pain, moaning. Timber stopped at the door and turned around, wanting to make sure Charlotte was okay.

"*Now!*" Charlotte yelled.

Timber did as she was told, bursting out of the dwelling and running as fast as she could across the compound, weaving through younglings and elders, until she reached the Nursery Dwelling. There were about a dozen or so infant younglings inside, some of them crying for attention, while others were being soothed to sleep. Timber lingered for a moment, wrinkling her nose at the hybrid odor of shit and milk, until she spotted Carpet, who was busy patrolling around with her arms crossed. After Timber told her that Charlotte was fixing to push out a youngling, Carpet barked out a few orders to the women under her watch, letting them know how things were to run in her absence.

When Timber arrived back at her dwelling with Carpet, they found Charlotte lying on the floor, weeping. Carpet kneeled down beside her, stroking her bald head and speaking soft words that Timber couldn't quite make out. Charlotte nodded in response and Carpet gently helped her up to her feet. She snapped her fingers at Timber, calling her over to Charlotte's side, so she could help walk her down to Marlow Stream.

Upon arriving at Marlow Stream, Carpet helped Charlotte out of her dress, before leading her into the water, crouching down with her into the gentle current. Timber was sitting on the bank, hugging her knees, letting her feet dangle in the cool stream, when she heard Jupiter calling out for her. Turning around, she saw him running her way.

"What do you need?" Carpet asked.

"Just looking for Timber."

"Quit making so much noise, then," Carpet said.

Jupiter squatted down beside Timber, resting his chin on her shoulder.

"They're going tonight," he whispered.

"What are you talking about?"

"Daddy Marlow's Boys."

"Tonight?" she said.

"It's okay if you changed your mind."

Timber hesitated.

"What do we have to do?" she asked.

"We need to talk about it in private."

Timber took a deep breath, letting it all sink in, before stepping ankle deep in the water, to get Charlotte's attention.

"Just stay where you are," Carpet snapped. "What do you need?"

"Charlotte?"

"Yes, Timber?" she replied with as much honey as she could muster.

"Would it be okay if I went back to the dwelling?"

"Of course."

She managed to lift her head, smiling at Timber, reassuring her that she would be okay. Timber smiled back, before running off with Jupiter, entirely unaware that this was the last time she would ever see her Charlotte again.

Timber and Jupiter sat on the floor, beside the window, neither wanting to hint at just how scared they were. He told her about a wooden trunk in the back of the rusty orange pickup truck, which stretched all the way across the bed, lengthwise, beneath the rear window. This would be her escape pod.

"There should be enough room to fit you inside," Jupiter said, "but we gotta empty it."

"What's in it?"

"Tools and such," he said. "When we empty it, we can't let Daddy Marlow's Boys find out."

"What do we do?"

"Well, I'll have to hide the tools somewhere good and, when we get back, I'll have to get them back in. Of course, if I get caught doing any of this—"

"You won't get caught."

"But if I do," he said, pausing to find the right words, "it won't be good."

"Do they use their tools in the Outside?"

"Sometimes."

"What happens if they need them, then?"

"Let's just hope they don't."

This was the only moment where Timber genuinely considered backing out of the whole thing. It just seemed that there were too many unknown variables, too many blind spots. It didn't feel like there was anything calculated about the risk they were taking, they were simply hoping not to get caught. But, Timber chose not to let on about her second thoughts and Jupiter went on talking about the plan.

"There's one other thing," he said. "Once you're inside that trunk, you've gotta *stay* inside."

"For how long?"

"The whole time," he said. "I'll leave the lid unlocked so you can peek out some, but that's all."

"What's the point of me going then?"

"I'd rather you stayed, myself."

"Well, don't count on it," she said.

"That's fine," he said, "just don't go getting any big ideas about getting out while you're out there."

After their secret meeting, Timber and Jupiter went on with the rest of their day like normal, if only to keep up appearances. Timber went back to the Sustenance Dwelling, while Jupiter spent the day with Daddy Marlow's Boys, assisting them with some minor maintenance on their rusty orange pickup truck. When nightfall came, Daddy Marlow's Boys went to the Main Dwelling—which was their new home since Daddy Marlow had moved into the New Dwelling—and sat around a candle-lit table, playing cards until it was time to head out. Jupiter stayed behind, despite an invitation to join them. It was while they were playing cards that he snuck away to the rusty orange pickup and, under the cloak of night, removed the tools from the wooden trunk.

When he was done, Jupiter casually walked to Timber's dwelling, where she was telling stories to Oakland and Syracuse. He didn't tell her it was time to go, nor did he have to. Tucking the two younglings into bed, Timber kissed them each on the forehead, before leaving with Jupiter. When they reached the rusty orange pickup truck, Jupiter surveyed the scene to make sure nobody else was around, before climbing into the back. He waved for Timber to join him and she quickly jumped in, sounding a metallic squeak. They each looked around, making sure the squeak hadn't alerted any unwanted attention.

A simple hook latch laced through the eye of a loop bolt was what locked the lid of the wooden trunk in place. Jupiter unhooked the latch and lifted the lid for Timber. She hesitated a moment, looking down into the dark, empty space inside.

"Well," he whispered, "what're you waiting for?"

Timber climbed into the trunk and found that, while there was enough room for her to fit, she couldn't comfortably stretch out. She curled on her side in the fetal position, her body pressed at various angles against the cool wood, which felt damp against her skin. Jupiter closed the lid and Timber heard the scratch of the hook as he locked her in.

She felt the weight of the truck lift as Jupiter jumped out, his footsteps grinding in the dirt, quieter and quieter, until the only remaining sound was the pounding of her heart. The air inside was dense, making it difficult for her to breathe. As a wave of anxiety washed over her, Timber squeezed her eyes shut, concealing herself in her own darkness, doing her best to forget about her wooden cell.

Timber wasn't sure how much time had passed—it could have been an hour, it could have been a week—before Jupiter returned to the truck with Daddy Marlow's Boys. She heard both doors open, followed by the level of the truck dropping as they got in, slamming the doors behind them, the sound of which echoed inside of the wooden trunk. Timber then heard the sound of Jupiter jumping into the back of the truck, followed by the sound of his knuckles lightly rapping the lid of her escape pod.

The rusty orange pick up truck roared to life, engine growling like a jungle cat. Locked in the darkness, Timber could hear the sound of dirt and pebbles crunching beneath the truck's tires as it moved forward, gradually picking up speed. They hit a bump in the road, lifting the truck off its shocks and sending Timber airborne into the lid of the trunk. She inadvertently yelped when her head connected with the wood.

As they picked up even more speed, Timber heard Jupiter unlatch the hook, lifting the lid just enough for his eyes to appear through the sliver of moonlight that snuck in. He asked if Timber was okay, but his words were barely audible as the rush of wind flying past the truck diluted the volume of his voice.

"We're out of the Divinity now," he said. "We're driving down the mountain."

"Can I look?"

"Hold on."

Jupiter lifted his head, making sure Daddy Marlow's Boys were all facing forward, which they were. He gave her the okay and, with her fingertips, Timber pushed the lid slightly open, increasing her view to about three inches, all the way across. Sitting up on her elbow, she pressed her face up against the mouth of the wooden trunk, watching as the moonlit road stretched out behind them, further and further, until it was swallowed up by the vanishing point like a black hole.

Soon the road changed from dirt and rocks to cracked asphalt and yellow divider lines and the large rush of trees thinned out, until only the large jagged wall of the mountain could be seen. On the driver's side there was no mountain at all, just the pale light of the midnight sky. Soon enough, the cracks in the asphalt became less and less, and the strips of paint became more pronounced. Other cars started driving past, opposite the rusty orange pickup truck, their brake lights glowing like demon eyes in the darkness. All of the mountains eventually melted away, replaced instead by large industrial structures—buildings and warehouses, tract homes and shopping centers.

Soon the road got smaller and the truck slowed down. While they had spent the entirety of their journey moving in a seemingly straight line, they now engaged in hard turns, leading them into a suburban neighborhood where the homes were bigger and more impressive than any dwelling Timber had ever seen. Slowing down to a crawl, the truck entered through an open gate, which led onto the driveway of a large house. The tall walls in front of the yard concealed the house from the rest of the houses, isolating it like an island in the middle of suburbia. Parking beside a yellow Cadillac in the driveway, the rusty orange pickup truck's engine rumbled into silence. The roaring rush of wind, which had become the soundtrack of Timber's journey, was replaced by an unfamiliar silence. Jupiter dropped his face down, meeting Timber's eyes with his own.

"We're here."

Daddy Marlow's Boys exited the truck, lifting its level in relief of their massive bodies. Jupiter pressed the lid of the wooden trunk down, before leaping from the bed of the truck, leaving Timber alone. She waited a few moments, listening for the footsteps to get quieter, before pressing her fingers to the lid of the trunk and pushing it up just enough to see out. She watched Jupiter and Daddy Marlow's Boys walk up to the porch and knock on the door. A few moments later the porch light turned on and the door opened with Billy D. Luscious waiting on the other side. He shook hands with Daddy Marlow's Boys and gave Jupiter a long hug, before welcoming them all inside.

No sooner had the front door closed, did Timber lift the lid of the wooden trunk just enough to slink out onto the rusty steel bed. Her bent knees and elbows were stiff, having been set in place for at least an hour. Lying on her back and staring up at the same moon she had come to believe existed only above the Divinity, Timber gingerly worked out her joints. Rolling over onto her knees, she peeked over the edge of the truck, insuring that nobody had come outside, before jumping onto the concrete driveway, and taking a few steps over until she was standing on Luscious' large front lawn.

While Timber knew from grass, she had never seen a lawn before—all healthy and manicured, sharp and precise. She kneeled down and ran her hand over the cool wetness of the blades, a million tiny feet dancing on her palm. She walked back and forth across the pristine blades, listening with a buoyant fascination as they crunched beneath her feet.

Suddenly wary of getting caught, Timber went back to the truck, though she wasn't ready to get back in the wooden trunk yet. She walked around to the passenger side window, cupping her hands around her eyes and pressing her face to the glass, close enough to taste the dirt. She looked at the steering wheel and the gear stick, the worn seats and the thick pieces of foam pushing through the upholstery. On the floor, beside the passenger door, was a magazine. Timber had never seen a magazine before, nor, for that matter, had she ever seen a photograph.

On the exposed pages of the magazine was a woman, completely naked, lying on a bed; one leg falling off, while the other bent up towards the ceiling, her toes pressing into the mattress. Her hair was long and straight, spreading across a pillow and falling off the bed like a blond waterfall. Timber had always assumed that a woman with grown hair like that would be a hideous sight, but, in that moment, she found the opposite to be true. As she gazed at all the most intimate parts of the woman's body, she found herself with a pleasant ache in her loins.

A car approached from behind, entering the long driveway from the open gate, its headlights flashing off the rearview mirror into Timber's eyes. Seized with panic, Timber leapt into the bed of the truck, laying flat on her back, as the car pulled up in front of the house. Timber heard the doors open, followed by two sets of footsteps walking towards the house. As the footsteps moved past the rusty orange pickup truck, a man peered over and looked down at Timber, who was lying on her back.

"Give my regards to the stars," he said, smiling.

Once they were past, Timber lifted herself up enough to get a better view. The man who spoke was wearing bright red cowboy boots, with heavy heels that clicked on the pavement as he walked up the steps to the front porch. Luscious opened the door, welcoming both men with a handshake and letting them inside. A few minutes later, the front door opened again and Three Marlow stepped outside, heading for the truck. Timber slinked over the side and onto the concrete driveway; lying flat on her back, she quickly shuffled herself beneath the bed of the truck.

She was staring at Three Marlow's shoes as she listened to him open up the wooden trunk, cursing to himself when he found it empty. Growling under his breath, he kicked the side of the truck, inadvertently sprinkling dirt and debris onto Timber's face, stinging her eyes and tickling her nose. As he walked away, back towards the house, Timber let out a sneeze, stopping Three Marlow in his tracks.

Methodically, cautiously even, he walked back to the truck. Timber's heart raced as she stared at his shoes, which weren't any more than a foot or two away from her face. Her nose tickled again and she could feel another sneeze building up. She held it as long as she could, staring at Three Marlow's shoes. When she couldn't hold the sneeze any longer, Timber brought her T-shirt up to her face and sneezed into it, muffling the sound as best she could.

Despite her efforts, the sound caught Three Marlow's attention. He crouched down, about to look beneath the truck, when the front door opened and Two Marlow was standing in the frame.

"What's taking so long?"

"Our tools aren't here."

"Let's worry about that later."

Three Marlow walked back to the house, joining the others inside. Timber had no idea what to do. There was little doubt, in her estimation, that Daddy Marlow's Boys would examine the wooden trunk one more time before they left, which meant she couldn't be in it when they did. So, she remained hidden beneath the bed of the truck.

A sudden commotion came from inside of the house, followed by yelling and banging. The front door opened and the man in the red cowboy boots crawled out onto the porch, his shirt torn and his face bloody. Three Marlow pounced on him, putting the defenseless man on his back and punching him in the face until his fists were slick with blood.

While Three Marlow beat the life out of him, One and Two Marlow worked together to carry the lifeless body of his partner to the rusty orange pickup truck, tossing him in the back. Luscious stood in the doorway with Jupiter, watching the violent scene play itself out. As Three Marlow gathered up the man in the red cowboy boots, who was almost definitely dead, Luscious gave Jupiter a hug, followed by a long kiss on the lips.

Three Marlow dragged the limp body of the dead man towards the truck, the thick heels of his red cowboy boots pulling through the grass before reaching the concrete of the driveway. Luscious stepped back into the house, closing the door and turning off the porch light. Jupiter ran to the truck to help Three Marlow lift the dead man into the bed. Like his partner before him, the dead man's limp body landed hard on the steel bed, echoing a loud bang beneath. Timber watched as all the feet in her view quickly disappeared into the truck.

The engine roared to life, its sound jarring in Timber's ears, causing her to scream; muffled by steel and horsepower, her screams went unheard. Her body tensed as the tires began to roll and the greasy bottom of the truck passed over her. She rolled over onto her knees, kneeling as she and Jupiter locked their eyes on one another, until the rusty orange pickup truck disappeared through the open gate and into the darkness, leaving Timber stranded in the Outside.

chapter**fourteen**

Of Angels and Orange Juice

Timber awoke the next morning in a strange bed, surrounded by bright colors and framed pictures; the bed was very comfortable, unlike any in the Divinity, and she was covered beneath three layers of the softest, most welcoming blankets she had ever felt. A large painting on the wall caught her eye; there was nothing particularly unique about it, beyond the fact that she had never seen one before. On a small bedside table, lit candles and burning incense delighted her olfactory senses.

She was still sleepy enough that she didn't immediately question where she was, yet she felt more rested than she had in a very long time. Sitting beside her on the edge of the bed, legs crossed, with a steaming cup of tea in his hands, was Luscious. Timber panicked at the sight of him, quickly sitting up from her covers. Despite her sudden jerk of movement, Luscious managed to balance his tea without spilling a drop. He rested his hand on Timber's leg and smiled.

"Relax, love," he said, soothingly. "You're fine. Everything's fine."

The night before, when the rusty orange pickup truck was out of sight and Timber realized there was no reasonable way for her to get back to the Divinity, she panicked and began running after it. As she ran, wanting nothing more than for Daddy Marlow's Boys to see her, she was also coming to terms with the reality that, once she got back to the Divinity, she would have to face some severe consequences. In those moments, however, when she was chasing the rusty orange pickup truck, desperately wanting nothing more than to go home, Timber wasn't worried about consequences. Reaching the end of the street, she stopped running. The rusty orange pickup truck was out of sight. Gone. Leaning over with her hands pressed to her thighs, catching her breath, Timber was coming to the realization that, no matter what happened next, her life would never be the same again.

She walked back to Luscious' house, not knowing where else to go, and sat down on the large lawn in front of the porch where the man in the red cowboy boots had been beaten to death. She imagined how the following morning the naked bodies of he and his partner would be waiting in the large freezer for her and Luna— only Timber wouldn't be there. Luna would go to her dwelling, mad as all hell, looking to find out why she hadn't shown up. Charlotte wouldn't know where she was either and soon they would both be concerned. Charlotte would panic, before going straight to Daddy Marlow. Luna would go to the Sustenance Dwelling and get back to work. Daddy Marlow would go to Jupiter and ask what he knew. Timber wondered what would happen after that.

Would he keep their secret to himself for fear of his own wellbeing or would he tell Daddy Marlow what they had done? Would they send Daddy Marlow's Boys to look for her or would she be left to waste away in the Outside? Would she never see Charlotte or Luna again? Hugging her knees to her chest, scared and alone, a stranger in a strange land, Timber cried herself to sleep there on the grass. And, in the middle of the night, that's exactly where Luscious found her.

Luscious had an associate of sorts who owned a towing company. Whenever he had an abandoned car in need of picking up—which was more often than you might imagine—he called his associate. Luscious, in turn, paid his associate a handsome fee to both tow away the abandoned car and not ask any questions. That night, when he came by to pick up the car abandoned by the man in the red cowboy boots, Luscious' associate let him know that there was a young girl with a shaved head asleep on his lawn. Without missing a beat, Luscious lied and told him the bald girl was a friend of Joseph Goldstein; this was good enough for his associate, as Luscious knew it would be.

Luscious carried Timber into the house, removing her shoes and laying her in his bed, covering her up. He left her alone, checking up on her periodically, not wanting her to wake without anybody to explain where she was. And when she finally did awake, jerking up in the bed, nearly causing him to spill his tea, his only concern in the whole world was making her feel at home.

"Do you remember me?"

She nodded.

"Your name is Timber, right?"

She nodded, again.

"Do you remember my name?"

She did remember his name, as well as the shiny rings he wore, the diamond encrusted chain that hung from his neck and the platinum watch that adorned his wrist. This morning, however, he wore none of his shiny accessories. Neither did he wear a fancy suit with alligator shoes. Instead he wore a black kimono with wide sleeves that hung like a grandfather's jowls. His legs were bare, but for a pair of slippers on his feet. He had no hair on his legs—or his hands or his arms for that matter. There was a silk handkerchief wrapped around his head, tied just above his meticulously plucked eyebrows.

"Luscious," she said quietly, practically under her breath.

"Right," he said, pleased. "Does Daddy Marlow know you're here?"

All at once, Timber felt the weight of her situation and began to cry.

"Please don't cry, love," Luscious said, caressing her bald head. "It breaks my heart."

Setting his tea down, Luscious scooted closer to Timber and gently set her head on his lap, cradling her and humming something pleasant in her ear. Gradually, her tears dried and she began to relax. It was then that Ginger Falls arrived.

Ginger was eighteen years old at the time Timber first laid eyes on her. She had auburn hair, which was pulled back into a lazy ponytail. Her skin was fair, almost white as a sheet of paper in the glare of morning that came in through the window. Her cheeks were dotted with freckles and her face, without makeup, was the prettiest Timber had ever seen. While she and Luscious were friends, their primary relationship was as employer and employee. Ginger served as the centerpiece of Luscious' very own porn website.

Ginger wasn't scheduled to do anything for the website that particular day, but Luscious called her up in the morning and asked her to come over anyway. Though she didn't know the extent to which Luscious was involved with the Divinity—and, for her own safety, he hoped she would never find out—she *did* know that the Divinity existed and Luscious, by way of Joseph Goldstein, was acquainted with them. She understood that they were a cult up in the mountains and that everybody there shaved their head and body. She *didn't* know, however, that they were cannibals. And, more importantly, she didn't know that, aside from chaperoning Outsiders up to get laid, Luscious helped provide bodies for them to eat.

Luscious asked Ginger to come over that morning in part because he didn't know exactly what to do with Timber, but also because he thought it might be less threatening to have a female there when she woke up. Ginger, for her part, was more than happy to help, as she had always been curious to meet someone from the Divinity. She had become resigned to the idea that this would never happen, so when Luscious called her that morning to tell her that a girl from the Divinity had turned up on his lawn, Ginger felt like she had just won some sort of surreal lottery.

"Come on in," Luscious said to Ginger, as she lingered in the doorway.

Ginger walked up to the bed, mesmerized by Timber, looking her over like an exotic zoo animal.

"Timber, this is my friend, Ginger," Luscious said. "Ginger, this is Timber."

Ginger reached out to shake Timber's hand, but Timber didn't immediately reciprocate.

"It's okay, love," Luscious said. "She's my friend. She won't hurt you."

When Timber at last took Ginger's hand in her own, there was an almost audible chemistry in the air. Without knowing exactly why, Timber was suddenly—*thankfully*—at ease.

"It's nice to meet you, Timber," Ginger said, a little too slowly.

"She's not retarded," Luscious said. "She's just not from around here."

"I'm sorry," Ginger said quickly.

Timber smiled her appreciation, though she had no idea what Ginger was apologizing for.

"You hungry?" Luscious asked Timber. "Thirsty, maybe? You want some orange juice?"

Timber shrugged.

"Oh, orange juice is good," Ginger said, "if you've never had it, I mean."

After a brief hesitation, Timber said, "I've never had it."

"Let me go get you some," Luscious said. "I'll be right back."

In his absence, Timber and Ginger were left alone together. Ginger sat down at the foot of the bed, crossing her legs.

"How did you get here?" Ginger asked.

"Jupiter," Timber answered.

"The planet?"

"My friend."

"You're friends with Jupiter?"

"Yes," Timber said.

So far as Ginger could tell, the people in the Divinity might've been a little crazier than she thought. A minute or so later, Luscious returned with Timber's orange juice.

"Here you go, love," he said, handing her the glass.

Timber, hesitant at first, took the glass to her lips and lightly sipped, letting the juice linger on her tongue. Its thick, pulpy resolution was interesting, but not unpleasant; whatever hint of bitterness threatened to offend her taste buds was overwhelmed by the sweetness. Timber brought the glass back to her lips, slowly tilting it to the ceiling until the orange juice was all gone.

"Didn't I tell you it was good?" Ginger said.

Timber smiled, wiping her mouth with the back of her hand.

"Would you like some more?" Luscious asked.

"Of course she would," Ginger said.

This made Timber smile even bigger.

Luscious left and quickly returned with another glass of orange juice, this time bigger and filled to the brim. As she did before, Timber brought the glass to her lips and downed it in a matter of seconds.

"Are you hungry?" Ginger asked.

Timber nodded, yes.

Looking to Luscious, Ginger said, "Let's go get some breakfast at Kathy's Diner."

"I don't know if it's such a good idea to take her out," he said.

"What's the big deal?" Ginger asked.

Luscious honestly didn't know. He just didn't want to make anything more complicated than it had to be. Soon enough he realized that no real harm could come from taking Timber outside, so he asked Ginger to help get her cleaned up. She took Timber into the bathroom, where she saw her reflection in the mirror. While Timber had seen her reflection before in her dwelling window and in Marlow Stream, she had never before seen herself in a mirror before. Running her fingers over the stubbles of her bald head, she smiled at the novelty of seeing her face so clearly.

Next she was caught up with the novelty of seeing running water come from the sink. She put her hands under it and let the warm water run though her fingers. With Timber's permission, Ginger wet a small towel and cleaned the dirt from Timber's face, much of which she'd accumulated during her trek into the Outside. Timber loved the gentle touch of the towel on her face, but, more than that, she loved that it was Ginger doing the touching. Ginger, for her part, wasn't yet aware that Timber was attracted to her, though she was entirely aware that being so intimate with Timber—who was still a virtual stranger—felt both pleasant and natural.

When Ginger took Timber back to the bedroom, Luscious had some clean clothes waiting for her; though they were slightly big for her, they would do the job. He stepped out long enough for Ginger to help Timber change, though, for the most part, Timber was able to dress herself. After Luscious got himself dressed into a polyester tracksuit, he led Timber and Ginger out to the front yard where his yellow Cadillac awaited them. Timber had never sat inside of a car before, let alone a luxury vehicle such as Luscious'. Luscious settled her in the back seat, putting her seatbelt on. When he started the ignition, Timber was startled by the radio.

"Do you guys have music where you come from?" Ginger asked.

"We sing songs sometimes," Timber said.

"Do they sound like this?"

"No."

"I'm sure they don't," Luscious chuckled.

Driving through the residential suburb of Rancho Cucamonga, the city Luscious called home, he made his way into downtown, where Timber marveled at the many cars. She looked on with wonder at a man walking his dog, which she assumed was a coyote or a wolf. She saw a woman with an infant youngling strapped to her chest. She saw her first elderly person ever, a woman with white hair and hanging skin.

They soon arrived at Kathy's Diner, which was tucked away in the corner of a small shopping center, where its large sign with its big red letters was visible from the 210 freeway. Because Timber was illiterate, the letters in the sign were just a bunch of abstract shapes. Inside, Luscious, Timber and Ginger sat in a booth, where Kathy, the diner's namesake and proprietor, greeted them, handing them each a laminated menu.

"That's a nice haircut you've got there," she told Timber.

Timber looked at her, confused.

"If I had the nerve, I'd do the same thing myself," she said, smiling. "And how are you doing, Luscious?"

"I'm doing just fine."

"And you, Ginger," she said, "looking pretty, as always. How are you, dear?"

"Good, thank you."

"So, who is this lovely young lady, anyhow?"

"This is my friend, Timber," Luscious said. "She's visiting from out of town."

"It's nice to meet you, darling," Kathy said. "You on a break from school or something?"

Timber looked to Luscious for an answer.

"Her parents are old friends of mine," he said. "They're going through sort of a thing right now, so, you know, they asked if I wouldn't mind looking after her for a bit."

Kathy seemed genuinely moved by the lie.

"Well, let me get your orders."

"We'll take two short stacks with sausage and eggs. Over easy for me, scrambled for Timber."

"I reckon you'll be getting the usual?" Kathy asked Ginger.

"*Huevos a la Mexicana*," Ginger said, smiling.

"I don't even know why I bring you a menu anymore," Kathy said. "How about drinks?"

"I'll have a coffee, black and strong," Luscious said. "For Timber, bring out the biggest glass of orange juice you have in this joint."

"And I'll just have some water with a lemon slice, please," Ginger added.

"All right," Kathy said, scribbling it all down, "I'll get this order right in for you."

After Kathy was gone, Luscious decided it was time to address Timber's situation.

"So," he said, as gently as he could, "I can't help but wonder how you got down here."

"Jupiter," Timber said.

"Oh," Luscious said, "I guess that makes sense."

"It does?" Ginger asked.

"Jupiter is a friend of mine from the Divinity," he told Ginger.

"So we're not talking about the planet?"

"No," Luscious laughed, "not the planet."

"By friend," Ginger said, "I take it you mean he's a...*friend*?"

"Sort of," Luscious said. "It's complicated."

"I'm sure it is," she said.

"So if you came down with Jupiter," Luscious asked, "how did you get left behind?"

"Daddy Marlow's Boys didn't know I was in the truck."

"I see," Luscious said, "so Luscious snuck you out."

"Who's Daddy Marlow?" Ginger asked.

"He's the leader," Luscious said. To Timber, he said, "Daddy Marlow's Boys probably don't know you're here then, huh?"

Timber shook her head, no.

"We'll need to get you home at some point," he said, "but I won't be hearing from Daddy Marlow's Boys for at least a few days. Until then, you'll just have to hang out with us, I guess."

Timber smiled.

Kathy brought out their breakfast on large plates. Timber had never eaten anything like what she was looking at; only the sausage patty looked remotely like the food she ate in the Divinity. She picked it up with her hand, unaffected by its hot temperature, and tentatively brought it to her mouth. Though nobody at the table that day knew it, pork is purported to be the closest approximation to human flesh with regards to flavor and texture. This might help explain why Timber took such an immediate liking to it; that and the sausage patty was packed with exciting flavors, on account of the spices and seasoning. Within three bites the sausage patty was all gone.

"Well done," Luscious said. "Should we order you another?"

Timber nodded her head, as she drank down half her orange juice.

She watched Luscious spread a small scoop of butter across his pancakes, before pouring the syrup, lifting each one to make sure they all got efficiently covered. Timber picked up her butter knife to do the same, but, despite her expert hands, found the task somewhat awkward; Ginger helped her out, before pouring the syrup for her. Having already been pleasantly surprised with the orange juice and the sausage, Timber was looking forward to trying the pancakes, which didn't disappoint, especially since there were no sweets in the Divinity. Timber quickly adjusted to eating with a fork and knife by watching how Luscious and Ginger ate, mimicking their mechanics. She couldn't even remember eating the eggs, but they were gone too, with everything else.

Kathy came by to drop off the check and was delighted by Timber's empty plate.

"My, my," she said, "that's some appetite, Miss Timber."

Timber smiled.

"I only wish I could eat like that and still have a cute little shape like yours," she said, picking up their plates. "Must be nice."

Without looking at the check, Luscious left a fifty-dollar bill for Kathy.

"I sure hope I get to see you again, before you go home, Miss Timber."

"Okay," Timber said, smiling.

"Okay it is, then."

All told, Timber spent three days with Luscious in the Outside. During her three days, Timber grew comfortable enough to speak casually with him, engaging in pleasant conversations and even telling him about her role in the Divinity working in the Sustenance Dwelling. Luscious was grateful that she shared this story when Ginger wasn't visiting. He let Timber know that Ginger didn't know everything about the Divinity and it was important they keep it that way.

"Certain people wouldn't like it if she found out too much," he said. "They might want to hurt her if she did."

"Hurt her?" Timber said. "How bad?"

"Really bad," he said.

Luscious also warned that, should she meet any other Outsiders, she shouldn't talk about the Divinity at all.

"Why not?"

"People out here don't know about the Divinity."

"Really?" she said. "Then why do people in the Outside hate us?"

"Nobody out here hates you guys," he said. "I'm one of the only people who knows you exist."

"And Ginger," Timber said.

"Yes, Ginger knows, too," Luscious said. "And she doesn't hate you, does she?"

Timber smiled.

"I guess not," she said.

On the first day, Luscious took Timber to her first movie. He bought her popcorn, licorice and a soda, loading it in her lap as they sat down in the theater. He explained to her, before the movie began, that what they were about to watch was make-believe; none of it happened for real and all the people she was going to see were simply pretending. Despite his preface, Timber found herself hopelessly captivated by the larger than life images on the screen. She chomped on her popcorn, nervously watching as the hero battled his foes. Her heart raced when he was captured and placed into an inescapable situation that would surely spell doom. She cheered out loud, spilling her drink, when he overcame his final obstacle, defeating the enemy. And when it was over, the credits having rolled and the lights back on, she asked Luscious if they could watch it again. So they did.

On the second day, Luscious and Ginger had to work on the website. Timber watched as Ginger did her make up in the bathroom and got dressed into a sexy outfit for the photo shoot. In the beginning of their partnership, Luscious hired a photographer to do the photo shoots, until he figured out that the quality of the pictures didn't seem to make much of a difference to the subscribers of *Introducing Ginger Falls*; so he started taking the pictures himself. Timber found the whole process fascinating, especially when she got to see the pictures uploaded on Luscious' computer. Later that night, they all sat in front of the TV, watching cartoons and old movies. Luscious ordered out for pizza and made root beer floats, both of which Timber loved.

On the third day, when Daddy Marlow's Boys pulled up in front of the house, Timber was curled up on the couch, her head on Luscious' lap. Ginger wasn't there. Luscious and Timber were in the living room, across from the front window, which framed the rusty orange pickup truck as it rolled to a stop in the driveway. Timber watched Daddy Marlow's Boys march in their familiar lockstep through the manicured lawn and up onto the porch.

As Luscious stood up to open the door, Timber grabbed him by the arm.

"They're going to punish me," she whispered.

With Daddy Marlow's Boys knocking on the door, Luscious held Timber's face in his hands, kissing her on the forehead.

"Everything will be fine," he said.

The knocks grew louder and Luscious made a face that expressed his helplessness to do anything but send Timber back into the mountains.

"It was a pleasure having you here, love."

Timber said nothing, holding back her tears as Luscious opened the door.

chapterfifteen

The Sacrifice
of Jupiter Marlow

I t was ruined. All of it.

Charlotte was dead. Having lost too much blood during her final labor, she was unable to survive the birth of her youngling; while her dead body lay limp in the water, Carpet Marlow held the newborn youngling in her arms, the gentle push of Marlow Stream passing through her quivering knees, taking with it the final crimson remains of Charlotte's life force. Timber hardly had a moment to grieve Charlotte's passing, before learning about the impending fate of Jupiter.

After spending the previous three days consulting the stars, Jupiter approached Daddy Marlow in the New Dwelling and told him everything, hoping to earn himself some level of mercy by being forthright. Jupiter had been placed in the Sacrifice Dwelling just before Daddy Marlow's Boys left to retrieve Timber in the Outside. So far as anybody was aware, Jupiter had nominated himself for a Sustenance Sacrifice. Timber herself would eventually be thrown into a prison dwelling, but not before Daddy Marlow dealt with her personally.

For the three days that Timber was gone, nobody was more concerned for her safety than Luna. She feared for Timber's life when she went missing without a trace. But, upon learning that she had been in the Outside and would be immediately retrieved, Luna feared even more for the wellbeing of her young apprentice. She knew better than anybody the wrath of Daddy Marlow; she had spent most of her life cleaning up after him. Time after time, Luna had taken the remains of her brother's anger, laid them across her heavy wooden table and turned them into sustenance, laundering the bloody remnants through the collective belly of the Divinity.

Luna stood outside, near the long dirt road that led out of the compound, arms crossed, waiting. She was there when the rusty orange pickup truck rolled in, all three of Daddy Marlow's Boys in the cab with Timber squeezed between them. Timber's demeanor was admirably stoic, holding a posture of strength, defying the tears that streaked down her face. Beyond the tears and the stoic demeanor, Luna noticed one very important detail—Daddy Marlow's Boys had neglected to blindfold her. Luna knew that any hope Timber had of surviving beyond the next few days rested on whether or not she took advantage of her unshielded eyes, applying her uncanny power of memory to retaining the secret route that connected the Divinity to the Outside.

Luna wasn't the only audience to Timber's return. There were many Divinity members out and about, tending to their chores and routines. They all watched as Daddy Marlow walked to the rusty orange pickup truck, yanking Timber out and throwing her to the ground. They watched him slap her across the face, hard enough to shoot blood from her mouth. They watched Luna run to her, stopping only when Daddy Marlow stepped in her way. They watched her attempt to push past him, only to back off when he lifted his hand, threatening to strike her down as well.

Timber lay flat on her belly, dragging handfuls of dirt into her fists, her blood turning black in the dirt.

"Don't you dare harm her," Luna told Daddy Marlow.

He didn't appreciate having his authority challenged, especially not in front of his people.

"Luna," he said, "your ignorance in this matter is both painful and embarrassing. Your efforts are best exercised in the Sustenance Dwelling, where you belong. This youngling has forsaken my goodwill and, therefore, must be dealt with appropriately."

Luna took a step forward, not yet willing to give up on rescuing Timber right then and there. But, thinking better of it, she stopped herself and walked back to the Sustenance Dwelling.

Daddy Marlow grabbed Timber by both wrists in one of his giant hands, dragging her along the ground, her heels plowing the dirt in protest, through Marlow Square and past Sustenance Cradle, past the Learning Tree and past the Main Dwelling, all the way to the New Dwelling. He dragged her through the small entryway, up the staircase, carelessly bouncing her off each step of his furious ascent. He dragged her down the hallway, past the wooden banister and into his bedroom.

On his bed, naked, was Bella Marlow. She was half asleep when they entered, her hands between her thighs, lying in the fetal position. Though groggy, she managed to sit up as Daddy Marlow entered, dragging Timber behind him.

"Leave."

Bella gazed at him, confused.

"*Now!*"

Bella jumped out of the bed, hastily grabbing her clothes from the floor and running out of the bedroom, past Timber and Daddy Marlow, shutting the door behind her. Daddy Marlow threw Timber onto the bed, but she immediately jumped off, attempting to run past him. Daddy Marlow grabbed her by the arm and punched her in the belly. Timber crumbled to the ground, curling into herself, desperately trying to catch her breath. He lifted her again, dropping her back onto the bed. This time Timber did not fight back, her body and spirit having been effectively worn down. All she could do was watch as Daddy Marlow removed his clothes, before kneeling beside her on the bed.

Soon thereafter, Timber lay in the corner of a prison dwelling, curled up, sobbing quietly to herself. There was a small window in the door, which provided the only light that entered the dwelling. Timber spent many hours staring out her window for the first day of her imprisonment, hoping to see a familiar face or witness a familiar scene. She saw plenty of both and soon realized that these sights didn't make her punishment easier. Standing guard outside her dwelling during any given hour of the day was always one of Daddy Marlow's Boys.

On the day of Jupiter's sacrifice, Timber lay curled up in the prison dwelling, falling in and out of consciousness. When the Marlow Bell tolled once, she didn't move. When it tolled a second time, she opened her eyes. And when it tolled the third time, she screamed out, pounding her fists on the concrete floor. Three Marlow, who was standing guard at the time, yelled for her to be quiet, banging on the door for emphasis. Timber pulled herself up to her feet and walked over to the door; stretching up on her tiptoes, she looked out the small window.

She saw the parade of Divinity members making their way to Marlow Square, all of them smiling and laughing, delighted to be an audience for yet another Sustenance Sacrifice. Soon, as a consequence of Timber's limited range of vision, the crowd disappeared, leaving only the chatter of their voices as evidence of their presence. Three Marlow looked into the window, locking eyes with Timber.

"Don't go anywhere," he said.

No sooner had Three Marlow backed away from the door, did his two brothers come into view, dragging Jupiter between them, his toes leaving a dual trail in the dirt. His head was slumped forward, concealed in that familiar burlap sack, his chin resting against his chest. Timber screamed out to her best friend, pushing her face against the small window. At the sound of her voice, Jupiter's head lifted from his chest for a moment, before dropping back down. Moments later, he was dragged beyond the window and out of sight. Timber could hear the chatter of the onlookers rising to frenzy, no doubt watching as Jupiter was strapped down to the Sustenance Cradle. The chatter grew louder and louder, pulsing like a collective heartbeat—and then, all at once, it stopped.

With their silence, Timber knew Daddy Marlow had made his appearance. Even isolated in the prison dwelling, Timber heard Daddy Marlow's booming voice carry through the air. She listened intently, following along with his familiar script like a countdown, her heart pounding harder and harder the closer he came to the end. So caught up was she in the trance of Jupiter's inevitable death, Timber hadn't noticed Luna appear in front of the window, until she whispered for her attention.

"Listen up," Luna said. "We ain't got but a minute or two. What they're about to do to that boy out there, I ain't gonna let happen to you."

Timber said nothing.

"Tonight, when it's good and dark, I'm busting you out of here."

"How?"

"Don't you worry about that," she said. "Just be ready to run."

Timber nodded.

"After tonight, you and me can't stay here no more," she said. "I'm gonna get the keys to that ugly, old truck and we're gonna hightail it out of here."

"Where will we go?"

"I dunno," Luna said. "But we can't never come back here. Not ever, you understand?"

Timber nodded.

"You just stay strong for a little while longer," Luna said. "It'll all be over soon enough."

Luna quickly left the prison dwelling and, presumably, joined the crowd of Marlows around the Sustenance Cradle. Timber could faintly hear Daddy Marlow's voice working its way through all his familiar beats and pauses. She couldn't make out his words, but she knew he was finished when his voice went silent, followed by the sickening thud of his ax striking down.

chaptersixteen

The Great Escape

Timber had been lying down beside the door, crying for the loss of Jupiter, when she heard a struggle erupt outside. It was a violent struggle that involved a body slamming into the door, followed by the loud cry of a male voice. As quickly as the struggle started, it stopped—and there was silence. Timber heard the lock outside her prison dwelling being manipulated until the door swung open, revealing Luna on the other side. She was breathing heavily, slouched over with her hands on her thighs; unable to speak, she waved her hand, signaling for Timber to exit.

Two Marlow was on the ground with Luna's cleaver embedded deep into the side of his neck. A pool of blood slowly radiated around his head, forming like a large crimson pancake. Luna planted her foot on his chest and pulled the cleaver free.

"Come on, youngling," Luna whispered. "We've gotta hide this big boy."

Just like they had with so many other dead bodies, Timber and

Luna collaborated to lift Two Marlow, carrying him into the prison dwelling and dropping him onto the floor, his skull sounding a crack as it bounced off the concrete. Stepping back out, Luna closed the door behind them.

"All right," she said, "let's get out of here."

"Going somewhere?"

Luna turned around and found herself face to face with Daddy Marlow. In a flash, his hands were wrapped around her neck, causing her to drop the cleaver to the ground. Daddy Marlow, still holding her by the neck, lifted Luna into the air; she held on to his powerful forearms, kicking her legs as she struggled. While Luna gasped for breath, Timber launched an attack on Daddy Marlow, punching him in the legs and ribs, her fists bouncing off of him like rubber balls against a brick wall.

Realizing there was nothing she could do to Daddy Marlow with her hands, Timber dropped to her knees and began feeling around the cold dirt until she found the cleaver. Standing to her feet, she held the cleaver in both hands like a baseball bat and swung it as hard as she could into the meat of Daddy Marlow's thigh, causing him to scream out in pain as he dropped Luna to the ground. Timber left the cleaver in his leg and checked on Luna. She was already dead.

"You feel brave without your blade?" Daddy Marlow said.

He was standing straight now, holding the cleaver beside his wounded leg, his jeans soaked with blood. Timber began walking backwards, away from Daddy Marlow.

"I asked you a question, youngling," he said, methodically limping towards her.

Timber kept moving, not saying a word.

Despite his injury, Daddy Marlow picked up speed.

"There's nowhere for you to run, youngling," he said. "You'd best accept your fate. Resign yourself to the inevitable."

Timber kept moving.

"You're going to die tonight," he said. "How does that feel?"

Timber kept moving.

"You are a brave one, though," he said. "I'll grant you that. But, bravery is an illusion of the mind. It convinces people to do things they know they can't do. Convinces them to fight battles they know they can't win. That bravery inside you, that fire you're feeling in the pit of your belly right this second, it's played you for a fool. And now you're dead."

Now Daddy Marlow began to run, moving at an impressive pace, despite his injured leg. Timber turned around and began racing for her life, past the Main Dwelling and the New Dwelling, past the Sustenance Cradle and through Marlow Square, past the lingering spirits of every Divinity man and woman who had ever been killed in the name of righteousness, running until her thighs burned with the exertion of her effort. Each time she looked over her shoulder, she saw that Daddy Marlow was never more than two or three long strides from catching up to her.

She ran all the way into the Sustenance Dwelling, past the heavy wooden table, stopping at the back door. As she put her hand on the doorknob, the lights turned on. Turning around, Timber saw Daddy Marlow standing on the other side of the table, smiling, still holding the cleaver.

"I could sink this blade into your back, before you ever made it outside," he said.

Timber slowly let go of the doorknob.

"Good."

Daddy Marlow started moving around the table, sliding his free hand along the surface. Timber did the same, moving away from him. Daddy Marlow smiled the whole time that they rounded the table, clearly enjoying himself. Timber had no doubt that he could have killed her whenever he pleased, but he chose instead to drag it out, giving in to the more sadistic side of his nature, savoring their little game of cat and mouse.

Emboldened by a bravery born of desperation, Timber leapt onto the heavy wooden table and ran across, leaping into Daddy Marlow's chest, catching him off guard. The weight of her momentum carried them both to the floor, causing him to drop the cleaver. Timber quickly got to her feet and, instinctively, ran into the freezer as far as she could go. Realizing there was nowhere left to run, she turned around and saw Daddy Marlow's silhouette in the doorway, cleaver in hand.

"I really have enjoyed this," he said, stepping inside. "I almost regret what must happen next."

With her back against the wall she slid down to the floor, resting her arms on her knees.

"For what it's worth," he said, stepping closer, "I'll carve you myself and eat you raw."

As he stepped ever closer, Timber resigned herself to her fate. She let go of any possibility of winning this battle, any possibility of walking out of that freezer alive. And in that moment she was at peace. Perhaps Daddy Marlow saw it in her eyes or maybe he simply felt it in the air—perhaps it was simply the pain in his gaping thigh. Whatever the reason, he stopped moving for just a moment. In that moment, Timber let her right hand fall from her knee onto the cold floor where, in the poorly lit freezer, her fingers discovered a stray meat hook.

When the moment passed, Daddy Marlow started moving again, dragging his bloody leg until he was standing in front of Timber, completely unaware of the meat hook in her hand. He raised the cleaver up over his head, preparing to strike and, in so doing, left his ribcage unprotected. Before he could bring the cleaver down, Timber swung the meat hook up, piercing it through Daddy Marlow's side. He screamed like a scolded child, dropping the cleaver behind him, clanking it off the concrete. Timber moved past him, retrieving the cleaver, and, before he could turn around, she buried it between his shoulder blades, splitting his long cape of hair.

Daddy Marlow dropped to his knees, his shoulders scrunched up around his neck, still screaming. Stepping on his back for leverage, Timber pulled the cleaver free. Holding it with both hands, she swung it into the side of his neck, shooting a stream of blood against the cold steel wall. Daddy Marlow fell flat on the floor, the meat hook still in his ribs and the cleaver in his neck. Timber turned him onto his back and, once again, pulled the cleaver free. He was still breathing, if only barely, just enough life left in him to hear Timber speak.

"Before this moment, your fear was blind. Now I give it eyes and it sees me."

That dark seed sprouted its charcoal branches around Timber's heart as she raised the cleaver over her head, bringing it down on Daddy Marlow's Adam's apple, over and over again, severing his head from his body. Timber picked up the decapitated head by its long, long hair and exited the freezer, stepping through the steaming puddle of blood, kicking the door closed behind her. Before walking out of the Sustenance Dwelling for the final time, she picked up a box of matches and slipped them in her pocket.

Outside, the Divinity was desolate, everybody quietly tucked away in their dwellings for the night. The moon was the only witness to Timber's short trek from the Sustenance Dwelling to the Learning Tree, where she climbed up the massive trunk with Daddy Marlow's head still in her grip. Straddling that long, horizontal branch, she shimmied along, stopping at the halfway point, her legs dangling on either side. She tied Daddy Marlow's long hair in a knot around the branch, letting his head dangle like a grotesque Christmas ornament.

Climbing down, Timber ran to the Garage Dwelling, gathering up all of the oily rags she could hold and took them to the New Dwelling. Careful not to make too much noise, she opened the front door and stepped inside. If, at that moment, Timber were thinking with her head, she would've just hit the road without looking back. But, as it were, she was thinking with her heart. She wanted to burn that place to the ground.

But for the moonlight floating in through the front window, it was completely dark inside the New Dwelling. With the rags bundled in her arms, Timber walked up the stairs and across the hallway, entering the bedroom where Daddy Marlow had perpetrated his ungodly deed. She dropped the rags on top of the bed and took the matchbox out of her pocket. Pulling out a match, she scratched it against the side of the box, but it didn't light. She dropped the dud to the floor and pulled out another, scratching it against the box, only to be met with the same result. As she was pulling out a third match, she heard the front door open.

A set of heavy footsteps came running upstairs, moving quickly down the hall. Timber, in a blind panic, dropped to the floor and slid under the bed. As she heard the doorknob turning, she realized that the oily rags were in plain sight. There wouldn't be enough time for her to pull them down and get back into her hiding place before the door opened, so she stayed put, her heart pounding against the floor.

"What are you doing?" came a voice from downstairs.

"I'm gonna tell Daddy Marlow," said the voice outside the door.

"You can't just walk in," said the downstairs voice. "Knock first."

Timber heard three polite knocks on the other side of the door. "Well?"

"He must be sleeping."

"Come down, then."

"He'll want to know."

"We'll tell him in the morning," said the downstairs voice. "For now, we need to take care of Luna's body."

"What about Two?"

"He'll turn up," he said. "Come on."

The heavy footsteps slowly receded in the opposite direction, back across the hall and down the stairs. Crawling out from under the bed, she took out another match and struck it against the box—this time it lit. She laid the small flame carefully against the pile of rags and watched them grow into a large bonfire, before leaving the room. Running down the stairs and through the front room, she quickly exited the New Dwelling, which would soon be engulfed in flames.

As she approached the Learning Tree, Timber heard Three Marlow yell out in horror and found him kneeled beneath the severed head of Daddy Marlow, sobbing into his hands. One Marlow was there too, but the fire in the New Dwelling captured his attention; running full speed, he moved right past Timber, oblivious to her presence. The fire had pushed itself out of the bedroom window, its flames curling up the wall, licking the moonlit sky.

Timber waited for Three Marlow to follow after his brother, but he did not. He just stayed on his knees, crying, completely vulnerable. Pulling the cleaver from the back of her pants, she took a step forward and thought briefly about killing him right then and there. She thought about how easy it would have been. But there was something about him kneeling there, crying like a child, all helpless and pitiful, that gave her pause.

From the darkness, a Divinity woman appeared, running past Three Marlow, toward the fire-engulfed New Dwelling. Three Marlow turned his head in the direction of her sprint, just as she ran past Timber. As the piercing scream of a Divinity man filled the air at the discovery of Daddy Marlow's hanging head, Three Marlow saw Timber, covered in blood, cleaver in hand. He slowly stood up, squaring his body towards Timber, like a couple of cowboys in the Old West, Daddy Marlow's head swaying between them.

More screams filled the air as more Divinity members made the gruesome discovery of their slain leader. They came out of their dwellings in droves, packing around the Learning Tree, each trying to claw past the next in order to see if what they heard was true. The bigger the crowd got, the further Timber and Three Marlow were pushed from each other. With the chaos in full swing, the crowd swelled to the point where Timber and Three Marlow could no longer see each other.

Timber turned and walked away, separating herself from the crowd of Marlows, away from their radiating circle of terror and panic, moving through Marlow Square entirely unnoticed, despite being covered in Daddy Marlow's blood. Reaching that lone dirt road, which lead out of the Divinity and into the Outside, Timber stopped to take one last look at the only home she had ever known, before running as hard as she could into the mystery and the darkness.

chapter**seventeen**

Red Letters in the Sky

The road ahead was dark, blending in the distance with the sky above, like one large black abyss. Were it not for the stars overhead and the soft glow of moonlight, Timber would have done just as well to travel with her eyes closed. She had stopped running when the burning fatigue in her muscles became too much to bear. Walking down that long, long road, Timber's body ached, physically and emotionally. Alone in the world, walking through the darkness, unsure of where she was going or if she would ever get there, Timber really and truly began to mourn the losses of those she loved.

The longer Timber walked, the more her grief weighed on her, until her knees buckled and she collapsed in the dirt, dropping Luna's cleaver; she didn't even realize she had been holding the cleaver, until it fell from her hands. Pulling herself into the fetal position, Timber began to cry. The tears rolled ceaselessly down her face, falling into the dirt road, forming tiny craters of sorrow and regret. She coughed and heaved, inhaling dust into the back of her throat. Time and space were nonexistent in that vacuum of darkness and grief. She didn't know quite how long she had spent crying into the dirt before her nose twitched with the smell of smoke.

Standing up and looking into the distance, Timber saw a wall of orange flames growing out from the blaze she had ignited in the heart of the Divinity. And so, with Luna's cleaver in hand, Timber once again began running down that dark road, away from the fire that she knew, despite having given it life, would not take mercy on her.

Timber spent two days traveling down the mountain, sleeping only once during her sojourn. By the middle of the second day, long after the aches and pains in her legs had become an afterthought, the dirt road Timber traveled down turned to gravel and soon to asphalt; dashed yellow lines were painted down the center and there was a regular flow of cars driving on either side. All the while, the large wall of fire remained in the distant background, its smoke billowing into the sky, thick and black.

Were it not for the fire, Timber may have spent the rest of her life on that mountain, trying to find her way down; but as night fell, a truck driver pulled off to the side of the road and opened his door to her. Not knowing enough to question his motives, Timber willingly climbed into the eighteen-wheeler, relieved to be off her feet. If the driver noticed the blood on Timber's clothes, he didn't say anything about it; as for the cleaver, Timber had it tucked in the back of her pants. As soon as she relaxed, her legs hurt even more; she pulled them up to her chest, resting her feet on the edge of the seat. The truck driver, an older man with a thick white mustache, asked Timber where she was headed.

"The Outside," she said, pointing out the window.

This made the truck driver chuckle.

"Lucky for you," he said, "that's exactly where I'm going."

He leaned his body towards Timber, reaching his hand into the glove compartment, and pulled out a granola bar.

"I was saving this for my midnight snack," he said, "but it looks like you need it more than I do."

Timber held the granola bar in her hands, not knowing what to do with it.

"Go ahead and eat it," he said.

Timber brought it to her mouth, biting into the wrapper.

"You need help with that?"

Timber nodded.

The truck driver deftly opened the wrapper, without ever letting go of the steering wheel.

"There you are," he said, handing it back.

After taking one small bite for safety, Timber devoured the granola bar.

"You certainly were hungry," he said. "What's your name?"

"Timber."

"Pleased to meet you, Timber. My name is Dalebert Thomas Bonner the Third. My friends call me Dale," he said, "so I reckon you can too. Where you from, Timber?"

"Back there," she said.

"I know how that goes."

Dale turned on the radio and Timber settled into her seat, quietly listening to the music as she traveled further and further away from the great fire that was once the Divinity of Feminine Reproach.

As they reached the freeway, Timber pressed her face to the window, trying to take in the exciting setting of the Outside as it rushed past her eyes. Out in the distance, not far from the freeway, Timber saw the large, glowing red letters of Kathy's Diner floating in the air.

"There," she said, slapping her palm against the window. "There! There! There!"

"What is it?"

"I want to go there!" she said, pointing at the red letters.

"Kathy's Diner?" he asked. "Is that where you're going?"

"Yes."

"Okay," he said. "I can drop you off if you like, but I can't stick around. I've gotta keep moving, you know?"

Timber pressed her face back to the window, not saying another word. Dale pulled off the freeway and drove along the local streets, eventually reaching the modest little shopping center where Kathy's Diner resided.

"You gonna be all right?" he asked.

Timber nodded.

"Okay," he said, reaching over her lap and opening the door for her. "I certainly enjoyed the pleasure of your company, Timber."

"Thank you," she said.

Hopping out of the truck, Timber turned around and watched Dale drive away. She walked through the parking lot, stopping in front of Kathy's front window. Kathy was inside wiping down the long counter, when she saw Timber standing outside. A look of recognition flashed across her face, as she pulled the ring of keys from her apron to open the door.

She invited Timber to sit on one of the tall stools at the counter and served her a slice of hot apple pie. Timber dug in without reservation. While she ate, Kathy made a phone call and, soon thereafter, there was a knock on the glass door. Timber turned around and saw Luscious standing outside. Kathy opened the door to let him in and Timber met him halfway, throwing her arms around his waist, crying into his shirt. Luscious hugged her back, kissing the top of her bald head, telling her she was okay. Everything was going to be okay.

parttwo

The Outside

chapter**eighteen**

The Inland Empire

T he Inland Empire is an eclectic region of Southern California—encompassing most every city north of San Diego and
east of Los Angeles—with a rich history that nobody knows about,
including most of the people who live there. I didn't know an awful
lot about it myself until I started this project and decided that, in
order to properly tell Timber's story, I needed to learn more about
where she grew up.

San Bernardino is one of the anchor cities of the Inland Empire,
as well as the gateway to the San Bernardino Mountains. It's had
many faces over the last 150 years or so, from farming community
to saloon hangout and eventually to the city that birthed the Hell's
Angels and became one of the foremost manufacturers and suppliers
of crystal meth. It used to be a place of railroad trains and horse-
powered ambulances, acres of orange groves and magnificent brick
buildings. It was a place where children could go to class barefoot in
overalls and grow up to drive Model T automobiles. It was a place

where Hollywood studios used to bring their movies, making it the preview capitol during the first half of the twentieth century, ushering in all the top stars of the time to take a look at their latest films. It was the place where McDonald's first opened its doors, selling fifteen-cent hamburgers. It's a place where grapes were squeezed and wine was had. It's a place where great and devious men laid the seeds of history, where schools were named to honor them and streets named so as not to forget them.

San Bernardino is a place synonymous with the historic Route 66, that long stretch of road that will take you across America and back, which was traveled by gamblers and lounge singers with Vegas in their sights, by hippies and surfers with dreams of the Pacific, by teenagers intoxicated by the innocent danger of the road and by weary travelers looking for a place to sleep. Route 66, as it passes through the Inland Empire, is locally called Foothill Boulevard, a major street that connects the neighboring cities like a candy necklace: San Bernardino, Rialto, Fontana and most notably, as it concerns Timber's story, Rancho Cucamonga. There is no emperor who rules over the Inland Empire, but, if there were, his kingdom would be Rancho Cucamonga.

Rancho Cucamonga is a large community, the crown jewel of the Inland Empire, easily the richest of the surrounding cities and, without question, the most conservative. The high schools are built like universities and Chaffey College, the local two-year institution, was deemed important enough to host a speaking engagement for President Bill Clinton. Even still, despite the overwhelming prosperity of this community built on grapes and wine, Rancho Cucamonga has clear socio-economic divisions with the proverbial line drawn in the sand separating north and south. In the northern half, the houses are big, the schools are clean and everybody has a manicured lawn. In the southern half, the houses seem to shrink, like some alternate universe; the schools exist in outdated buildings and the street corners are less inviting when the sun goes down.

It was in the northern, more prosperous, half of Rancho

Cucamonga where Timber found refuge from the Divinity, where she spent five years salvaging her life with the help of Billy D. Luscious and Ginger Falls. In Timber's happier moments in Rancho Cucamonga, when she was most at peace with her life and the tragic circumstances that informed it, she wouldn't know that Three Marlow was out there lurking, biding his time, waiting for the perfect moment to take it all away.

chapternineteen

In the Beginning

For the first week of Timber's return to the Outside, all the local news media was fixated on the wildfires that had erupted overnight in the San Bernardino Mountains, spilling over into the San Gabriel Mountains that served as the backdrop of Luscious' home. He and Timber spent many hours sitting on his front porch, watching the bright orange flames burning through the mountains, large clouds of smoke filling the sky like an oil spill, helicopters and small airplanes flying back and forth. A light layer of ash and soot coated the Inland Empire for the days that followed. With sirens wailing in the distance, Luscious taught Timber how to play Tic-Tac-Toe on the hood of his yellow Cadillac.

Firefighters from California, Arizona and Utah put forth a collective effort to combat the fires, which had spread from Big Bear all the way to San Jacinto. There were fires in Malibu and San Diego County, likely the work of inspired arsonists. By the end of the week, the California wildfires had become a national story and coverage of them could be seen on most every major network with a satellite in the sky. Timber's first real initiation with television was dominated not by watered down cartoons or benign sitcoms, but by men and women standing in the mountains, surrounded by smoke and fire, discussing the most recent neighborhood to be evacuated or the current number of homes that had burned to the ground.

By the second week, despite the fires still burning, albeit to a lesser degree, the national media had moved on to other news, most of which concerned the lives of celebrities and disgraced politicians. Soon enough, even in Southern California, media coverage of the wildfires died down as the efforts of the firefighters began to pay off. All that was left to do was count the losses and marvel over the skeletal forests of leafless black trees. Stories spread about coyotes and mountain lions with nowhere else to go, roaming through cities and neighborhoods, snatching small dogs right in front of their owners.

Once the fires were snuffed out completely, the evacuees either went back to their homes or began the long, hard process of starting over. The Divinity was burned to the ground, Timber was sure of it, and with that thought she experienced an overwhelming catharsis. Daddy Marlow and Two Marlow were definitely dead. She assumed that One Marlow and Three Marlow were also amongst the dead. And the rusty orange pickup truck, she imagined, was just a shell of black metal.

She was confident that nobody would come looking for her to take her back, as there was nobody left and nowhere to go. Gripped in a vacuum of relief, Timber cried hard and often. Luscious held her throughout, stroking the soft stubble that had begun to grow from her head. He made her hot tea, sweetening it with honey, and they watched movies together, usually old ones, black and whites or Technicolor musicals. *The Wizard of Oz*, *Singing in the Rain* and most anything by Billy Wilder. She curled into his side as they sat on the couch, her arms hugging his waist, her ear against his heart, thinking about how far she had come and wondering how far she had left to go.

Luscious hadn't yet told Joseph Goldstein about Timber's escape from the Divinity and, if he could help it, he hoped he wouldn't have to. Goldstein was the reason Luscious was connected to the Divinity at all. He profited from the Divinity in more ways than one and so Luscious knew he would be a little more than disappointed to find out that it was no more. He wasn't afraid of what Goldstein would say when he found out, so much as what he would do. Either way, Luscious knew he couldn't keep the news away from him forever, but that wouldn't stop him from stalling for as long as possible.

Nonetheless, Luscious knew it was inevitable that Goldstein would find out the Divinity was gone. It was simply a matter of him calling up Luscious with a new assignment, at which point Luscious would have to tell him that the assignment in question couldn't be completed. Goldstein, of course, would want to know why, at which point Luscious would have to come clean. The only thing Luscious didn't know was how long it would be before he got that phone call. Sometimes it would be just a few days between assignments, while other times it could be weeks. There was never any rhyme or reason to it all. All told, Luscious would have a month with Timber before he had to tell Goldstein what was going on—but it would be Luscious who initiated the call, not Goldstein.

During her first month with Luscious, Timber spent much of her time in front of mirrors. Whether standing in the middle of the bathroom or pausing in the hallway, anytime she could contemplate her reflection, she did. Her eyebrows had grown in first, square and thick. Her scalp slowly followed suit and, by the end of her first month, Timber's hair had grown in, short and boyish. One day at a time, the girl she saw in the mirror was changing, slowly becoming someone that she didn't quite recognize.

Ginger began spending more time at Luscious' house after Timber arrived. She was mostly there at Luscious' request, as he figured that a female counterpart would help with Timber's transition into the Outside; but beyond Luscious' request, Ginger simply enjoyed spending time with Timber. As it turned out, it would be with Ginger's help that Timber encountered her first truly confusing conflict with Outsider culture when, while taking a bubble bath, Ginger offered to shave her legs.

Though it wasn't Timber's first bubble bath, she was still getting acquainted with all of Ginger's sweet smelling soaps and shampoos that she kindly donated to Luscious' bathroom. Ginger wasn't there everyday to help Timber with the bath, but when she was around she was happy to hang out and assist in any way necessary. On the day in question, Timber was soaping up her bent leg, balancing it with her wet toes fanned out on the edge of the tub, when Ginger noticed that her hair had noticeably grown in.

It wasn't thick or dark, but it was certainly there, so she offered to show Timber how to shave it off. Up to this point, Timber had assumed that, because people in the Outside were essentially opposite of everything she knew in the Divinity, she would grow all the hair on her body in order to assimilate; so she didn't quite understand why Outsiders chose to shave specific parts of their body, while letting hair grow on others.

"It's just something women do," Ginger said.

"Why?"

"It looks better," she said. "Sexier."

Timber didn't really have a grasp on when or why something was sexy—though she did find Ginger to be very sexy, even if she didn't yet know there was a word for it.

"Do men shave their legs?"

"Not really, no," Ginger said. "I mean, sometimes, I guess. But, traditionally, men don't shave their legs, no."

"Why wouldn't they shave their legs, if it looks better?"

"It doesn't really make *their* legs look better," she said.

"But some men do it?"

"Yes."

"Do *they* think it looks better?"

"Yes, probably."

"Do *you* think it looks better?"

"Depends on the man, I guess."

"So, not all the time?"

"Right."

"But sometimes."

"Yes."

"Does hair sometimes look good on women's legs?"

"No," Ginger said. "Not ever."

"Never?"

"Never ever."

"Why?"

"Having hair is masculine," she said.

"Masculine?"

"That means manly," she said. "You know, traits that are associated primarily with men."

"Does the hair on your *head* make you masculine?"

"No, men and women can both grow hair on their heads," she said. "Though women generally grow their hair longer and men keep their hair cut shorter."

"But I thought having more hair made you masculine," Timber said. "Why would a woman grow her hair long and a man keep his hair short?"

"I guess it doesn't make a whole lot of sense, when you think about it, huh?"

"No," Timber said. "Not really."

"At any rate, let's get to work on those legs, shall we?"

And so they did.

Timber had never known from vanity. In the Divinity everybody simply went on from day to day, going about their business, completely oblivious to how they looked. As she gently ran a pink disposable razor up Timber's leg, Ginger explained that vanity, in general, was about building up your self-esteem from the outside, with the hope that it would eventually work its way to the inside. This meant very little to Timber. What she knew for sure, however, was that she found Ginger very attractive, despite the fact that she looked nothing at all like the women she grew up around in the Divinity.

Despite being a mature fifteen years old when she escaped the Divinity, beginning her life in the Outside—having not only experienced tremendous personal loss, but also knowing what it was to take a life with her own hands—Timber was enamored with cartoons. *Tom and Jerry* was her favorite, mostly because the characters didn't speak; all of their stories were told through action, which made it easier for her to follow. Because she loved *Tom and Jerry* so much, Luscious thought it would be nice to get Timber her very own cat, which she promptly named Tom; for what he imagined were obvious reasons, getting her a pet mouse was not an option. But when Luscious found Timber chasing Tom around the house with a skillet, he decided that it was probably too soon for a pet of any sort. So far as Timber knew, Tom had run away in the middle of the night, never to return.

On the days that Ginger was at the house to do photo shoots or webcam appearances for her website, she enjoyed sitting with Timber and watching cartoons, both before and after her work. At eighteen years old, Ginger had mostly grown out of cartoons, with the exception of anything produced by Disney, which she always loved and never grew out of—in fact, it would be Ginger who eventually showed Timber her first Disney cartoon. But even when they were watching cartoons that Ginger would otherwise find boring, she found that she loved watching them with Timber—or, to be more precise, she loved watching them through Timber's eyes. For that matter, Ginger discovered she enjoyed experiencing many things with Timber for the very same reason.

On any given day during her initial assimilation into the Outside, it would not have been at all uncommon to find Timber, Luscious and Ginger sitting on the couch and watching television together. And when they were done watching TV and it was time to call it a night, Ginger would go home to her lonely apartment, while Luscious tucked Timber into bed, reading to her until she fell asleep.

When they weren't watching cartoons, Luscious spent a lot of time with Timber watching educational programs on public television, such as *Sesame Street* and *Mr. Roger's Neighborhood*, as they helped Timber get acquainted with letters and numbers. Timber's uncanny ability to memorize information, which had already served her many times in her young life, became her most indispensable tool.

Luscious and Ginger were amazed at how quickly Timber managed to pick up the alphabet. When they ate breakfast at Kathy's Diner, which was often, Timber regularly applied what she had learned when looking at the menu, trying very hard to figure out what to order without Luscious or Ginger's assistance. Though she failed often in her preliminary attempts, Luscious and Ginger stood in awe of her rapid improvements. Within a month, Timber was able to read some of the simpler items off the menu and order an entire meal all on her own.

Timber's teeth were a light shade of yellow and her gums were receding, so Luscious made an appointment for her with his dentist. In the mean time, he got Timber into the routine of rinsing her mouth with peroxide and mouthwash, before brushing and flossing. Flossing was Timber's least favorite part of the routine, as it was tedious and made her gums bleed.

When he took her to the dentist, he lied and said she was his niece. He asked the dentist if he could stay with Timber for the entire appointment, as she had never been in a dentist's office before. Timber had her teeth X-rayed, before sitting down for a cleaning that lasted over an hour. She writhed in pain through much of it, while Luscious held her hand, trying to keep her relaxed.

After the cleaning and a brief examination of the X-rays, the dentist determined that, all things considered, Timber's teeth weren't that bad. Amazingly, she had no cavities. This came as a shock to Luscious, who was certain that Timber would have a lifetime of dental issues to deal with. The dentist got Luscious' assurance that he would bring Timber back for another cleaning in six months and twice a year thereafter.

While sitting in front of the television, Timber talked Ginger's ear off about the dentist and how awful it was. Ginger assured her that nobody in the Outside enjoyed going to the dentist, but it was an important part of keeping yourself healthy. Oddly enough, Luscious had attempted to tell her the same thing following her visit, but Timber wasn't terribly amenable to listening. But when Ginger told her, it just sounded better somehow.

Since the night he brought her home from Kathy's Diner, Timber had been wearing clothes from Luscious' wardrobe—mainly sweatpants and T-shirts—and Ginger had brought over some modest outfits of her own for Timber to wear, despite being slightly taller and more physically developed than Timber. Luscious had discarded the clothes Timber had been wearing that night, being that they were filthy and covered in Daddy Marlow's blood. After a few weeks, Ginger decided it was time to take Timber on a proper shopping trip. So one day after breakfast at Kathy's Diner, the three of them headed over to Victoria Gardens, Rancho Cucamonga's state of the art outdoor mall.

While she sat in the corner of a dressing room in Forever 21 watching Timber change, it occurred to Ginger that neither she nor Luscious, she presumed, had asked Timber if she'd ever had a period. So, while Timber tried on a skirt for the first time, showing off her smooth legs, Ginger asked. Confused by the terminology, Timber didn't immediately know what Ginger was asking; of course, it only took a few specific details before she figured it out. Timber confirmed that she had indeed had her first period while still living in the Divinity. Ginger asked Timber if she'd had a period since coming into the Outside. She had not.

Timber had been in the Outside for over a month at this point, so naturally Ginger was concerned that there might be an unforeseen issue for them to contend with. Not wanting to concern Timber right away, Ginger waited until they were done shopping before telling Luscious what she had learned in the dressing room. When they got home, Luscious, as tactfully as he could, asked Timber if she'd had any recent sexual contact before she arrived in the Outside. With a certain hesitation, Timber told him and Ginger what Daddy Marlow had done to her after Daddy Marlow's Boys had taken her back up to the Divinity. Luscious gave Timber a hug, kissing her on the forehead and apologized profusely. He then asked Ginger if she wouldn't mind hanging out with Timber, as he was ready for bed.

And so, while Timber and Ginger watched television together, Luscious went into his bedroom and cried himself to sleep. He was in over his head and he knew it. His grief stemmed not just from the tremendous guilt he felt for allowing Timber to be taken back up into the Divinity in the first place, only to have Daddy Marlow do what he did, but also because it was time to face the inevitable. Luscious needed help and the only person he could ask was Joseph Goldstein.

chapter**twenty**

The Disappeared

To her knowledge, Timber never saw Joseph Goldstein in the Divinity, though he had made more than one trip up there. If she ever *did* see him, she would have had no reason to assume he was anything but another Outsider. There would have been no way for her to know that he was the reason she and her fellow Divinity members always had enough to eat. Goldstein was the smartest and most powerful man Luscious knew, which was why he decided to ask for his help with Timber's situation. He just dreaded telling Goldstein everything else that went along with it, including the fact that the Divinity—which, up to that point, had been pivotal in many of Goldstein's business affairs—no longer existed.

Before Luscious became Goldstein's apprentice, of sorts, he was a seventeen-year-old kid turning tricks for gay men in San Bernardino. Born William Kennedy Jones to a mother whom he never met, Luscious spent his whole life, up until his seventeenth year, growing up in foster care. He ran away from his last foster home—though, being he was so close to turning eighteen, it's doubtful the system went out of its way to find him. After roaming around the streets of San Bernardino for a few weeks, sleeping on benches and eating abandoned leftovers from fast food restaurants, Luscious was charmed into the company of a brutal pimp named Big Daddy Johnson.

Big Daddy Johnson plied his trade on the streets of San Bernardino and, upon meeting Luscious—who, at the time, was going by the name Billy K.J.—invited him to live in his apartment, which wasn't nearly as big or glamorous as the personality he projected. They met at a bar called Leroy Blue's, which wasn't a gay bar per se, but, for those in the know, it was understood to be a relatively safe environment to have gay encounters. Though he was only seventeen, Luscious managed to get inside Leroy Blue's on more than one occasion—and it was on one such occasion that he met Big Daddy Johnson.

So far as Luscious knew, Big Daddy Johnson was his boyfriend, because he invited Luscious to stay with him in his apartment, where he promptly relieved him of his virginity. Luscious knew without question how Big Daddy Johnson earned his living, as he watched him deal with his prostitutes—men and women alike—both on the streets and occasionally at home. Big Daddy Johnson was a large figure, with broad shoulders and heavy knuckles. He knew how to be charming, which Luscious enjoyed, but he also knew how to get his way using brute force. Luscious knew the brutal side of Big Daddy Johnson existed, as he'd seen him use it on more than one of his prostitutes, but he always assumed that he would be spared such treatment.

Luscious found out that he himself was one of Big Daddy Johnson's prostitutes on the night he dropped him off in front of Leroy Blue's and told him to go make him some money. Luscious laughed, clearly under the impression that Big Daddy Johnson was joking. He took Luscious' scrawny arm into his huge hand, squeezing so hard that Luscious would find a bruise there later in the night, and told him that he'd better not make him repeat himself. So, Luscious got out of the car, wandered into the bar and, without a clue of what to do, attempted to turn his first trick.

Inside of a three hour period, to his astonishment, Luscious actually did manage to turn a trick. The john was an older man with white hair and a worn baseball cap. They went across the street to a dirty motel, where Luscious' trick knew the man at the front desk by name and left him a tip after he got his room key. Inside the room, the old man spent twenty minutes talking about his wife who had passed away five years earlier and his two sons who lived back in Utah—where he himself had spent his formative years—before asking Luscious, ever so cordially, to suck his dick.

After they were done, Luscious figured he was free to go home, having successfully earned some money, as per Big Daddy Johnson's request. He called Big Daddy Johnson, but couldn't reach him, so he took a cab. Inside the apartment, he found him sitting on the couch getting a blowjob from a teenage boy whom Luscious had never seen before.

"Who the fuck is *he*?" Luscious asked.

Big Daddy Johnson pulled the teenager's face from his lap and walked over to Luscious, slapping him to the floor with one swing of his massive knuckles. Lifting him to his feet by his collar, Big Daddy Johnson threw Luscious across the room, tumbling him over the couch, where he hit the back of his head on the coffee table, opening a gash that would require nine stitches to close. Reaching into Luscious' pockets, he pulled out the money he'd earned earlier in the night. Disappointed with the amount, he kicked Luscious in the stomach, before leaving with his teenaged friend. Luscious pulled himself up onto the lip of the couch, hugging the cushion like a man lost in a storm.

On the night that would mark the beginning of Luscious' march to freedom from Big Daddy Johnson, a squat man with curly salt and pepper hair walked into Leroy Blue's. At this point, Luscious had been turning tricks for a few months and had become quite popular with the local clientele—primarily closeted men with wives and children at home. The squat man removed his camel silk overcoat, laying it over his lap, before taking a seat beside Luscious at the bar. Without a word spoken, the bartender set a gin and tonic in front of the squat man. Pulling a pack of Pall Malls from his breast pocket, he slipped a cigarette into his mouth, which the bartender promptly lit. He took a long drag, exhaling a plume of smoke from the side of his mouth.

"Billy K.J, right?"

"Do I know you?"

"The name's Joseph Goldstein."

"Nice to meet you."

"I hear you've become quite the attraction."

"How'd you hear that?"

"This sort of information usually makes its way to my doorstep."

"I guess that makes you important."

"I don't know about that," he said, sipping from his gin and tonic. "I own a few bars and motels, including *this* dump and that hole across the street. They're not consequential to my lifestyle, but I like to keep my money busy. The real money is in dirty movies."

"Makes sense."

"Billy, I'm a man who loves people. They fascinate me to no end. As a businessman, it behooves me to understand them. I've come to learn that people love two very simple things—and sex is one of them."

"What's the other?"

"Making their problems disappear."

"I didn't realize that was for sale."

"Sure it is," Goldstein said. "Just figure out what people want, then give them a price. You like dirty movies, Billy?"

Luscious dropped his eyes, feeling suddenly shy.

"Me too," Goldstein said. "I have to admit, I never thought they would be as profitable as they are, but they contribute handsomely to my fortune. How much do you make doing what you do, Billy?"

"Depends, I guess."

"On a good night," Goldstein said, "what can you take home?"

"Six or seven hundred dollars, maybe."

"Not bad," Goldstein said, taking a drag from his cigarette. "How much of that goes in your pocket?"

"What do you mean?"

"You know what I mean."

"I keep enough."

"There's something else I know about people," Goldstein said. "Enough is never enough."

Goldstein pulled a business card from his coat, handing it to Luscious.

"You have a handsome face, Billy. I think you'd look good on film. I produce both straight *and* gay pictures, so if you're ever interested in earning some extra money, you give me a call."

It was a Saturday afternoon while Big Daddy Johnson was gone for the weekend visiting family in St. Louis, that Luscious called Goldstein. As luck would have it, Goldstein was in the middle of setting up a porn shoot in his backyard and told Luscious he was welcome to take part, if he were so inclined. Luscious jumped at the offer and, within an hour, there was a car in front of his apartment ready to take him to Goldstein's Beverly Hills mansion.

Being that he had never been there before, Luscious was surprised to find that there literally were hills in Beverly Hills, with palm trees lining the streets and big, beautiful houses of varying styles and decor. Entering Goldstein's mansion, he saw two large, curving staircases, which met at the second floor like a giant horseshoe. Overhead was a crystal chandelier and on either side of him were a couple of tall, vintage mirrors. The driver took Luscious through the large house, past any number of paintings and glassware, sculptures and antiques, into the backyard where a small film crew was set up around the swimming pool.

Luscious sat with Goldstein at the glass table beside his large pool, where the shoot was taking place. From the pool, you could look out over all of greater Los Angeles, which was a sight to behold when the stars were out and you had a cool drink in your hand. Goldstein allowed Luscious to watch some filming take place for about thirty minutes or so, before encouraging him to get involved. There were any number of legalities Goldstein was bypassing for the time being by throwing Luscious into the mix, but he wasn't immediately concerned with all of that.

"We'll take care of the paper work later, Billy," he said. "You just go and have fun."

Luscious gingerly approached the pool and, with the help of the three men who were waiting for him, began removing his clothes. He vaguely heard the director say action and, before he knew it, one of the men was giving him head. By the end of the afternoon, Luscious had been with all three men in every conceivable position and circumstance. Goldstein gave him a thousand dollars in cash for his performance.

"This is more than the other three made," he said as he walked him to the car, "so don't go comparing notes."

Back at Big Daddy Johnson's apartment, Luscious found an empty jar and dropped his money roll inside, watching it unfurl as it hit the bottom. Screwing the top on, he stuffed the jar in the back of his sock drawer.

Luscious made three more movies with Goldstein before the month was over, steadily filling his money jar. He figured in a few months he would have enough to break away from Big Daddy Johnson. But one day, having returned from Goldstein's mansion, Luscious walked into the bedroom and saw his glass jar sitting empty on top of the dresser. Big Daddy Johnson was sitting on the edge of the bed counting his money.

"That's mine," Luscious said.

Big Daddy Johnson laughed.

"What's yours is mine," he said, "or didn't you know that?"

Overcome with a bravery fueled by anger, Luscious leapt on top of Big Daddy Johnson, scattering the money on the floor. Landing a few punches about his face and neck, Luscious was filled with a false sense of victory—naïvely believing that, in the end, all he ever had to do was stand up for himself. Reality set in when Big Daddy Johnson threw Luscious from the bed, into the dresser. From there, he delivered a brutal beating that was all alligator shoes and gold rings. Luscious lost consciousness before it was over.

He woke up on the floor with a horrible throbbing in his head and stiffness in his jaw. Sitting up against the dresser, he saw that all the money was gone, along with Big Daddy Johnson. When he tried to push himself up, a sharp pain shot through his shoulder. Without using his arm, he managed to stand up in front of the dresser mirror. His eye was swollen shut, rounded over like he was hiding a billiard ball. His right arm hung awkwardly, dislocated at the shoulder. And the sharp pain of his cracked ribs accompanied every breath he took. Not wanting to be home when Big Daddy Johnson got back, Luscious called up Goldstein and asked if he could please pick him up.

He spent the next couple of days in one of Goldstein's guestrooms, his ribs wrapped and his arm in a sling. It wasn't until almost a week had passed, and the two of them were eating breakfast by the pool, that Goldstein addressed Luscious' situation. He asked about his relationship with Big Daddy Johnson, wanting more details than he had given him the night of the beating. Goldstein smoked a Pall Mall, while Luscious spoke. When he finished, Goldstein looked out over the clear blue water of his swimming pool.

"Would you like me to take care of this situation for you?" he asked.

"What do you mean?"

"This Big Daddy Johnson fellow," he said, taking another drag from his cigarette, "would you like it if I handled him for you."

"Handle him?"

"Would you like me to make it so that he can never hurt you again?"

"You can do that?"

"It can be arranged," Goldstein said. "Would you like that?"

Luscious nodded.

"Okay."

A few nights later, Goldstein had his driver take Luscious and himself to Big Daddy Johnson's apartment, parking across the street. They sat in the back of his long black car, the windows cracked, letting the cool night air seep in. Soon enough, Big Daddy Johnson's car drove up the street, turning into the apartment complex. A few moments later, a rusty orange pickup truck drove slowly up the street, turning into the same apartment complex, disappearing into the darkness.

Luscious lived with Goldstein from then on. There was no official offer made by Goldstein, nor a request made by Luscious. He simply never went back since, really, there was no place for him to go back to. Goldstein provided food and spending money for Luscious, while also continuing to pay him to perform in movies from time to time. Billy D. Luscious became his porn name only after Goldstein suggested he needed one. None of the movies Luscious was in were particularly big hits, but they did generate money and Goldstein always made sure he received royalties, a rarity in the porn industry. Even after he stopped making movies—which, as with so many other things around Goldstein, seemed to happen organically, even when they were by design—Luscious held onto his porn moniker.

The whole situation really did seem too good to be true and yet month after month passed by and Goldstein never asked Luscious for anything beyond his friendship and loyalty.

"It's important to have people around you that you can trust," Goldstein said. "I understand people, Billy. I know them well. When I come across good people, I like keeping them around. You're good people."

"Thank you."

"And if one day I should ever ask a favor of you," Goldstein said, "it will most likely be of a sensitive nature, so you can imagine how important trust is to me."

"Of course, Mr. Goldstein."

More than a year would pass after that conversation before Goldstein finally called on Luscious for a favor. He didn't explain the favor, but simply told Luscious he needed his help with an urgent situation.

"I can count on you, right, Billy?"

"Of course, Mr. Goldstein. I'd do anything for you."

"*Anything* is a big word, Billy."

"Anything," Luscious said again.

"Tomorrow, I'm gonna get you started with one of my businesses," Goldstein said. "You'll make some money and learn what it is to be your own boss. Sound good?"

"Yes, Mr. Goldstein."

The following afternoon, Goldstein had one of his drivers take he and Luscious to Leroy Blue's. In front of the bar was a young man, no more than sixteen or seventeen, sitting on the hood of a Volkswagen Beetle. Goldstein let him into the car and the young man quickly dug into his pocket, pulling out a wad of bills, handing them over like they were on fire.

"He's a virgin," Goldstein told Luscious.

The young man blushed, dropping his eyes.

"No need to be embarrassed, kiddo," Goldstein said. "There's a first time for everything."

Luscious gave Goldstein a concerned look.

"And don't *you* worry, either," he said. "The boy wants to fuck a woman, not you."

The rusty orange pickup truck pulled up across the street, with Daddy Marlow's Boys waiting inside. Goldstein patted his driver on the shoulder and told him they would be back in a few hours. He, Luscious and the virgin all got out and walked across the street to the rusty orange pickup truck, where Goldstein introduced everybody.

"This is the client," Goldstein said, referring to virgin.

"Who's *he*?" Three Marlow asked, looking at Luscious.

"My business associate."

Three Marlow grabbed three bandanas from the glove box, before stepping out of the truck. He instructed Goldstein, Luscious and the virgin to get in the back, before blindfolding them.

"What's this all about?" Luscious asked Goldstein.

"It's okay, Billy," Goldstein said. "It's just how they do things."

"Who are *they*?"

"Business associates."

However uneasy he was with all of it, Luscious trusted Goldstein not to put him in harm's way. Blind to the world, he heard the doors shut and the engine roar to life. Within moments, the truck was racing down the road, wind whipping in his face.

"Where're we going?" Luscious asked.

"Just a little business trip," Goldstein said.

They rode for over an hour in the back of the truck, before it slowed down, rolling to a stop. The doors opened and moments later Luscious' blindfold was removed. Looking around, he found himself in the middle of a strange village, populated by crudely built houses and curious looking people with shaved heads. Daddy Marlow's Boys led the three of them into the largest of the houses, where they met with Daddy Marlow. Three Marlow led the virgin out soon thereafter.

Goldstein introduced Luscious to Daddy Marlow, who briefly stood up to shake Luscious' hand. Luscious was struck both by Daddy Marlow's size—he was both tall and impressively muscular—as well as his long hair, which hung nearly to the floor. Before he sat down, Goldstein handed Daddy Marlow the virgin's money; Daddy Marlow handed the money to Two Marlow, who left the room with it. With that settled, Goldstein told Daddy Marlow that Luscious was to be his new liaison to the Outside. Both Luscious and Daddy Marlow were hearing this for the first time.

"Has something happened to Blank?" Daddy Marlow asked.

"Not yet," Goldstein said.

"I see," Daddy Marlow said. "Will you be requiring the assistance of my boys?"

"Yes," he said. "But it's complicated."

"How so?"

"He's going to attack your boys."

"Why would he do that?"

"Because I asked him to."

"My boys will kill him dead."

"That's what I was hoping for."

"You *want* Blank dead?"

"Yes."

"Why not have my boys complete the service in a more straight forward manner?"

"I have my reasons."

"And this is to be his replacement?" he asked, referring to Luscious.

"Yes."

"Do you trust him?"

"I trust him, yes," Goldstein said.

When Three Marlow returned to the Main Dwelling, Daddy Marlow explained that Luscious was to be their new liaison.

"Did something happen to Blank?" Three Marlow asked.

"Not yet," Daddy Marlow said. "Mr. Goldstein has asked him to attack you and your brothers, at which point you are to kill him."

"Shouldn't we kill him first?" Three Marlow asked.

"No," Goldstein said.

"Mr. Goldstein has his reasons," Daddy Marlow said. "And I trust him. This is to be Blank's replacement. I want you to take him to the Sustenance Dwelling. Luna should be preparing the day's final Sustenance Portions."

"Come with me," Three Marlow said.

Luscious looked to Goldstein, who simply nodded his head for him to go. So Luscious got up from the couch and allowed Three

Marlow to lead him out into the Divinity, through Marlow Square, passing by a series of bald heads and curious faces, until they reached the Sustenance Dwelling, which looked somewhat like a small barn from the outside. Inside, however, it was impressively well kept and easily the most modern spot in the Divinity.

They stopped when they reached a heavy wooden table, which was in the middle of what appeared to be a kitchen of sorts. Lying on the table was a naked man. Luscious didn't realize the man was dead until he noticed his head was missing, at which point he tried to turn and run outside. Three Marlow caught him in his arm, like a parent catching an wandering toddler, pulling him back. Three Marlow turned Luscious towards the heavy wooden table; by the strength of his grip, Luscious knew any further escape attempts would be useless.

Behind the heavy wooden table, cleaver in hand, was Luna Marlow.

"Who's he?" she asked.

"He's replacing Blank."

"Did something happen to Blank?"

"Mr. Goldstein wants him dead," he said. "Go on with your work."

With a weak stomach, Luscious watched Luna take hold of the dead man's ankle, holding his leg steady, before swinging her cleaver down on the back of his knee. Every time the cleaver struck down, creating a sickening thud that Luscious hoped he would never hear again, his stomach turned a little more. Of course, once Luna progressed to the next phase, Luscious would miss the time when she was merely chopping off body parts. Using the point of her cleaver, Luna split open a long slit along the back of the dead man's thigh. While that was unpleasant enough to watch, it wasn't until Luna dug her fingers beneath the skin and started pulling it back off the muscle, creating an audible tearing sound, that Luscious finally threw up.

He leaned over, retching onto the sawdust-covered floor, resting his hands on his knees as he tried to compose himself; while a stalactite of saliva hung from his lips, Three Marlow grabbed Luscious by the back of the neck and pulled him up, slinging the rancid stalactite back onto his face. Squeezing Luscious' neck hard enough that he wouldn't dare bend over again, Three Marlow simply, but sternly, said, "Watch."

For the next forty minutes, or so, Luscious watched Luna dismember and carve the headless man on the table. When she finished, Luna wrapped up his parts into burlap, along with various selections of squash and vegetables. As she took the wrapped flesh and vegetables out the back door, Three Marlow led Luscious back to the Main Dwelling.

Daddy Marlow had one of the women retrieve a wet rag for Luscious, which he used to clean the vomit from his face and hands. With his elbows on his knees, Luscious remained bent over, unable to look either Daddy Marlow or Goldstein in the eyes. Goldstein massaged the back of Luscious' neck with one hand, a pleasant paternal gesture that, under most any other circumstance, would have made him feel loved and comforted. Daddy Marlow sat back in his chair, taking in his new liaison, watching as he struggled to come to terms with what he had just been made to witness.

"We exist on the sustenance of human flesh," Daddy Marlow said. "What you have just been allowed to watch is the process by which our sustenance is prepared."

Daddy Marlow paused.

Goldstein continued to massage.

Luscious said nothing.

"Not many have ever seen what you have just seen," Daddy Marlow said. "Not even Mr. Goldstein."

Luscious turned his head just enough to see Goldstein nodding.

"Anybody who has ever seen what you have seen without my permission did not live long enough to spread the word of what their eyes witnessed. This is true for both my people and Outsiders alike. Because you have now seen what we do in such an intimate manner, I have an investment in your life. You live now because I allow it. And when you die, it will be because I made it so. In this way, I have assured your loyalty. I know that nobody else in the Outside knows what you now know. And so, if it should come to my attention that this knowledge has been passed along, I will have no doubt that you were the source. Your death will follow swiftly thereafter, though I can assure you it will not be painless. Have I made myself clear?"

Luscious looked up at Daddy Marlow and nodded his head.

"Now, Mr. Goldstein has told me you are to be my new liaison to the Outside. However, if Mr. Goldstein tells me that he has made a new choice and you are no longer my liaison, then for the reasons I have already outlined, you will not be allowed to live. Is this clear?"

Luscious nodded.

"I've said enough," Daddy Marlow told Goldstein. "My boys will now take you and your companions back into the Outside."

"Thank you," Goldstein said.

Three Marlow led Goldstein and Luscious out to the rusty orange pickup truck, where One and Two Marlow were already waiting with the former virgin blindfolded in the back, a distant smile on his face.

Luscious spent about ten years as the Divinity's liaison to the Outside, before Timber burned it down. In the beginning he was resentful of the position Goldstein put him into for all the obvious reasons. But, in the end, Luscious' loyalty to Goldstein won out— that and Daddy Marlow's threat to kill him if he didn't want the job. As time passed, Luscious found that the job didn't require all that much of him, beyond an ability to desensitize his conscience. As liaison, Luscious had two main responsibilities. First, he coordinated trips for men looking for sex; the price Daddy Marlow asked was far more reasonable than what most of these men would pay for sex in the Outside. Second—and most importantly—Luscious helped make people disappear.

For all the time Luscious spent with and around Goldstein,

he didn't know everything about him. Nobody knew more about him than he wanted them to know—and that's the way Goldstein wanted it. One thing Luscious came to understand, however, was that Goldstein was connected to a criminal element. What sort of criminal element, Luscious never knew, because, until the day he died, Goldstein managed to keep this a secret. Even still, Luscious was involved with a part of Goldstein's criminal element, if only peripherally, because that was what his job description as Divinity liaison entailed.

Goldstein made people disappear. And, so far as Luscious could tell, he earned a lot of money doing it. The way it worked was people would pay Goldstein to get rid of other people whom they didn't want around. Goldstein handled the particulars, which involved setting up a time and place for Daddy Marlow's Boys to kill the target (or targets) and take them back up to the Divinity where they were turned into sustenance. And just like that—*poof!*—they joined the ranks of the disappeared.

The money Goldstein got was his to keep, as the Divinity collected its payment in dead bodies. The people who paid for the service were never present for the disappearing act. They didn't know where the disappeared went or what became of them. This was all part of the arrangement. Luscious' job, where it concerned the disappeared, was to be the contact person. He was a middleman for whatever they thought they were getting—be it a drug score or a rare baseball card. So far as the target understood things, Luscious was always the guy who knew the guy.

Luscious' charm was his main asset. He kept them smiling, kept them laughing, made them feel comfortable and secure. He always met them in remote locations, usually Leroy Blue's, preferably during a late hour. When Daddy Marlow's Boys showed up, they finished the job. It was usually quick and violent and, to his surprise, Luscious eventually grew accustomed to watching it happen. So long as he could report back to Goldstein that the transaction was complete, Luscious' work was done.

As a result of Timber's rebellion, Luscious' work with the Divinity was done for good. Despite the small fortune he earned as liaison, he was as happy as anyone—save for Timber—that the Divinity was gone; while he grew accustomed to his role, he never enjoyed it. And now he was sitting at the glass table beside the pool, wondering what his life would look like after he gave Goldstein the bad news. He was also hoping against hope that Goldstein would help him figure out a solution to Timber's situation. Luscious would find himself both incredibly relieved and profoundly disturbed by Goldstein's response.

chapter**twenty-one**

Goldstein's Solution

T imber loved Luscious' yellow Cadillac. It was big and spacious, with leather seats and tinted windows. She loved leaving the house just for the fun of sitting in the passenger seat, her knees pulled to her chest, her head leaning gently against the window. Driving made Timber happy, which was why Luscious decided to tell her during their drive into Beverly Hills that she would have to start working for Goldstein. Luscious wasn't particularly thrilled with the idea, but the way Goldstein had laid everything out, it was clear that neither he nor Timber had a choice.

They were driving west on the historic Route 66 when Luscious told Timber that Goldstein was going to help them with her pregnancy; Timber had only just learned she was pregnant a few days before, after Ginger gave her a pregnancy test. She didn't understand the ramifications of being a pregnant underage girl who, according to any state or federal records, didn't exist. There would most certainly be some intimidating government agencies with a lot of questions about who she was, how she got pregnant and what she was doing with Luscious—who, so far as public record was concerned, was an Internet pornographer. In any event, Luscious couldn't imagine a scenario that ended without Timber being taken away, which he didn't want to happen. Goldstein, for his part, agreed with Luscious' assessment of the situation. Of course, before he could even allow himself to discuss Timber, Goldstein had to wrap his brain around the realization that the Divinity was gone.

As they merged onto to Interstate 210, Luscious told Timber about his conversation with Goldstein by the pool. He told her about how nervous he was sitting there, watching Goldstein swirl his gin and tonic, listening to the ice clink against the glass. He told her how he just blurted it out, like tearing off a Band-Aid, telling Goldstein that the Divinity had burned to the ground, that Daddy Marlow was dead and that the only survivor was pregnant with his child. He told her about how impressively Goldstein concealed his emotions and the closest he had to a reaction was when the ice cubes stopped clinking.

"You sure it's gone?" Goldstein asked.

"I haven't seen it for myself or anything," Luscious said, "but yeah. Timber came down and there were the big fires up in the mountains. And I haven't heard anything from Daddy Marlow's Boys for weeks."

"You know for sure Daddy Marlow is dead?"

"Yes."

"How do you know for sure?"

"Timber killed him."

"That's a little hard to believe," Goldstein said, "but if it's true then Timber is a pretty impressive young girl."

"She is."

"Be that as it may," Goldstein said, "the Divinity being gone isn't good news."

"I'm sorry."

"You have nothing to apologize for," he said. "You're just the messenger."

Luscious couldn't believe how well Goldstein was taking the news. It was all going so much better than he had imagined.

"Of course, Timber's pregnancy is the main reason you're here," Goldstein said. "Right, Billy?"

"Yes," Luscious said, taking a deep breath.

"I shouldn't be surprised," he said. "You have a big heart."

Luscious smiled.

"If she weren't pregnant, is it safe for me to assume that you would've put off this conversation a little while longer?"

Luscious dropped his eyes, saying nothing.

"I can't blame you," Goldstein said. "But, I don't want you to worry. I have a heart too, you know. I'll help you with Timber."

"Thank you, Mr. Goldstein," Luscious said. "But how?"

"I don't know just yet," he said. "Give me a few days to think about it."

"Okay."

"But, Billy," Goldstein said, "whatever happens, you need to know tough choices will need to be made."

"Like what?"

"I don't know yet," he said. "But a situation like this won't have any easy solutions. I just want you to be prepared."

"Okay."

"You go on now and I'll get in touch with you in a few days."

"Thank you, Mr. Goldstein."

Merging onto Interstate 101, Luscious told Timber about the first part of Goldstein's solution. He told her that Goldstein wanted her to continue carving dead bodies, just as she had done in the Divinity. He wanted it to be as if she never stopped. He wanted her to help make them disappear. Luscious had just a few days prior heard this for himself, sitting again at the glass table beside Goldstein's pool.

"I don't understand," Luscious said.

"I thought you knew," Goldstein said. "She worked with Luna in the Sustenance Dwelling. You remember what that was, don't you?"

Luscious nodded.

"Daddy Marlow told me she was quite useful with a cleaver," Goldstein said. "Really knew her way around a body."

Luscious had discovered Luna's cleaver the night Timber escaped. He was changing her out of her bloody clothes when he saw it sticking out from the back of her pants. When he removed it, Timber panicked, worried he was going to dispose of it. He handed it back to her, understanding that it was important. He hadn't recognized it as the same cleaver he saw Luna use in front of him so many years before. And only when Goldstein told him about Timber's role in the Sustenance Dwelling did it make sense why she had it at all.

"You didn't think she was just sweeping in there, did you, Billy?" Goldstein said. "She was cutting up bodies, carving them like a butcher in a meat market."

Luscious dropped his eyes, shaking his head.

"She may still be a kid," Goldstein said, "but she's seen and done things that most people can't even imagine. And the thing is, Billy, she doesn't think of it as strange. To her, it's perfectly normal. It's all she knows. Business as usual."

"I still don't understand," Luscious said.

"I've got people beating my door down, Billy," Goldstein said, "begging me to take their money."

"What are you asking for, Mr. Goldstein?"

"I want Timber to work for me," he said. "I want her to be my magician."

"She's not a murderer."

"I'm not asking her to kill anyone," Goldstein said. "I just want her to deal with the bodies *after* they've been killed."

"No," Luscious said. "It's not right."

"Not for you, maybe," Goldstein said. "But you didn't grow up like she did. Think of the comfort it would bring her. Imagine, the only place she ever lived is burned down and now she has to live in a brand new world. She may as well be on Mars. Imagine the comfort it would bring her to embrace something she knows."

"It just doesn't feel right," Luscious said.

"Listen, Billy," Goldstein said, "I'm not a tyrant. At the end of the day, she's your responsibility. I can't force you to do anything you don't want to do."

"Thank you, Mr. Goldstein."

"If you don't want her to help me, then we're done talking about it."

"I appreciate that."

"It's just that now I'm in an awkward position."

"What's that?"

"If she's not going to help me, then I have no reason to help her."

"What're you talking about?"

"This whole pregnancy issue is going to get really complicated and fast," Goldstein said. "I had it all figured out, too."

"You did?"

"I worked out the details myself," he said. "I was even going to finance the whole thing."

"What were you gonna do?" Luscious asked.

"Doesn't matter," Goldstein said. "I just want you to do what you think is right. I'm sorry if I put you in an awkward spot."

Goldstein sipped from his gin and tonic.

"How long would you need her?"

"Somewhere between indefinitely and not forever."

"But you're not asking her to kill anyone?"

"Definitely not."

"Where would she work?"

"Those details will get worked out later."

"And you'll make sure she and the baby are safe and secure," Luscious said. "You can make sure that nothing happens, that they won't get taken away?"

"You have my word."

Just then, a tall, muscular man in sunglasses approached the glass table. He had grease-black hair and dark stubble on his chin. He acknowledged Luscious with a slight nod, before turning his attention to Goldstein. His name was Tom and he was a member of Goldstein's staff. He seemed to be something of a bodyguard, though his duties were generally ambiguous. Tom leaned over to speak into Goldstein's ear, whispering something.

"Thank you, Tom," Goldstein said. "I'll be right there."

Tom turned and walked away. Luscious had seen him around for years, but scarcely heard a word from him. That's the way Goldstein liked it.

"Something's come up," Goldstein said. "I have to tend to it. Bring Timber down this weekend so we can talk. I'm having a barbecue. She can swim in the pool if she likes."

Goldstein stood, grunting as he did; his corpulent body wasn't so easy to move around as he got older. He stood beside Luscious for a moment, placing his hand on his shoulder. "You're doing the right thing, Billy," he said, before walking away.

Timber, Luscious, and Goldstein all sat around the glass table beside the swimming pool. Standing behind Goldstein, still as a painting, was Tom; he appeared to being staring straight ahead, into nothingness—but his sunglasses were so dark it was hard to tell where his eyes were aimed. All around them in Goldstein's backyard were people, hundreds of them, enjoying the festivities of the barbecue. There was a world-class chef working the grill and a deejay playing music. People danced in the grass and swam in the pool. Nobody bothered Goldstein while he sat with Timber and Luscious, which was probably by design. A servant briefly appeared, setting a gin and tonic down for Goldstein, a bottle of water for Luscious, and a glass of orange juice for Timber. Timber and Goldstein had been formerly introduced a few minutes prior.

"How has your transition been, Timber?"

"My what?"

"How are you getting along here in the Outside?"

"Oh," she said. "Fine."

"I'm sure it's a lot to get used to."

"Yeah."

"Do you miss the Divinity?"

Timber shrugged.

"I'm sure it's better here," Goldstein said, "but maybe you miss it a little, huh? Parts of it anyway."

"Maybe," Timber said.

"I understand that things got bad for you there," Goldstein said, "before you left. I'm sorry about that. If I had known such things were happening, I would have gotten you out myself."

Timber smiled.

"Despite the bad, I'm sure you still have plenty of good memories," Goldstein said. "It's important to cherish those good memories, to remember the things that we loved, especially after they're gone."

Timber sipped from her orange juice.

"How do you enjoy our food?"

"It's good."

"But, different, right?"

Timber nodded.

"Do you miss eating human flesh?"

Luscious raised his eyes to Goldstein and was about to interrupt, but Timber spoke before he could.

"Yes," she said.

Luscious turned his eyes to Timber, unable to decide if he was shocked or disappointed.

"Would you like it if you could eat human flesh here in the Outside?"

Timber nodded, sipping from her orange juice.

"I can make that happen, you know?"

"You can?"

"The only problem is cannibalism—which is what we call that here—isn't accepted in the Outside," Goldstein said. "But I'm sure Billy already explained that to you."

Timber nodded.

"Since you already know cannibalism is frowned upon here," Goldstein said, "I'm sure you understand that you can't tell anybody, especially after I provide you with some human flesh to eat."

Timber nodded.

"You'll have to keep it a secret," Goldstein said. "Now, in exchange for me helping you, I need you to help me. Did Billy tell you about the job I have for you?"

Timber nodded.

"Good," Goldstein said. "It'll be just like it was in the Sustenance Dwelling. You'll carve up bodies for me."

"Okay."

"Good," Goldstein said. "I've got an assignment coming up that I'll need you for. I'll give Billy the details when it's time."

And that was that. Tom leaned over Goldstein's shoulder and took in whatever his boss whispered into his ear. Goldstein excused himself, but encouraged Luscious and Timber to stay as long they liked. Luscious told him that they had to go. Goldstein apologized for not being able to walk them out to the car, but insisted they let Tom see them out.

Walking just in front of Timber, Tom seemed like a giant, almost as big as Daddy Marlow. And even though she only met him briefly, Timber got the impression that Tom was very close with Goldstein, both personally and professionally, which was why she would find it so strange that, just days after their meeting by the pool, Tom would be laying naked in front of her—cold, dead and waiting to be carved.

chapter**twenty-two**

Suicide Missions

When they were sitting by the pool, Luscious didn't realize that Goldstein was planning on getting rid of Tom. He didn't know what Tom had done wrong, nor would he find out. This was how Goldstein liked it. Luscious wouldn't find out Tom was to be Timber's first disappearing assignment until after he was dead, but he was confident, even before Goldstein confirmed it for him, that Tom was the victim of a suicide mission.

Suicide missions were Goldstein's way of getting rid of people who worked for him without them knowing it. The point was to give them an impossible assignment that would all but assure their death. And if by some miracle they managed to survive, then Goldstein would have a good reason to reevaluate his decision. Luscious had seen this before, as the man he replaced as liaison to the Divinity was made to disappear in this fashion.

His name was Rene Alberto, but Goldstein called him Blank. It was a silly—and not altogether creative—nickname that he had gotten because, even when you had his undivided attention, his expression appeared to be blank. At the time Goldstein met him, he was selling ecstasy to high school kids in East L.A. Blank was tall, with broad shoulders; and though he was tough, he wasn't as tough as he looked. Luscious never met Blank personally and he never even knew he existed in the world at all, until he learned he would be replacing him as liaison to the Divinity. While they never met, Luscious did see Blank in person once, as Daddy Marlow's Boys beat him to death.

At the time, Luscious was sitting in the back of a black car parked across the street from Leroy Blue's, staring out through tinted windows. Goldstein sat with him in the back. A few days earlier, Blank had been given orders to kill one of Daddy Marlow's Boys. Blank probably knew as well as anybody that Daddy Marlow's Boys were essentially indestructible; the knowledge of their seeming indestructibility may very well have emboldened Blank to some degree, as, in his mind, it meant Goldstein had faith in his ability to kill one of the indestructible triplets. He could choose any of the three to kill, Goldstein told him, so long as he left him dead. He explained to Blank that this was a power play, that Daddy Marlow was preparing to make a move—Goldstein's explanations rarely got more detailed than this—and so they needed to strike first to make sure they maintained their leverage. However vague Goldstein's instructions were, he knew in the end that Blank would loyally do his bidding. If he hadn't known this to a certainty, then he never would've employed Blank in the first place.

So Luscious stared out the tinted windows, watching Blank pace back and forth on the sidewalk in front of Leroy Blue's. It was after two in the morning and the bar was closed for the night, so there was nobody around. Blank's fists were empty, barren of any weapon. Goldstein told him that in order to assure that Daddy Marlow didn't retaliate, he must kill one of his boys with his bare hands. This, Goldstein told him, was the only way to insure Daddy Marlow's respect. And so Luscious watched Blank pace back and forth, his heavy hands clinched into fists, pulsing like a couple of beating hearts with knuckles.

Blank stopped pacing when he heard the rusty orange pickup truck turn the corner. He stood with his hands at his sides, frozen like a statue, that same blank look on his face—and still, his fists pulsed in anticipation of the killing he thought he would do. Luscious watched as Daddy Marlow's Boys got out of the truck and approached Blank. After just a few moments of conversation, Blank threw himself into Three Marlow, tackling him to the concrete. He managed to get in a few punches, while One and Two Marlow stood aside. Three Marlow deftly protected his head with his massive arms, while Blank tried his best to beat him up. Neither One nor Two Marlow made a move to help, which Luscious found to be curious, until he saw Three Marlow push Blank up and back, as if completing a bench press.

When Blank charged again at Three Marlow, shoulder first, his face was met with an impeccably timed knee. Blank writhed around on the sidewalk, holding what Luscious assumed was a broken nose. Blood poured from his face, through his fingers, dripping down his forearms. With a nod of his head, Three Marlow signaled for his brothers to get involved. Like a pack of coyotes, they all three pounced on Blank, expertly—however brutally—beating the life out of Goldstein's former employee.

Just as Blank's body went limp there on the sidewalk in front of Leroy Blue's, Luscious was consumed with the idea that Blank's final thoughts were probably of guilt and disappointment for letting Goldstein down. Daddy Marlow's Boys each helped to lift Blank's large frame, heaving it into the back of the rusty orange pickup truck. Within moments, the truck was gone and the street was empty, with scarcely any witnesses to the carnage that had just taken place.

Upon taking over as liaison to the Divinity, Luscious moved to Rancho Cucamonga, a conservative area where the people generally voted Republican and most everyone went to church on Sunday. It wasn't necessarily Luscious' choice, though he wasn't disappointed with the change in scenery. Rancho Cucamonga, Goldstein had decided many years earlier, was a fine halfway point between Beverly Hills and the San Bernardino Mountains, so he purchased a nice house there in the suburban community. It was the house where Blank used to live while serving in the same position that Luscious now had.

No moving trucks were necessary for Luscious, as he would simply inherit everything in the house; he would, of course, dispose of Blank's wardrobe, giving his clothes away to Goodwill. From his new home, Luscious was a simple twenty-minute drive from Leroy Blue's and just over an hour's drive from the Divinity—not that he ever drove *himself*, nor knew how to get there.

While working for Goldstein did come with a steady and generous income, Luscious didn't actually earn a paycheck. He was paid in cash once a month, which he stored away in a small safe in his office. He didn't have much use for the office, as of yet, except for the safe. Since the house was paid for and all of the bills and utilities were taken care of, Luscious was able to live comfortably on money he had saved over the years from doing porn, as well as the modest royalties he still earned from his better selling films. Luscious was only called up to the Divinity a few times a month, whether it was to escort a couple of Outsiders into the mountains or to oversee a disappearance.

And that's how things were for the first year or so. It was all pretty seamless, which was how Goldstein liked it. But eventually, whether it was out of boredom or ambition, Luscious decided that being liaison to the Divinity wasn't enough for him. At his core, Luscious had an independent streak and in order for him to be completely satisfied with his day-to-day life, he needed something of his own. Because porn was an industry he felt he had a keen understanding of—not to mention, it was the only industry he'd enjoyed any sub-stantive success in—it made sense to Luscious that he should start up some sort of porn company.

In any given year, since the passing of the new millennium, adult websites generated between two and three billion dollars worth of revenue, as porn was purchased roughly at the rate of eighty-nine cents per second. Luscious believed that he needed only to tap into a fraction of that revenue to become a very wealthy man—far beyond the money he earned working for Goldstein. And thanks to the meteoric advancements of the Internet, he knew exactly where to start.

So after his first year of being the Divinity's liaison, Luscious met with Goldstein to announce he would be starting a porn website. Luscious was quick to assure Goldstein that he was in no way resigning from his position as liaison; he didn't have a death wish, after all, and he certainly didn't want to end up on Luna Marlow's heavy wooden table. He simply wanted something to call his own.

"That's good," Goldstein said. "You're thinking about your future. It's what young men are supposed to do."

"I didn't want you to think I was doing anything behind your back."

"I appreciate you being upfront," he said. "If you allow it, I'd like to help you."

"I think I have enough money to start it up myself, but thank you."

"I understand," Goldstein said.

"I hope that doesn't upset you."

"You have nothing to apologize for, Billy," he said. "I do want to make sure that, if you truly plan on doing this, you do it right. I want to make sure you're doing your homework and understand what you are getting involved in. For example, do you know what pornography is, as opposed to obscenity?"

"No."

"Do you know where the law stands on the issue of profiting from obscene material?"

"No."

"Excuse me just a moment."

Goldstein got on his cell phone and made a quick call, asking for some files from his office. A few minutes later, Tom appeared by the pool, handing Goldstein a manila folder. Goldstein thanked him, before shooing him off. He pulled some pages from the folder, before putting on his spectacles.

"If this is the business you want to get into, Billy, the first thing you're going to have to do is become familiar with U.S. Code 2257."

Goldstein perused the pages in his hand, until he found what he was looking for.

"It says here, 'Whoever produces any book, magazine, periodical, film, videotape, or other matter which, one, contains one or more visual depictions made after November 1, 1990 of actual sexually explicit conduct and, two, is produced in whole or in part with materials which have been mailed or shipped in interstate or foreign commerce, or is shipped or transported or is intended for shipment or transportation in interstate or foreign commerce, shall create and maintain individually identifiable records pertaining to every performer portrayed in such a visual depiction.'"

Goldstein lifted his eyes from the page.

"Does that make sense?"

"Kind of, I think," Luscious said.

Readjusting his glasses, Goldstein continued reading.

"'Whoever violates this section after having been convicted of a violation punishable under this section shall be imprisoned for any period of years not more than ten years but not less than two years, and fined in accordance with the provisions of this title, or both.'"

Goldstein lifted his eyes.

"How about that, Billy," he said. "That make sense, too?"

Luscious shrugged, staying quiet.

"Is that a no, Billy?"

"I guess."

"And do you know *why* it doesn't make sense?" Goldstein said, setting the papers down on the glass table.

Luscious shook his head, no.

"Because it's legal gibberish that's not meant for you to understand. That's the point. The point beyond that is you're going to be held up to these laws, as well as *others* you won't understand. How are you supposed to keep from breaking a law that you don't understand, Billy?"

Luscious said nothing.

"I'm not trying to scare you out of this idea of yours," Goldstein said. "I just want to protect you. I want to make sure you don't cut any corners or skip any steps. If you're going to go into business for yourself, you've go to take it very seriously."

"I understand," Luscious said.

"Especially if porn is the business you want to get into, then you really need to understand what you're doing, because you're only just barely not breaking the law."

Luscious found Goldstein's concern for the law interesting, if not entirely ironic.

"If you really plan on doing this, then you need to come to peace with the fact that local law enforcers will almost definitely get involved with your affairs—especially in Rancho Cucamonga. There's no way of knowing *when* it will happen or to what degree, but you need to know that district attorneys love tangling themselves in the affairs of pornographers, making their lives more difficult than they need to be."

"Is that legal?" Luscious asked.

"When the time comes," Goldstein said, "it won't really matter."

Luscious' efforts in the Internet porn trade were modest at first, as he opted not to provide original adult content, choosing instead to offer images he had purchased from wholesale retailers. The site itself was free to view and catered to a primarily heterosexual audience; he generated revenue by selling advertising space. After nearly a year of breaking even without earning a profit, Luscious decided it was time for a new game plan. The right idea seemed to be finding a female model and building a website around her, providing original and exclusive content. Luscious had no doubt it could work, but the only real challenge would be finding the right girl.

He began making the rounds at the various strip clubs between the Inland Empire and Los Angeles County, from San Bernardino to City of Industry. Among them: Club 215, Flesh, Déjà Vu, Hawaiian Theater, Miss Kitty's, Synn and The Spearmint Rhino. But it was at Tropical Lei, a club set along one of the seedier stretches of Route 66, where Luscious finally discovered Ginger Falls.

Tropical Lei was one of the more infamous strip clubs in the Inland Empire, primarily for the many police busts it endured for letting its dancers sell sex to the customers. Many of the men who frequented the club knew that they could buy sex for the price of a VIP dance; that dance would buy them roughly twenty minutes in a private room with the dancer of their choice. Regulars knew precisely what sort of things happened in the backrooms, while non-regulars came into the club completely ignorant. Before she met Luscious, this was how Ginger earner her living.

The element of surprise, when properly applied, was as seductive a tool as any in Ginger's repertoire. She would saunter over, shooting her hips from side to side, oozing sex; resting her hands on the mark's thighs, she would lean into him and ask if he wanted to buy a lap dance. If he acted coy, unwilling to immediately agree to a dance, Ginger pushed herself between his legs, pressing her weight against his crotch, and asked again. If his coyness continued, she would run her fingers up his ribs and around his neck, leaning her face into his, make-believing that she wanted to kiss him; pushing her breasts together and adjusting her top, she would almost—but not quite— reveal her nipples. Rare was the man who could resist Ginger at this point, but if he were still being particularly stubborn, she would take his hands and run them up her rock hard stomach, brushing them past her breasts; the mark, at this point, would usually take over, running his hands down her back and over her thighs. When he did this, it meant he was thinking about sex—specifically, with Ginger—and selling it to him was but a formality.

Because Tropical Lei was a hotbed for prostitution, it was usually on the radar of the local authorities. Sometimes they got raided, other times they were infiltrated by undercover cops. Whenever the club got caught red-handed, they simply paid a fine and put a squash on the backroom sex for a little while, letting things cool off before going back to business as usual. As for the girls caught during the raid, they were always cut loose; usually they spent the night in jail, heard from a judge, paid a fine and were back on their feet in another club. While Ginger never did get caught, she did have one of the most improbable close calls in the history of close calls, which ultimately convinced her that she needed to find a new way to make a living.

Ginger, unbeknownst to her at the time, had sidled up next to an undercover cop. She went through her seduction routine and was pleasantly surprised to find he wasn't the usual coy mark she was accustomed to. When she asked if he wanted to buy a dance, he immediately said he wanted to go to the VIP room. Holding his hand, she led him into the VIP room, laying him down on the bed. Straddling his lap, Ginger unbuttoned his shirt, running her fingers up and down his bare chest. Before she unbuttoned his pants and unzipped his fly, the undercover cop was supposed to stop her, he was supposed to tell her that she was under arrest for prostitution, she was supposed to spend the night in jail, hear from a judge, pay a fine and find work at another club—but this was Ginger Falls, the most seductive woman in Tropical Lei and, arguably, the Inland Empire. Few men, even an undercover cop who was supposed to know better, could resist.

Ginger pulled down his fly and held him in her hand. He smiled, putting his hands behind his head and relaxing. She pulled a condom out and rolled it down, before getting on her hands and knees in front of him. He worked hard and fast, his hands on her hips, pulling her into him with every thrust. When his twenty minutes were up, Ginger casually pulled away, letting the undercover cop fall out. She turned to him and asked if he wanted to buy twenty more minutes. When he agreed, Ginger lay down on her back and welcomed him back inside. Within a few minutes he was done.

When Ginger asked for her money, the undercover cop went through his wallet, but found his commanding officer had only given him enough to get into the VIP room, at which point he was supposed to make an arrest or leave. Leaving his wallet behind as collateral, the undercover cop went out to his car and called his commanding officer, confessing what had happened and letting him know that he needed extra money; the commanding officer showed up in an unmarked car, gave him the money and took him back to the station where he was immediately suspended from duty and eventually fired. As a matter of procedure, his mistake with Ginger had to be reported and he was made to testify in front of a judge and jury.

It was a sexy story in the local newspapers, which was how Ginger learned about it. She was paralyzed with the idea of what might have happened had she gotten arrested. It may have been routine for most of the girls there, but Ginger didn't consider herself to be like most of the girls. While she wasn't college educated, she was book smart; she loved to read and had insightful opinions about the world. She didn't mind working in the sex industry, she just didn't want to be a stripper anymore. And when Luscious showed up to Tropical Lei, she knew she had found her way out.

Their website was called *Inside Ginger Falls*, which could—and probably still can—be found at www.GingerFalls.com. Its success rested on a combination of Ginger's ability to transcend her sex appeal through the computer screen and Luscious' well-earned knowledge as an Internet businessman. By submitting *Inside Ginger Falls* to search engines, both locally and abroad, while also submitting it to key adult directories and strategically linking it to other adult websites, Luscious generated enough traffic to successfully make both he and Ginger very financially comfortable.

On the night Goldstein made the call requesting Timber to carve her first body in the Outside, Luscious was in the middle of a late-night photo shoot with Ginger, as they were preparing to put up a new set of pictures on the website. It was about the only time he regretted not having a photographer; instead he had to end the photo session without explanation and ask Ginger to trust that it was important. Of course, he couldn't tell her what it was that was so important.

Explaining to Ginger why he and Timber had to leave proved to be a bit awkward. The awkwardness Luscious felt wasn't so much that he and Timber leaving the house in the middle of the night seemed strange, so much as now there would always be a cloak of deception between them for as long as Timber had to work for Goldstein. And from that moment on, there would always be a quiet tension that only Luscious would be aware of, a fear of what might happen if Ginger ever found out the whole truth of Timber's existence. Ultimately, Luscious wasn't so much worried about what *Ginger* would do if she ever found out, but rather he feared what *Goldstein* would do.

While Ginger probably was curious about what was so urgent for he and Timber to do in the middle of the night, Luscious appreciated that she asked no questions of him. She simply collected her things, gave Timber a hug goodnight, and went back to her apartment. Before they left, Timber went into her bedroom and opened the bottom drawer of her dresser, where she retrieved Luna's cleaver, which was wrapped up in a white T-shirt. She held the cleaver in her lap as she and Luscious drove to Leroy Blue's. For his part, Luscious had actually forgotten that Timber held onto the cleaver upon her arrival to the Outside.

When they arrived at Leroy Blue's, Luscious saw Goldstein's black car parked on the street, which was otherwise empty. Luscious parked behind the black car before getting out and leading Timber inside of Leroy Blue's. It had been well over a month since Luscious had been to Leroy Blue's and as soon as he stepped inside he realized he hadn't missed it. Not the dirty floor nor the wobbly stools, not that unnamable musk that hung in the air nor the dim lights overhead, not the long strip of neon blue light that shone over the bar nor the booth in the back corner where he had given so many blowjobs beneath the table.

Goldstein was sitting at the bar, gin and tonic in hand, waiting. He smiled, greeting them both with a warm hug, before addressing Timber.

"So," Goldstein said, "your assignment is in the kitchen. I provided all the necessary tools for you, though I see you brought one of your own. You already know what you're doing, so I don't want to insult you with simple instructions. Just treat him as if you were in the Sustenance Dwelling. There're plastic bags for you to put the severed parts into. All of the parts that you would normally eat, place into the bags and set them in the freezer. Any left over parts, you can leave on the table. I'll have somebody in here after you to clean up, so don't worry about that. Any questions?"

"Does she have a time limit?" Luscious asked.

"No, not really," Goldstein said. "I'm sure she'll be plenty efficient. As long as you're done before sunrise, I'll be satisfied."

Luscious nodded, unable to speak on account of the queasiness he suddenly felt in his belly.

"Before I forget," Goldstein said, pulling an envelope from inside his jacket, "here's your payment for tonight's work. It's for both of you, of course. I won't tell you how to distribute it, as it's none of my business. I'm sure you'll find it more than fair."

Goldstein handed the envelope to Luscious. Looking inside, he saw a stack of bills at least an inch thick.

"You ready, kiddo?" Goldstein asked Timber.

"Yes."

"Okay," he said. "Luscious will lead you into the kitchen. I won't be sticking around, so good luck and I'll see you two very soon."

With that, Goldstein exited Leroy Blue's, leaving Luscious and Timber as the only living bodies in the joint. Leading her back into the kitchen, Luscious and Timber found the dead body of Tom lying fully clothed on a foldout wooden table. The table was draped with a long plastic sheet, which extended down to the concrete floor. While neither Luscious nor Timber knew who they would find waiting on the table, neither of them expected to see someone they had actually met; let alone someone who worked for Goldstein. But, as soon as he saw him lying there, Luscious knew Tom had been sent on a suicide mission. He didn't know what the supposed mission was, nor did he know exactly how Tom died, but the small, puckered holes in his chest and stomach were a pretty clear indication.

While Timber didn't really know Tom personally, she remembered him from her meeting with Goldstein. Suffice it to say, she was curious as to why he should be the one who Goldstein wanted to make disappear. While Luscious didn't know exactly why Tom had died either—and he knew Goldstein well enough to know he would never find out—he did his best to explain the nature and purpose of Goldstein's suicide missions. As part of the explanation, he told Timber about Rene "Blank" Alberto, sharing how he had watched Daddy Marlow's Boys beat him to death, before taking his body back up to the Divinity in the back of their rusty orange pickup truck.

Luscious' explanation reminded Timber of the Sustenance Sacrifices she you used to watch in the Divinity. She told him about how Daddy Marlow sometimes used them to get rid of people he didn't want around, like Idea Marlow and Jupiter.

"Jupiter?" he said. "Daddy Marlow killed him?"

"Yes," she said.

All at once, Luscious began to cry. He put his hands over his face, unable to compose himself. Setting her cleaver on the table, Timber went over to him.

"I'm okay, love," he said through his sobs. "I just didn't know, is all."

It was then that Timber remembered the kiss she saw Luscious and Jupiter share, before Daddy Marlow's Boys unwittingly abandoned her in the Outside. Timber hugged Luscious' waist, not knowing what to say—not that there was much she could've said. Even though Luscious hadn't held out any hope of seeing Jupiter again, not with the Divinity burning down and all, there was always a part of him that believed he could've survived. And even if he never did see Jupiter again, the thought of him being alive somewhere brought him comfort. So the news that he was not only dead, but had been murdered, was overwhelming for Luscious. Still crying, he excused himself from the kitchen. Timber started to follow him out, but Luscious assured her that he would be okay, that he simply needed some time to himself.

With nothing else to do, Timber went to work. Slipping the apron over her head, she walked around the foldout table, which seemed too flimsy to reasonably handle the weight of the large man—let alone the force it would have to withstand as Timber did her work—running her hands over Tom's cold, dead skin, stopping at his head and looking down at his face. Tom appeared to be looking up at Timber with his distant, unseeing eyes. Raising the cleaver over her head, Timber paused a moment to measure her swing, before bringing the cleaver down with all her might onto Tom's throat.

chaptertwenty-three

The Man in the Red Cowboy Boots

A week removed from Timber's first assignment, Goldstein invited she and Luscious over to his mansion for a barbecue by the pool. There were lots of people there, many of whom Luscious had never met before. Timber loved being in the pool and Luscious loved watching her enjoy herself. On the grill, the commingling aromas of various charbroiled meats could be smelled. When it was time to eat, the partygoers had their pick of steak, chicken or a mysterious meat that smelled and tasted just like pork.

Though the man working the grill—Goldstein's personal chef, as it were—would neither confirm nor deny anybody's guess as to what it was, the mystery meat proved to be quite popular. Timber especially enjoyed it, helping herself to two or three servings. Luscious, for his part, simply ate a salad.

Apart from the opportunity to relax and enjoy themselves, Goldstein wanted to use the barbecue to meet with Luscious and Timber about her pregnancy. The three of them sat around the glass table beside the pool, with Timber working on her second plate. Goldstein was enjoying a gin and tonic, a Pall Mall burning between his fingers.

"Does anybody else know about her?" Goldstein asked.

"Just Ginger."

"Does she know anything else?"

"She knows she's pregnant," Luscious said, "but that's all."

"Good," he said. "Make sure that's all she ever knows."

"Yes, Mr. Goldstein."

"Let's talk first about the particulars," Goldstein said. "As you already know, you're going to need to keep Timber and her child a secret from Uncle Sam."

"For how long?"

"Maybe five years or so," he said. "By then Timber will presumably be of legal age, or close to it, and her child will be of school age. Of course, we first need to deal with the particulars of the actual birth. "

"How will we get her in and out of a hospital without there being a record of it?"

"We don't," Goldstein said. "It'll have to be a homebirth. For that, we'll need a good midwife who knows how to keep her mouth shut."

"How does that happen?" Luscious asked. "And how much will it cost?"

"Listen, Billy," Goldstein said. "A deal's a deal, so I'll be taking care of the particulars. But more than that—beyond our gentlemen's agreement—Timber is family now. So, it will be my pleasure to employ all of the necessary resources at my expense."

"Thank you, Mr. Goldstein."

Ginger took on an active role in Timber's pregnancy, hanging around the house and helping out nearly everyday. It really did start innocently enough, their relationship. Ginger certainly wasn't looking for a girlfriend—she was usually busy enough juggling two or three different women at a time. Plus, she probably thought of Timber as a kid, as she couldn't have been more than fifteen years old to Ginger's eighteen. Despite her relative youth, Ginger had been on her own for nearly five years; she was never particularly forthright with the details of how she ended up on her own at thirteen. She started stripping when she was sixteen, finding most club managers to be suspiciously gullible when she lied about her age. I imagine she saw something of herself inside of Timber, kindred spirits as it were, a couple of girls forced to grow up far too early.

Luscious saw their romance blooming before either of them did. He watched the way they looked at each other, the way they laughed, the way they smiled. The way they sat near each other on the couch when they watched TV, the way Ginger was meticulous about making Timber's tea just the way she liked it, the way she spent hours at a time sitting with her in the kitchen, teaching her how to read. To anyone else, it all would have looked like nothing more than a couple of friends spending time together. But Luscious knew better.

To watch them slowly fall in love, even if neither of them knew it was happening, was bittersweet for Luscious, as he didn't have a partner to call his own. He didn't have a lover to wake up to in the morning, an ear to vent the day's frustrations, a hand to hold when the dark winds howled, a heart to curl into when it was all just too much. While it was absent from his life now, Luscious had once, however briefly, found what might have been love. It had all started one night when, during one of their trips into the Outside, Daddy Marlow's Boys brought a handsome new face with them named Jupiter Marlow.

The first time they met, Jupiter was quiet and shy. It was in the parking lot of Heritage Park in the middle of the night. Luscious was standing with three men beside their car, talking to them about whatever—nothing important. They were under the pretense that Luscious was facilitating a big drug score on their behalf. He stalled them as long as necessary, smiling and laughing as much as possible.

It was part of his technique. Keep them smiling. Make it fun. Goldstein hadn't taught this to him, Luscious figured it out himself. He was proud of this little wrinkle, his only minor contribution.

The rusty orange pick up truck entered the parking lot and Luscious smiled. "Finally," he said to the three men, keeping them at ease. Daddy Marlow's Boys pulled up behind the car. They got out and rounded to the back of the truck, lifting the lid of the wooden trunk. That's when Luscious saw Jupiter for the first time, sitting there in the bed of the truck, all wide-eyed, taking it all in.

"These guys skinheads or something?"

"No," Luscious said, laughing. "It's just a fashion."

Daddy Marlow's Boys pulled a couple of baseball bats and a crowbar from the trunk and headed toward the three men. Luscious took a step back onto the sidewalk. It was dark out and none of the three men noticed the weapons as Daddy Marlow's Boys approached. One of the three men said hello, almost laughing. He was in a good mood. He started saying what a character their pal Luscious was, before Three Marlow silenced him with a baseball bat to the side of his head. The other two men met similar fates, none of them quite knowing what was happening or why. Within a few minutes, they were dead, beaten to death. The blood they left on the asphalt would be all but unnoticeable when the sun came up.

Luscious didn't know what their crime was, what sin they committed to deserve such an ending. That was important, the not knowing. Goldstein taught him that early on. It wasn't his business to know. Knowing made it personal. Just assume they deserve it, Goldstein told him. Just assume they had it coming. Just assume that the world is a better place without them in it. These were all the thoughts that ran through his head as he watched Daddy Marlow's Boys collect the bloody, lifeless bodies of the three men, dumping them in the back of the rusty orange pickup truck. Jupiter, like Luscious, stood by and watched.

"Hello," Luscious said, walking up to him.

Jupiter looked his way, but said nothing.

"My name is Billy D. Luscious."

Jupiter nodded, seemingly more curious than anything else.

"You can call me Luscious," he said. "I've never seen you down here before. This your first time?"

Jupiter nodded, yes.

"I bet it's different than what you're used to."

Three Marlow approached, interrupting.

"Sit with the bodies," he told Jupiter.

Jupiter quickly walked back to the truck.

"So, who's the new guy?" Luscious asked.

None of Daddy Marlow's Boys offered an answer right away, momentarily giving Luscious the impression he had overstepped the boundaries of their working relationship.

"He's training," Three Marlow said.

"What're you training him to do?"

"What we do."

"Sounds reasonable," Luscious said. "Is he special, then?"

"He's young," One Marlow said.

"And strong," Two Marlow said.

"What's his name?"

"He's called Jupiter," Three Marlow said.

"When can I expect to see you guys again?"

"We'll come to your home in two days."

"I've got a couple of first-timers who want to go up," Luscious said. "We can all go up together."

"Daddy Marlow will be made aware," Three Marlow said.

Daddy Marlow's Boys each nodded and walked away without another word.

"Nice meeting you Jupiter!"

Jupiter lifted his head and smiled. Luscious waved and Jupiter began to wave back, but dropped his hand when he got a look from Three Marlow. As Daddy Marlow's Boys got in the cab of the truck, Jupiter looked back to Luscious and waved goodbye.

Two days later, Luscious sat in the back of the rusty orange pickup truck. He was more than ready to remove his blindfold, but knew the appropriate etiquette was to wait and let Daddy Marlow's Boys do it for him. He told his two customers the same thing, insuring they didn't cause any riffs. Luscious was pleasantly surprised when Daddy Marlow personally removed his blindfold, before helping him out of the truck. Together they walked to the Main Dwelling with Luscious' two customers following behind.

Luscious was dressed a little flashier than usual, wearing a yellow business suit, with stocking socks and matching alligator shoes. He didn't know if Jupiter would care for any of it, but he hoped he would. He felt like a teenager, all nervous and giddy inside. He wasn't sure how to go about making his request to Daddy Marlow. He wasn't even sure he liked the idea of calling it a request. Certainly, he wouldn't want Jupiter to feel pressured into doing anything he wasn't comfortable with. It was just that he sensed a connection, something deeper than the general pleasantries that come with meeting somebody for the first time.

Luscious briefly introduced Daddy Marlow to his two customers. He had learned to keep such introductions brief, as Daddy Marlow had no particular interest in mingling with Outsiders any more than was necessary. Still, Daddy Marlow was, in his own way, a gracious host. As they sat in the Main Dwelling, Three Marlow opened the front door and in walked Timber carrying a platter of food. Everything about her seemed chiseled from stone. Three Marlow took the platter from her, setting it on the large, wooden trunk in front of the couch where Luscious sat with his two customers.

"You've brought Sustenance Portions," Daddy Marlow said. "What a pleasant gesture. Gentlemen, please fill your bellies."

Luscious looked at the cubes of cooked meat smoking off the

platter and could barely keep himself from gagging.

"I'm not hungry," Luscious said. "However, my friends are more than welcome to partake at their discretion."

Luscious couldn't stop thinking of Jupiter. He wanted desperately to ask Daddy Marlow where he was and if he could see him. However, he didn't want to speak out of turn and he certainly didn't want to discuss such a thing in front of his customers. As his mind raced, trying to figure out the best way to broach the subject to Daddy Marlow, Luscious noticed Richard, one of his two customers, staring at Timber. She was barely a teenager, thirteen or fourteen from what Luscious could tell; laws of consent didn't apply in the Divinity, however, which was often what lured Outsiders.

"Timber," Daddy Marlow said, "come meet our guests."

Luscious stood and offered his hand.

"It's a pleasure to meet you, Miss Timber," he said. "My name is Luscious."

Timber took his hand and squeezed, surprising him with her strength. It felt to Luscious like she could've broken every bone in his hand if she wanted.

"My, my," he said, "that's quite a grip you've got."

"She's one of my prize younglings," Daddy Marlow said.

"I don't doubt it."

Luscious looked to Richard, raising his eyebrows, letting the gesture ask if she was his choice. Richard nodded, smiling. Luscious introduced the two of them, after which Daddy Marlow excused her, telling her to go back to the Sustenance Dwelling. In her absence, Two Marlow led Richard out to wherever it was they took Outsiders to have sex. Three Marlow left to retrieve Timber, while One Marlow led the other customer out to look around for his own choice, leaving Luscious with Daddy Marlow.

"There's a young man," Luscious said, almost blurting it out. He didn't know exactly where he planned to go with it. He hadn't actually thought about the exact words, hadn't rehearsed anything in his head.

"A young man?"

"Yes," Luscious said, "his name is Jupiter."

Daddy Marlow nodded, but said nothing.

"He's different, I think."

"He's a strong boy," Daddy Marlow said.

"I think he might be gay," Luscious said, his voice rising on the word "gay," as if it were more of a question than a statement.

Daddy Marlow neither spoke nor nodded, but simply looked hard into Luscious' eyes.

"Does this offend you?" Daddy Marlow asked.

"No, no," Luscious said, "not at all."

"Whatever he is," Daddy Marlow said, his volume rising, "he is one of my own."

"I mean no offense," Luscious said.

"What *do* you mean then?" Daddy Marlow said.

"I like him."

And there it was.

Luscious' cheeks warmed and he was almost certain he was blushing.

"Is that so?"

"Yes."

"Is this the purpose of your visit?"

"Yes."

"Well," Daddy Marlow said, "Jupiter is a man and men shall do as they please. It's the way it is and has always been. I shall have him retrieved for your company."

"Thank you."

Luscious and Jupiter spent their first afternoon together in the Outside on a Wednesday. Daddy Marlow's Boys were retrieving supplies from the hardware store for the construction of the New Dwelling. Jupiter was sent down with them. Daddy Marlow told them to leave Jupiter with Luscious and not to pick him up until they were on their way back to the Divinity.

They sat in his living room and talked, drinking beers. Jupiter had never had a beer before. Luscious didn't know how old he was at the time, but figured he was old enough. Jupiter was fascinated with the cool, fizzy nature of the beer. Whether or not he actually enjoyed the flavor, Luscious wasn't sure, but he finished his bottle before the dew could settle on the glass. Jupiter relaxed after that. He giggled a lot, too. He told Luscious how much he liked his dwelling, how it was like nothing he could have ever imagined.

He smiled a lot, Jupiter did. Luscious loved his smile. He wondered if Jupiter knew why Daddy Marlow sent him down. It didn't matter, of course. He was there and that's all Luscious cared about for now. Jupiter asked for another beer. He stood at the window and looked out into the backyard. He commented on how spacious it was, how it was almost like it's own world back there. Luscious came up behind him with beer in hand, reaching it over Jupiter's shoulder. He took it, before turning to face Luscious and they were simply there, their breath on each other's mouths. He couldn't even remember the moment their lips touched—one moment they weren't, the next moment they were.

They made love in Luscious' bed, barely a word spoken between them. All of it wild and unorthodox, clumsy and sensual. When they finished, Jupiter lay on his belly, arms crossed beneath his face, while Luscious ran his fingers along his back, gently tracing the long scars Daddy Marlow had given him. Luscious asked how he got the scars. Jupiter told him he had been punished as a boy for causing trouble. There was a hard knock on the front door. Luscious knew it was Daddy Marlow's Boys, so he threw on his robe and went downstairs.

In order to insure another chance to see Jupiter, Luscious scheduled a disappearance at his home. Goldstein wouldn't have approved of this, as they were always supposed to take place somewhere neutral, like Leroy Blue's, so Luscious decided not to tell him. Daddy Marlow's Boys showed up first, which wasn't supposed to happen. This didn't bother Luscious, though, because there was Jupiter. He led them inside to the living room. None of them spoke, but simply sat and waited. Luscious offered them drinks, but Three Marlow declined on behalf of everyone. He then asked Luscious where it would happen. Luscious didn't know, he hadn't thought about it. Three Marlow asked if they would be doing it inside of his home, but Luscious told him he would prefer they didn't.

Then came a knock at the door. Luscious hurried to answer it, finding the two men whom Daddy Marlow's Boys would soon make disappear. One of them wore red cowboy boots, which Luscious found interesting. He welcomed the men inside, into the living room where Daddy Marlow's Boys and Jupiter were sitting. There was an immediate tension in the air when the two men who would soon disappear saw the four bald men in Luscious' living room. Luscious introduced everybody and wasn't sure what to do beyond that.

The timing was simply off. Three Marlow looked displeased. Luscious spoke with the two men, making them laugh. Three Marlow stood from the couch and Luscious stepped over to meet him. He knew what Three Marlow was thinking, but he didn't want it to happen in his home.

"Can I get you anything?" Luscious asked.

"I need something from my truck."

"The stuff?" said the man in the red cowboy boots, clapping his hands together. "Right on, let's get down to business."

Three Marlow moved past Luscious, nearly knocking him over as their shoulders bumped. He was outside for at least a few minutes, during which time Luscious continued to do his job, making the two men comfortable, keeping a smile on their faces. The man in the red cowboy boots was doing exactly that, when Three Marlow came up from behind and punched him in the back of the head. One and Two Marlow pounced on the other man, beating him with their bare fists.

Three Marlow sat on the man in the red cowboys boot's chest, punching him in the face over and over, before standing up and telling Jupiter to finish him. Jupiter sat frozen on the couch. Three Marlow glared at him, but Jupiter didn't move. He walked over to him then, yelling at him to do as he was told. The man in the red cowboy boots turned over onto his hands and knees and crawled to the front door, tracking a thin trail of blood as it dripped from his face. He got as far as the front porch, before Three Marlow pounced on him. Luscious stood in the doorway with Jupiter and watched as Three Marlow beat him to death.

Three Marlow gathered up the man in the red cowboy boots and dragged him to the truck. One and Two Marlow had already moved the other dead man. Luscious pulled Jupiter into his chest and kissed him hard on the lips. As they parted, Jupiter smiled. Luscious went back inside the house without waiting for them to drive off. He had to make arrangements to have the man in the red cowboy boot's car towed away. One of his lamps lay broken on the floor and he needed to clean the blood while it was still wet. Within a few hours, Luscious would find Timber asleep on his front lawn.

chaptertwenty-four

Beverly Hills in December

Goldstein continued to have Timber work for him, butchering bodies in the kitchen of Leroy Blue's for the first few months of her pregnancy. And every time, he left Luscious with an envelope filled with money. Luscious always took the money home, removed it from the envelope, and placed it in the safe inside his office. He didn't do this because he was saving up for anything, nor did he do it to keep the money safe. He simply didn't want it—or, more precisely, he didn't want to benefit from it.

Luscious was willing to take responsibility for the choices he had made in his life, for the things he had done for money; but he wasn't comfortable profiting off of Goldstein's exploitation of Timber. He also didn't think it was right to simply get rid of the money, since it was as much Timber's as it was his. So he kept it in the safe and let it pile up. He had no plans for it, except to let it collect dust.

In the meantime, Ginger took a great deal of joy in transforming Timber's bedroom into a nursery, collecting every stuffed animal she came across, putting up wallpaper with every letter in the alphabet and compiling a library of everything from Dr. Seuss to Shel Silverstein. She helped Luscious pick out a crib, as well as a small chaise lounge for Timber to nurse in.

When it was decided that Timber could no longer work until after she gave birth, Goldstein proved to be a man of his word. At his own expense, he found a perfectly capable midwife who didn't ask any questions and agreed not to report anything she saw. Goldstein insured her cooperation by way of a generous paycheck—and a word or two about what might happen should she ever tell anyone of their arrangement. The midwife went to Goldstein's mansion once a week, where she gave Timber a private Lamaze class.

Because Timber was such a young girl, the pain and discomfort experienced during childbirth would be amplified beyond that of a more physically mature woman. For this reason, the midwife recommended a waterbirth, explaining that being immersed in water during labor would reduce the pressure on Timber's abdomen, promoting more efficient uterine contractions and better blood circulation. Not only would Timber's pain be reduced, but being in the water would also give her a certain buoyancy and mobility during her contractions, helping with the descent of the baby.

Goldstein had a large whirlpool bathtub, which he decided would be the best choice. Once the decision was made, Goldstein made arrangements for Luscious, Ginger and Timber to stay in his mansion during the last month of her pregnancy. Ginger and Timber went in the swimming pool everyday, as Goldstein kept the water warm throughout the winter months. Ginger would rest her hands on Timber's round belly beneath the surface, caressing her skin while they kissed. Luscious often wondered when the two of them figured out what he had already seen blossoming, but chose not to ask as it was none of his business.

About a week before Timber gave birth, Goldstein told Luscious that he had begun construction on a shed-like structure in his backyard. He said it would be complete by the time he and Timber were ready to go back home with the baby. Instead of Leroy Blue's, Goldstein told him, this shed would be where Timber would do her work. Luscious worried that having Timber carve dead bodies in their backyard was a terribly dangerous risk, but Goldstein assured him it would be fine. For one thing, his backyard was huge, practically it's own world. And beyond that, Goldstein would make sure all necessary precautions took place to insure nothing bad would happen.

When Timber finally went into labor, Goldstein declined an invitation to be present in the bathroom. Timber sat screaming in the bathtub, with Luscious and Ginger by her side holding her hands, pushing her little girl into the world. It wasn't until she held the child in her arms inside of Goldstein's large bathtub that Luscious realized they had neglected to pick out a name. He asked Timber if she had any names for a girl in mind. This sounded funny to Timber, since, in the Divinity, names weren't gender specific.

"Were there any women in your life that were important to you?" Ginger asked.

"Yes," Timber said, smiling down at her newborn child.

And so, in the middle of December, amidst the palm trees of Beverly Hills and the general desert that was Southern California, I was christened Charlotte Luna Marlow. While my new family hovered around me, enveloping me in their love, none of them knew—or could have possibly known—that Three Marlow was out there somewhere, driving around in his rusty orange pickup truck, just five years away from making his deadly return into Timber's life.

partthree

The Fifth Year

chapter**twenty-five**

Three Marlow

Three Marlow survived the fire. I don't know how he survived, nor do I know why he waited so many years to confront Timber. All I know for certain is he *did* survive and he *would* confront Timber and before this story ends someone very close to her will be dead because of it.

I would only ever have one conversation with Three Marlow. I was a little girl when it occurred, five years old at the time. I didn't really know who he was, nor did I understand why he sought me out. I look back on that conversation with any number of regrets—none of them reasonable—and more than anything, I simply wish I had the omniscient wherewithal to ask him all of the questions that have haunted me for most of my life.

It's not difficult for me to imagine Three Marlow's escape from the fire. I imagine that once it was clear to him that Daddy Marlow and his two brothers were dead, he got into his rusty orange pickup truck and raced down the mountain, driving fast and reckless, knowing the fire was not far behind, threatening to swallow him up into its merciless flames. When I watch him in my mind's eye, racing down that long stretch of road, weaving through the trees and around the boulders, winding about until he ended up on Highway 173, through Rim of the World and onto Interstate 15, ultimately leading him into the Outside, I wonder if, by chance, he passed Timber, who would've been eating her first granola bar, safely in the confines of an eighteen-wheeler.

Upon his arrival, I imagine Three Marlow treated the Outside like a new, untamed frontier, with little regard for human life. However, I would not call Three Marlow a serial killer. There would have been no psychological satisfaction accompanying his murders, no rhyme or reason beyond the pragmatics of survival. He was simply a cannibal. In the years that followed, only a handful of his killings would reach the public consciousness by way of the media, but I'm certain that he killed far more people than were actually discovered. It stands to reason that if there was a five year gap between Timber's escape into the Outside and her tragic reunion with Three Marlow, then he would have had to have killed hundreds of people to survive.

Of course, while Three Marlow was born and raised in the Divinity, he was not without initiation to the Outside. I imagine he knew enough to take caution when killing somebody, picking his prey wisely. The homeless might've made good targets for him, as they were mostly loners, with nobody to miss them or even know they were gone. Soon enough, however, he probably got brave and at night—always at night—he hung around the bars where so many lonely men and women got drunk in each other's company. In the darkness, Three Marlow would wait. All he needed was one, just one man or woman to walk out alone and vulnerable.

I imagine he would crouch in the dark shadows of alleyways, eating the flesh of his victims raw from the bone; he would have preferred cooking the flesh over an open fire, but not at the expense of drawing attention to himself. In time, however, as he grew comfortable with his surroundings, he would find places and ways to cook the flesh—hanging it over a flaming garbage can or charbroiling it in the barbecue of a public park. Since he couldn't reasonably drag dead bodies around with him, I imagine Three Marlow carved the flesh of his victims and packed up what he could carry, dumping the remains in the nearest garbage bin.

Three Marlow probably traveled all around the Inland Empire, aimlessly filling one day after another. Because he would have continued to live his days by the principles of his faith, as taught to him in the Divinity, Three Marlow would have seen the people around him as evil, which means he would have made no friends. Void of even the simplest companionship or the possibility of avenging the losses he suffered, I just can't imagine what motivated him to go on day after day.

And yet he did.

I have no doubt that, where money was concerned, he survived by robbing his victims. He would have little use for money, except for filling his truck with gas and buying razors and shaving cream. Maybe he treated himself to a candy bar every now and then or, perhaps, a clean set of clothes. I wonder if he knew enough about the Outside to take in a movie or go to the beach. I wonder if he ever traveled beyond the invisible borders of the Inland Empire, perhaps driving three hours east into the bright lights of Las Vegas or, maybe, six hours north to San Francisco. I wonder how many bodies lay lifeless in his path, mangled and butchered, entrées to any scavenging wildlife fortunate enough to find them.

I wonder when it finally occurred to him to look up Luscious and, more importantly, I wonder why. I wonder if he had any intention of seeking friendship from him or, perhaps, he was simply in desperate need of a familiar face. I wonder if he recognized Timber right away and if he wanted to kill her on the spot. I wonder if he knew he was called The California Cannibal, a nickname the media gave to the faceless murderer who left behind fingerprints for which there was no traceable identity. I wonder how long he savored the vengeance that would soon be his, letting that backlog of delayed joy build up, higher and higher, until the day he finally chose to strike.

chapter**twenty-six**

The First Five Years

My first five years passed like a blur and, as it is with most people, the early details of my childhood blended all together. By the time I celebrated my fifth birthday, Timber was twenty years old and Ginger was twenty-three. Luscious, who was very much the father figure in my life, was somewhere in his mid-to-late-thirties, though he was never fond of telling anyone exactly how old he was. All three of these lovely grown-ups played significant roles in my adolescent development.

Timber, along with being my mother and the source of all the love I could ever need, was something of a best friend. She introduced me to *Tom and Jerry* early on, which we loved watching together; when I was old enough to appreciate the story, she told me about the cat Luscious bought her, which she named Tom, and how Luscious got rid of it after she tried to smash its head with a frying pan. Because Timber was still learning how to read and write, we also watched of lot of *Sesame Street* together.

Timber and I loved watching Disney movies together. It was Ginger who introduced us to all things Disney, as she herself was a lifelong fan. The first movie she showed me—which, coincidently or not, was also the first movie she showed Timber—was *Sleeping Beauty*. And just like most any kid lucky enough to be raised in Southern California, Disneyland became a regular fixture in my life. When I couldn't be at Disneyland, I was usually sitting in front of the TV watching the Disney Channel.

Beyond creating a Disney-centric atmosphere that defined a large part of my childhood, Ginger also thought it important to introduce me to classic literature, as she herself was very well read. And in this way, she instilled in me a voracious appetite for not just reading, but for stories in general. For the rest of my life, I would be something of a perpetual audience, always ready and waiting for another great story to engage my imagination. For Ginger, this was all part of the plan. She had a keen understanding of the incredible capacity a child has for learning, so from the time I was an infant, she would read to me from Shakespeare's plays.

Ginger always took the time to explain to me what was happening in whatever given play she was reading, usually equating it with one or another Disney movie. "Iago is a bad man who tricks Othello into thinking he is a friend, but really he wants bad things to happen to him," she told me, "just like Honest John and Gideon, who convinced Pinocchio they were his friends, but they led him into harmful situations." Or, "Hamlet is mad at his Uncle Claudius for murdering his father and wants revenge, like Simba and his Uncle Scar in *The Lion King*."

From Charles Dickens to Tim O'Brien, Ginger relished in assimilating my imagination into the canon of great literature. Despite my aptitude for learning—which even amazed Ginger—I still needed to hear stories that appealed to my adolescent sensibilities. Stories about princesses and toads, gingerbread houses and big bad wolves. Stories that paralleled reality, flirting with the surreal, offering me a world that could only ever exist on the page. And so, in this vain, my favorite story from the literary canon Ginger loved so much was Franz Kafka's classic novella, *The Metamorphosis*.

It's the story of Gregor Samsa, a man who's forced to live a life that he hasn't chosen for himself. A life he hates so much that one night, after awaking from unpleasant dreams, he discovers his whole body has morphed into a giant cockroach. You can only imagine what a spell this put me under, imagining Gregor Samsa as a cockroach, laying on his back and trying to work all of his new legs, eating rotten leftovers like they were fine cuisine, watching his family suffer under the burden of his new form.

The new Sustenance Dwelling was built and ready for Timber to begin working in by the time she returned from Goldstein's, following my birth. Goldstein insisted Timber stay at his Beverly Hills mansion for an extra month after giving birth, both to insure she and I got proper round-the-clock care, but also to make sure the Sustenance Dwelling could be built without any interference. And, of course, knowing Goldstein, he probably had other ulterior motives, which he never shared with Luscious or Timber. When they returned home with me in tow, the first thing they did was go out to the backyard.

Luscious' house—which, technically, was Goldstein's house—was in plain view of the foothills of the San Gabriel Mountains, which neighbored the San Bernardino Mountains. While it was located in the middle of a whitewashed Rancho Cucamonga suburb, surrounded by tract houses built in the late 1970s, Luscious' home was built on a large piece of land, isolated from any immediate neighbors. The house was perched on a pleasant corner, surrounded by tall trees and adjacent to an orange grove across the street. Even with the large amount of space, the house still had fences around it, as well as a steel gate in front of the long driveway.

While every other house on the block had modest backyards, squared off against the property limits of their neighbors, Luscious' house had a sprawling backyard that felt endless. It had dirt and weeds and grass and trees, like a wild little forest in the middle of civilization. While Goldstein missed sending the disappeared into the Divinity, Luscious' backyard was the next best option. Among other things, nobody would suspect that bodies were delivered to the house in the middle of the night. Not to mention the fact that nobody knew the Sustenance Dwelling was out there at all, with the exception of the small handful of people who needed to know.

While Ginger knew it was there, she wasn't counted amongst that small handful who *needed* to know. Neither did she know the purpose of the Sustenance Dwelling, nor had she ever been inside. She was, of course, curious. A little too curious, as it turned out. The real trouble wouldn't begin until Ginger's curiosity was finally satisfied. In the mean time, she was reasonably held off by Luscious' simple—if untrue—explanation that it was a shed Goldstein had built to store some private items.

Luscious told her nobody was allowed inside, including himself. He swore to her that he had no idea what Goldstein kept in there. And he told her he preferred it that way. This explanation wouldn't satisfy Ginger's curiosity, but it would deter her from making an effort to see inside—at least for the first five years, that is.

During those first five years, the process was pretty simple. Two men named Marcos and Jared, whom Timber and Luscious formally met only once, would deliver the body—or bodies—to the Sustenance Dwelling in the middle of the night. Other than Timber, Luscious and Goldstein, Marcos and Jared were the only two people who could get inside. Goldstein would contact Luscious the night before a drop was scheduled, which usually occurred three to four times a month. The body—or bodies—were kept in the freezer until Timber could get to them. As often as she could, Timber tried to carve up the bodies on the same night they arrived; but being a young mother made it impossible for her to focus solely on her work.

Apart from her responsibilities as a mother, there was also the issue of Ginger's occasional sleepovers to contend with, as they kept Timber from sneaking off into the backyard to do her work. Luckily for her and Luscious, Ginger was fiercely independent, and while she was never invited to move in, she was never tempted to abandon her one-room apartment, which was only five minutes away.

Just as she did in the Divinity, Timber carved up bodies on a heavy wooden table, putting the pieces away in the freezer. She put the excess skin and fat into large garbage bags, setting them beside the freezer, as per Goldstein's instructions. Neither she nor Luscious ever knew what happened to the bags, except Marcos and Jared picked them up in the middle of the night, along with the carved flesh in the freezer. Usually on the first weekend that followed a night of Timber's work, Goldstein would host a backyard barbecue, which, for a five-year period, he did with more frequency than anybody seemed to remember him doing in the past.

Along with the other barbecued treats, there was always the mystery meat that both befuddled and delighted Goldstein's guests. So much of the fun for his guests, Timber noticed, was to try to figure out amongst each other what the mystery meat was. Was it camel? Or lion? It couldn't be zebra, could it? Or elephant? The more exotic their guesses became, the more they seemed to enjoy it. So far as she knew, Timber was the only guest at these barbecues who both enjoyed the mystery meat, while also knowing what it actually was. Luscious, for obvious reasons, never partook. And Ginger, thankfully, was a vegetarian.

While the barbecues were held primarily so Goldstein could keep his promise to Timber of providing her an avenue to continue eating human flesh, it was also an opportunity to pay Luscious for Timber's work. As always, Goldstein didn't concern himself with what Luscious did with the money; he simply wanted to be sure that both he and Timber were paid a fair wage for the service they provided. As he did with all of the payments that came before, he placed it in the safe in his office, letting the money pile up. Over the five-year period that elapsed before Three Marlow returned, Luscious had inadvertently saved over a half-million dollars.

All during the time Timber was working for Goldstein, Luscious and Ginger continued their work with *Inside Ginger Falls*. The website continued to maintain a high level of popularity, which could be accounted for both by Ginger's striking beauty and transcendent sexuality, but also her willingness to go out and promote herself. While this included going to sex expos to sign autographs and take pictures with fans, she primarily kept herself relevant by working as a feature dancer at all the various strip clubs between the Inland Empire and Las Vegas; most other clubs didn't offer enough money to make it worth her while to travel any further than that.

But her main work she did at Luscious' house. That's where she modeled for photo shoots, as well as videos that generally began with a sensual striptease and ended with her climaxing with a sex toy. A couple times a week, Ginger also did a webcam, where her subscribers could chat with her live on the Internet; and, for the fans willing to pay a generous per-minute fee, they could get a private sex show where Ginger would do most anything they asked of her.

More times then not, when Ginger and Luscious finished their work, we would all do something together as a family, like watch a movie or go to Disneyland. It was on such a day, after they took me bowling for the first time, that Officer Kirkland entered our lives.

chaptertwenty-seven

Officer Kirkland

I was almost five years old the first time I went bowling. I think my first exposure to it was in a cartoon, though I can't for the life of me remember which one. Not long after that, on a random Sunday morning, I discovered *real* bowling on television. I can't explain what it was that attracted me, but as soon as I saw it I knew it was what I wanted to do. Timber, Luscious and Ginger were all very amused by my sudden fascination with bowling, so they promised to take me sooner rather than later. The day I finally got to engage in what would quickly become my favorite pastime was the same day Officer Kirkland entered our lives.

Luscious was finishing up his most recent photo shoot with Ginger, while Timber and I were downstairs in the living room watching *Snow White*. Luscious joined us on the couch, while Ginger showered. When she came downstairs, into the living room, she leaned over and kissed me on the forehead, before kissing Timber on the lips.

"Are we ready to go bowling or what?" she asked.

Standing up from the couch, Timber lifted me up into her powerful arms. I wrapped my arms around her neck, stroking her long hair, which hung nearly to her waist. Even though I had been long since capable of walking to the car myself, Timber still enjoyed carrying me—and I still enjoyed letting her. Piling into Luscious' yellow Cadillac, we headed out for my first trip to the bowling alley.

The Brunswick bowling alley was on Haven Avenue, just off Route 66. When we arrived, I jumped out of the car before everyone else, unable to contain my excitement. Leading the pack, I raced to the sliding doors of the entrance, waiting as they parted much too slowly. Tremendous thunderclaps of sound exploded all around me, seizing my attention. Luscious rented a lane, as well as four pairs of bowling shoes; the exchange of one of my shoes for a pair of Brunswick's made the experience all the more exotic, like I was being indoctrinated into a secret society.

We searched out the different balls, a different color for every weight. I found a pink ball, which I liked, but, because it was twelve pounds, Luscious said it was too heavy. But after an adorable protest on my part, he eventually relented. We got to our lane and each put our shoes on. Despite being the only two among us who had ever stepped foot in a bowling alley before, neither Luscious nor Ginger knew how to input our names onto the screen that would display our scores; after a brief wait, one of the Brunswick attendants came by to help us out. And since my name was on top, I got to go first.

The holes in the twelve-pound ball were too big for my fingers, so I held it with both hands instead. Luscious stood up so he could walk me up to the lane and help me roll it, but I was already running full speed, throwing it in the air like a basketball as I reached the foul line. Because it was a twelve-pound ball and I wasn't yet five years old, it traveled just a foot or so before dropping with a loud bang, slowly rolling for a few more feet before veering off into the gutter. Timber, Ginger and Luscious all enjoyed a good laugh over this, though I didn't understand what was so funny.

After a few more gutter balls, the same Brunswick attendant

who had inputted the names, suggested we put bumpers in the gutters—so we did. The next time it was my turn, Luscious walked me up to the foul line and, standing behind me, told me to swing the ball between my legs before releasing it forward. I did as he told me, lightly releasing it down the lane, where it bounced back and forth along the bumpers before finally making contact with the pins, nudging a few over like lazy dominoes.

After we finished bowling a few games, Luscious bought us hamburgers and fries from the snack bar. The food was served in red plastic baskets, which was new and exotic to me, making the whole experience all the more fun. We sat at our table eating and laughing, watching other people bowl. As we ate, the same Brunswick attendant who had helped us twice before stopped by our table and dropped off a flyer for Cosmic Bowling. He told us it was very popular on Friday and Saturday nights, as they turned down all the lights, replacing them with special black lights that lit up the balls and the pins into various fluorescent colors.

I was very excited about this and desperately wanted to go. Luscious suggested that we plan on doing Cosmic Bowling for my fifth birthday, which was right around the corner. I loved the idea, but Ginger pointed out that it would conflict with our annual trip to Disneyland, which we always took on my birthday. Timber said I could do both, so long as I knew we couldn't stay at Disneyland all day, as we usually did. I was more than happy to make the compromise.

When we got home, there was a police car parked on the street in front of our front gate. As Luscious opened the gate and drove in, the police car followed behind us, parking in the driveway. The officer got out of his patrol car and walked towards us. He was tall and fit, with a chiseled jaw and a handsome smile. His uniform was clean and pressed and he was suspiciously polite. He introduced himself as Officer Kirkland, shaking each of our hands with both of his, gently as if handling an egg. He repeated each of our names as he learned them, insuring that he heard them all correctly. He asked if he could come inside and Luscious obliged, leading Officer Kirkland through the kitchen, offering him a seat at the table. Timber, Ginger and I followed.

"You have a very nice home, Mr. Jones," Officer Kirkland said.

"Pardon me?"

"It's very nice, very clean," he said. "Well kept. I appreciate that. Not enough people take pride in their homes."

"You called me Jones."

"I did, yes."

"My name is Billy D. Luscious," he said. "My friends call me Luscious."

"Not to be a *contrarian*," he said, smiling, "but your name is William Kennedy Jones."

At this point, Luscious asked Timber to take me up to his office. I didn't get the impression anything was wrong, nor was I aware that he didn't want me around for whatever he thought was going to happen next.

"What's the purpose of your visit, Officer?" Luscious asked.

"Straight to the point," he said, flashing his smile. "I appreciate that. I'm here on behalf of District Attorney Robert Michaels. Do you know of him?"

Robert Michaels has long since retired from his career as District Attorney of San Bernardino County, but at the time we met Officer Kirkland, he was completing his first term in office. Before that, he had served as Deputy District Attorney, as well as an attorney with the Major Crimes Unit. Early in his career, he worked as a probation officer for San Bernardino County, as well as a group counselor for the county's Probation Department. In between all his other duties, he spent seven years as a member of the San Bernardino Board of Education, focusing on the Chaffey Joint Unified School District. That he accomplished all of this in the course of a twenty-four year career points to a man of tremendous ambition and exceptional professional discipline. But ambition and discipline alone were not the secret to his success. Politics is a cutthroat business and Officer Kirkland was about to give Luscious a firsthand lesson.

"As you probably already know," Officer Kirkland said, "Robert Michaels is currently running for re-election for the office of District Attorney. I've been sent here on his behalf to request a financial contribution to his campaign."

"With all due respect," Luscious said. "I've never heard of Robert Michaels, so why would I contribute to his campaign."

"You're a pornographer, Mr. Jones," he said. "As District Attorney of this county, Robert Michaels is obliged to look into any legal misdeeds on the part of you and your company. But, as a favor to you, he is prepared to overlook his obligations in exchange for financial support to his re-election campaign."

"Well," Luscious said, "I hate to burst your bubble, but I've done nothing wrong. Everything about my business and the practices I employ are all well within the boundaries of the law."

"That will ultimately be up to District Attorney Michaels to determine," he said, "should you choose not to contribute to his campaign."

"That's extortion," Ginger said.

"Is it?" Officer Kirkland asked, smiling.

"Yes," Ginger said. "What you're talking about is an egregious disregard for the law."

"You don't say?"

"Don't think for a second I won't report this," Luscious said. "I'll tell anyone with a tape recorder what you're trying to do."

"Be my guest," Officer Kirkland said. "Rancho Cucamonga is a conservative town and pornography goes against everything its good people believe in. With all due respect to you, Mr. Jones, your word wouldn't look all that impressive against the word of District Attorney Michaels."

"Suppose I end this conversation right now and ask you to leave my home," Luscious said. "What happens then?"

"Well," he said, "under those circumstances, I could only assume that you've chosen not to give any money to District Attorney Michaels' campaign. In that case, he would have no choice but to prosecute you for breaking every obscenity law in the book."

"But I've broken no laws."

"That's not for you nor I to decide," he said. "You would, of course, get your day in court—*eventually*—before a jury of your peers."

"If I've broken no laws," Luscious said, "then no reasonable jury would convict me."

"That may very well be true," Officer Kirkland said, smiling, "but I hate to think about how much money you'll have to spend on legal fees in order to defend yourself. In fact, it's not hard for me to imagine you bankrupting your entire fortune in the vain of fighting a futile legal battle. Of course, you could save yourself the trouble by simply agreeing to make a monthly contribution towards the re-election efforts of District Attorney Michaels."

"What happens when the campaign is over?"

"We'll let you know."

Luscious shook his head, disgusted, but said nothing.

"Once a month," Officer Kirkland said, "I'll show up to your home. We'll sit down at the kitchen table, exactly as we're doing now. You'll leave the money, in cash, in an unmarked envelope on an empty chair. We'll exchange a few pleasant words and when I leave you'll find that the envelope will no longer be on the chair."

"How do I know you're not making this all up?"

"You don't have to believe me," he said. "But I think you'll acknowledge I've been nothing but forthright up to this point. If you choose to disregard our arrangement in an attempt to prove that I have somehow invented this whole scenario for my own personal gain, then you'll be left to suffer the consequences as they have been outlined for you."

"Why me?" Luscious asked.

"I'm not privy to such information."

"You just do his dirty work then, no questions asked?"

"I'm but a loyal foot soldier, Mr. Jones," Officer Kirkland said. "I believe in the system and I simply want to do my part."

Luscious set up a meeting with Goldstein as soon as he could, so he could get some advice regarding Officer Kirkland and his proposed plan of extortion. Sitting beside his pool at that familiar glass table, Goldstein sipped from a gin and tonic, listening to Luscious explain to him how he was being blackmailed to "contribute" to District Attorney Michaels' re-election campaign. Goldstein laughed long and hard, working himself into a brief coughing fit. As he gained his composure, he sipped from his gin and tonic.

"What's so funny?" Luscious asked.

"Contributing to a re-election campaign," he said. "I haven't heard that one before. It's good."

"What do I do?"

"You pay them the money."

"That's not fair."

"I told you many years ago that this was what you were to expect," Goldstein said. "I'm only surprised it took this long for them to finally get to you."

"They don't have a right to my money," Luscious said. "*I* earned it, not them."

"Listen, Billy," he said, "I've paid off my fair share of politicians over the years. It's part of the business."

Luscious found it hard to believe that for all the people Goldstein had ever had killed—for far lesser offences than extortion—his answer was simply to do what Officer Kirkland asked of him.

"You're doing very well with your business," Goldstein said, "are you not?"

"Yes."

"So, even after you've given the bullies your lunch money, you're still going to live comfortably. Correct?"

"Yes."

"Then there's your answer," Goldstein said. "You more than any-body understand the nature of my business, Billy. I have no doubt that over the years you've probably come to look at me as a callous man. And, I suppose in some respects, you wouldn't be wrong."

"I don't think that of you," Luscious said.

"Well you probably should," he said. "So, unless I'm mistaken, you've come here today because you would like me to make Officer Kirkland disappear."

Luscious lowered his eyes, saying nothing.

"While it would be fair for you to think of me as callous, you should also know that I don't call for death easily," Goldstein said. "In the end, it has to make sense. There has to be no better option. The people who you're now dealing with, Billy, are very powerful. This Officer Kirkland might only be one man, but he represents something far bigger. Not only would killing him not solve your problem, it would simply make it worse. And, anyway, he's a police officer. To try and kill him would be beyond difficult. So in the end, the best thing you can do for you and your family is to give them the money and be glad that's all they've asked for."

chapter**twenty-eight**

It's a Small World

The trip Timber, Luscious and Ginger took me on to Disneyland for my fifth birthday was the last time we ever went together. If I had known this ahead of time, maybe I could've concentrated harder, committed more of it to memory. But, as it is, when I try to remember that last trip together, the details get blurry. I'm never quite sure if I'm remembering my fifth birthday or my fourth birthday or maybe even some random trip we made in between birthdays. And the peculiar thing is, when I concentrate hard enough, managing for brief moments to make it all clear in my mind, Three Marlow is always there, my own personal bogeyman, forever present, lurking just out of sight. Watching. Planning. Waiting. Of course, he wasn't really there—and yet I imagine it. And not because I want him there, but I suppose that's the point.

On the morning of my fifth birthday, as we were walking out to the car, I see Three Marlow standing behind one of the large trees in our front yard in his blue jeans and dirty T-shirt. He's not looking at me, however. He never looks at me. Always Timber. He stares with scorn and hurt, that poisonous need for revenge coursing through his body, a timer in his head counting down the days, the minutes, the seconds until he can introduce Timber to true pain. True hurt. True sorrow.

The drive into Anaheim never took more than forty minutes or so and, no matter how many times we went, I always got giddy when we reached the outskirts of Disneyland, where everything was designed to make you feel as if you were already there. We parked on the Donald Duck level of the parking garage and rode a tall escalator down to a waiting area where we caught the tram that dropped us off in Downtown Disney.

At the entrance, just in front of the small hill of grass with his face shaped in flowers, Mickey Mouse was wandering about, posing for pictures and hugging children. Without any trepidation, I ran straight to him, hugging him around his waist, either not knowing or not caring that inside he was just an employee working his way through another shift. As we passed through the stone tunnel, which opened up to the park itself, the first order of business was going into the Main Street Cinema on Main Street, USA.

I loved the circular theater with its six different screens, each showing an old black and white Disney cartoon, including Mickey Mouse's debut in *Steamboat Willie*. It was dark inside the Main Street Cinema, except for the lights flickering off the screens, a panorama of cartoons all playing at once. Inside of that lonely little theater, forgotten by all but those who still appreciated the yellowed pages of days gone by, were glimpses of Mickey's past, his roots, his first infant steps, a history of where he came from, presented in sketchy black and white, offered right up front for anyone to see, though it was usually overlooked or simply never considered at all.

Leaving the Main Street Cinema, back onto Main Street, we saw a horse-drawn trolley, accompanied by the rhythmic sounds of clicking hooves as they moved past. Next we saw a small music band in candy-striped vests, playing banjos, trumpets and clarinets. Walking down Main Street, we passed most of the shops without even peeking in the windows, with a few exceptions, such as the Main Street Magic Shop, where I always insisted on going inside.

We moved along, past the Candy Palace and Candy Kitchen, the Main Street Photo Supply Company and the Penny Arcade, past a marching band parading down Main Street in white uniforms and red-feathered caps, past the families and their strollers, past the natives and visitors from other lands, moving straight ahead to Sleeping Beauty's iconic castle. It was much smaller up close than it looked from a distance, but it still remained the first and only castle I'd ever seen in person. I had, of course, seen the castle many times at the beginning of every Disney cartoon I'd ever watched, so standing before it was not unlike standing before a celebrity of sorts.

Luscious handed off his camera to Three Marlow and asked him to take our picture in front of the castle. There we were—Luscious, Timber, Ginger and I—our very own happy little family. Three Marlow gave the camera back, our happy little memory stored inside, and watched us walk away, through Sleeping Beauty's castle, into Fantasyland. I turned to look at him as we walked forward, watching him stare at us, his arms at his side, the sunlight glinting off his bald head, his muscles barely contained in his raggedy clothes. His hands balled into fists, squeezing, pulsing, tense and angry, a mounting rage, barely contained, ready to explode. His bite hard, his jaw set. He stares, unblinking, watching Timber—always Timber—until we move out of sight towards the King Arthur Carousel and Mr. Toad's Wild Ride, Alice in Wonderland and Peter Pan's Flight, the Mad Tea Party teacups and Snow White's Scary Adventure, until finally we reach It's a Small World.

We all piled into a little boat, curving around a bend of water, passing the topiary animal sculptures—giraffe, elephant and hippopotamus, among them—into the tunnel that led us to the alternate reality of It's a Small World. A world of bright colors and dancing animatronic doll children, their collective of international voices pumped in overhead, singing the ride's self-titled theme song.

From there we went into Tomorrowland to go on my favorite ride, Space Mountain. We waited in line for nearly two hours, which didn't bother me so much, as I was always fascinated with the space station interior and the fluorescent lights. Getting on to the train, I sat beside Timber, while Ginger and Luscious sat behind us. It moved slowly at first, entering a tunnel of pulsing blue lights, before bursting forward into darkness. Timber and I screamed as we zipped along the track of the indoor rollercoaster, our voices joining the collective whole that bounced off the fake stars overhead. My cheeks fluttered as the dual force of inertia and speed pressed against my face. I squeezed Timber's hand, wetting her knuckles with the sweat of my palms, until the train burst into a tunnel of pulsing red lights, suddenly slowing down into one last stretch of darkness, stopping in the calming florescent of the space station.

After a brief lunch in the Tommorwland Terrace, we headed off to New Orleans Square, where Disneyland offered a sterilized version of Mardi Gras and the French Quarter, replete with wrought iron balconies, gumbo, jazz and ghosts. After touring through the Haunted Mansion, we went on Pirates of the Caribbean, sailing through thick fog and past mountains of stolen treasure, battling pirate ships and invisible cannonballs. Amongst the animatronic pirates who auctioned off wenches and dunked men in water wells, drank ale and sang songs, there was Three Marlow. He sat atop a cobble stone tunnel beside a pirate who's dirty barefoot hung over the edge. Three Marlow stared down on us as we passed under him, but I was the only one who looked up, the only one who saw. I thought for a moment I caught his eye, but, as usual, he was not looking at me.

Because we were going Cosmic Bowling later that day, we couldn't stay at Disneyland for as long as usual, which meant we didn't have time to visit Adventureland or Frontierland, though we did manage to squeeze in a quick tour of Mickey's Toontown. Heading out of the park, back into Downtown Disney, we caught a tram back to the parking garage and rode the tall escalator up to the Donald Duck section. Timber held me in her arms, kissing my forehead, as we made our way to the car, Ginger and Luscious walking beside us. Just behind us was Three Marlow, walking slowly, keeping pace, not even trying to hide his presence. As we piled into Luscious' yellow Cadillac, Three Marlow got into his rusty orange pickup truck. And as we exited Disneyland, into the real world, Three Marlow followed behind us, forever haunting my memories.

chaptertwenty-nine

It's a Very Small World

However much I enjoyed the first half of my fifth birthday, the real highlight was Cosmic Bowling—both because it was my first time doing it, and it was the night I met my first real friend. Inside Brunswick, it was dark like a nightclub, with loud music, chatter and exploding bowling pins. The bowling alley was so crowded that night that we had to be put on a waiting list for a lane; the wait, they told us, would be more than an hour. Going home was definitely not an option for me and I think everyone knew it, so we sat by the snack bar and waited.

As soon as we sat down, I saw Officer Kirkland. He was bowling on the lane directly in front of us. I pointed him out to Timber, who then pointed him out to Ginger and Luscious. Because I was only five and had no idea what our relationship with him was, it didn't occur to me that seeing Officer Kirkland might be a bad thing.

"What should we do?"

"I'm not sure."

"You think we should go home?"

"I'd hate to disappoint Charlotte Luna."

At this point, they all looked to me, but I was no longer sitting at the table. I had gone to say hello to Officer Kirkland; not that I was concerned with being polite or social, so much as I just wanted to be nearer to the lanes. He flashed his big, bright smile and was extremely polite—he even remembered my name. He looked different out of his uniform, like a normal person. Luscious, Timber and Ginger figured out where I was pretty quickly and came around to get me. It was then that his wife and little boy stood up and joined Officer Kirkland.

"Mr. Jones," Officer Kirkland said, shaking Luscious' hand. "What a pleasant surprise. Ginger, Timber," he said, shaking each of their hands, "so nice to see you as well."

His wife stepped forward, smiling and saying hello. She was probably in her early thirties, blond and pudgy.

"You guys," Officer Kirkland said, "this is my better half, Rita."

Rita shook each of our hands, before nudging her little boy forward to be introduced.

"And this little man is our son, Winston."

Winston held out his hand and we each shook it, saying hello.

"So, what brings you out here tonight?" Officer Kirkland asked, before laughing at his own question. "Well, I guess I should know what you're doing at a bowling alley, huh?"

"It's Charlotte Luna's birthday," Luscious said. "She wanted to come bowling."

"That's wonderful," Officer Kirkland said. "Happy Birthday, young lady!"

He bent down and gave me a high-five.

"We have to wait an hour," I said.

"An *hour*? What for?"

"There's a waiting list," Luscious said. "We didn't realize how crowded it would be."

"Well," Rita said, "we can't let this little one wait an hour to bowl on her birthday. You'll just join *us*."

"Oh, we really couldn't impose," Luscious said.

"Nonsense," Officer Kirkland said. "I'm going to go take care of it right now."

And just like that, we were bowling with the Kirkland's. Officer Kirkland even insisted on paying for our shoe rentals and he refused to take a dollar from Luscious for the lane. When we all got settled, Rita finally asked how we all knew each other. Luscious looked at Officer Kirkland, unsure as to how he was supposed to answer.

"I was doing a little leg work for District Attorney Michaels," Officer Kirkland said. "I met these fine folks at their home where we talked about possibly having them donate to his campaign."

"Oh, that's wonderful!" Rita said. "Mr. Michaels is really a lovely man and he's done such a wonderful job."

"Well, we haven't actually decided if we can donate yet," Luscious said.

"Oh?" Rita said.

"Times are tough, honey," Officer Kirkland said. "We can't always afford to donate, even if it's the right thing to do."

"Right," Luscious said.

"Well enough political talk," Rita said. "We have a birthday girl here who is ready to bowl."

And bowl I did, for the next couple of hours. For anybody who didn't know better—such as Rita—we looked like a couple of friendly families enjoying a night of Cosmic Bowling together. The funny thing is, it wasn't long before that's really what we were. Rita chatted up Timber and Ginger most of the night, seemingly happy to have a couple of women in the fold. She didn't mind that Timber and Ginger were a couple and, in fact, she seemed almost overly supportive, as if she wanted to make a point. Luscious and Officer Kirkland also chatted, mostly over beers, and the elephant in the room remained in his corner for the whole of the night.

While the grownups kept each other company, Winston and I concentrated on bowling. He was already five years old and was much closer to his sixth birthday. He was in kindergarten, which I found interesting since I hadn't yet started school. I looked forward to starting school the following year, though I had no idea this was a source of mild concern for Timber and Luscious, since, so far as legalities were concerned, I was never born. Winston wore a Dodgers cap that nearly swallowed his head and he had his very own bowling ball, which I thought was amazing, as I didn't realize you could own your own ball.

At some point, he and I were the only ones bowling, as the grownups sat around, drinking beers and talking; though they occasionally stopped to watch Winston and I playing together, each of them overwhelmed by the adorable nature of our blossoming friendship. Timber especially found herself getting a little choked up watching me play with my new friend, as it reminded her of her friendship with Jupiter. Five years had passed since she saw Daddy Marlow's Boys dragging him to the Sustenance Cradle, but when she closed her eyes, it was like no time had passed at all and they were running free, climbing the Learning Tree, playing in Marlow Stream.

When it was time to go home, Officer Kirkland shook everybody's hands and said goodbye, while Rita chose instead to give us each a hug and say how wonderful it was to meet us all. Then the grownups made sure to put Winston and I together, so we could hug and say goodbye. Luscious expected Officer Kirkland to say something quiet that only he would hear, some sly allusion to what had prompted their initial meeting. But that didn't happen. Officer Kirkland simply put his arm around his wife, took Winston by the hand and walked out into the parking lot with his family.

Just a few days later, Officer Kirkland made his return visit to Luscious' home. Luscious invited him in, leading him to the kitchen where they took a seat at the table. He asked him if he could get him anything, a glass of tea perhaps. Officer Kirkland said that would be delightful, so Luscious asked Timber to put some water in the kettle. There was no mention of District Attorney Robert Michaels or his re-election campaign. As Officer Kirkland and Luscious each drank a glass of tea, they made small talk about work and family and the difficult balance of it all.

"Speaking of family," Officer Kirkland said. "Rita is awfully fond of your family."

"Is she?" Luscious said.

"She hasn't stopped talking about you all since Saturday."

"Well, we all liked her very much too."

I walked into the kitchen as Timber sat down at the table. I climbed up on her lap, before saying hello to Officer Kirkland.

"Timber," he said, "Rita wants to invite Charlotte Luna to bowl with Winston in a bowling league."

"What's that?" she asked.

"It's just a small league where some kids can get together once a week and bowl," he said. "They provide lunch and even have a coach, since most of the kids have never really bowled before."

"Can I mommy?" I asked. "*Please!*"

"How can you say no to that?" Officer Kirkland said, smiling.

"I guess I can't," Timber said.

Officer Kirkland left Timber with the information for the league, before finishing his tea and thanking us all for the pleasant company. Reaching over to the chair beside him, he retrieved the unmarked envelope that Luscious had left for him. We all walked him to the front door to say goodbye, before watching him get into his patrol car and drive down the long driveway, through the open gate, disappearing onto the street.

chapter**thirty**

Houdini's Cell

A few days removed from Officer Kirkland's most recent visit, Luscious dropped off Timber and me at the bowling alley for the first day of my new league. Rita and Winston were already there waiting for us. Rita took Timber to the front counter to help her get me signed up and to make sure Winston and I were on the same team; because the league was so small, there were only about ten teams, two kids per. While it was a competitive league—in so far as scores were kept and winners declared—it was designed primarily for beginning bowlers to learn the fundamentals.

Before we started league play, all of us kids huddled around Matilda, who both ran the league and coached the kids. A semi-pro bowler herself, Matilda spent part of her time struggling for relevance on the women's end of the Professional Bowler's Association, while also running The Little Lebowski, which was the pro shop inside of Brunswick. Matilda spoke to us kids about the importance of sportsmanship, as well as the importance of hard work and dedication; beyond that, she made sure to emphasize fun. After she spoke to us, she told us to watch her bowl a few practice frames.

Matilda's salt and pepper hair stayed perfectly still in its short, gelled spikes as she took her rhythmic steps towards the lane. She wore a shiny black brace on her wrist, which kept her hand straight, allowing her to better cup the ball before her release. It was like a magic trick, the way she controlled the ball. Upon her release, Matilda rolled the ball towards the gutter and, just as it seemed destined to drop inside, it curved back towards the pins, crushing them like a bomb had been set off. She bowled two more frames, crushing the pins in identical fashion. From that moment on, I was prepared to listen to anything she had to say.

The first thing Matilda told me was I couldn't use the pink bowling ball I loved so much, because it was too heavy.

"You've got to use a ball you can hold in one hand, with just these three digits," she said, tapping her two middle fingers to the tip of her thumb. "Let's find you a six or a seven."

Once all the kids were set up with their balls and shoes—Winston, of course, had his own bowling ball and shoes—we got started with league play. Each of the ten teams was paired off, so there were five matches going on. For this first day, Matilda just wanted us to bowl and have fun. She would watch and, perhaps, offer a few small pointers here and there; but she didn't want to make it all about coaching and learning on the first day.

"This is a fun game," she said. "Always remember to have fun."

And I was having fun, too—loads of it. I didn't know right away that a large part of why I was having so much fun was I now had a friend to engage with. Winston and I didn't necessarily talk each other's ears off, but we didn't have to, either. Just bowling and laughing together was good enough most of time. It didn't hurt that he was the best bowler in the league—which was probably a dubious honor at best—so in that inaugural match-up, we were handily beating our opponents.

Just as he did when we met during Cosmic Bowling, Winston was wearing the oversized Dodgers cap, which covered his whole head and the tops of his ears. It was about halfway through our second of three games that Winston fell to the floor in a relatively dramatic fashion. From the foul line to the pins, each lane was oiled down, as it was standard practice in every bowling alley across the country. What Winston did—which was a common mishap for many casual bowlers—was inadvertently slide his foot just over the foul line upon his release, slipping on the oil and falling backwards onto his butt.

The fall itself didn't do any physical harm; and really, outside of the loud buzz that sounded from the sensor at the foul line, it wouldn't have been very dramatic at all if Rita hadn't panicked the way she did. Upon his fall, Winston's hat fell off, revealing his completely bald head. Rita, who was sitting with Timber at a table behind the lanes, jumped up and ran to her little boy, quickly replacing his hat and lifting him into her arms. As for Winston, for all I could tell, he wasn't nearly as concerned as his mom; he was more upset about getting a foul.

After letting Winston get back to bowling, Rita excused herself outside. Timber followed her out, where she found Rita crouched down, crying with her back to the wall. Timber crouched beside her, gently stroking Rita's shoulders as she sobbed. Within a few minutes, she was able to compose herself, at which point she sat all the way down on the concrete, resting her head against the brick wall. She took a deep breath and, looking up into the clouds, began telling Timber about her family.

Winston had Leukemia. He'd been diagnosed about a year or so earlier. Timber had never heard of Leukemia, but, after five years spent in the Outside, she had at least heard of cancer, which was how Rita put it into context. Winston had his most recent chemotherapy treatment just a few weeks back, which, Rita said, was terribly tough for him. The good news was Winston's Leukemia was in remission, so his last two or three treatments were what the doctors called maintenance chemotherapy. But, as Rita explained, once your child gets sick like that, it's hard not to see them as extra fragile.

But Winston's health wasn't the only thing weighing on Rita. The medical bills were piling up and her husband, Officer Kirkland, was having trouble keeping up with them. In the last year, she said, they sold one of their cars and cancelled a family vacation. Now, more and more, they could no longer afford groceries, so she had to buy their food with credit cards. Most recently she learned that they were way behind on their mortgage payments and the bank was threatening to foreclose on them. Added to all of that, their health insurance premiums had shot way up with Winston's illness; of course, with Winston needing continuing treatment, they had no choice but to continue paying for the insurance.

"It just seems like my whole world is crumbling around me," Rita said, "and I feel like there's nothing I can do about it."

Timber simply nodded, not knowing what to say.

"All I can really do is make sure Winston is the happiest little boy I can make him," Rita said. "Even bowling is too expensive for us. But he loves it and for everything he's been through, I wouldn't dream of taking it away."

Rita laid her head on Timber's shoulder and took another deep breath.

During the previous five years, since Timber moved in with Luscious, there had been a precarious balance between the life she shared with Ginger and the work she did for Goldstein. Being that they were a sexually active couple, it stood to reason that Timber and Ginger would spend entire nights together, which they often did. But they couldn't *always* spend the night together, especially when Timber had work to do in the Sustenance Dwelling. Of course, she didn't always have to do her work in the middle of the night; even still—on Goldstein's order—nobody besides Luscious,

Timber and myself could be at the house when Jared and Marcos were delivering dead bodies. And he made it very clear that Ginger was no exception. Goldstein didn't say what would happen if Ginger ever found out about the work they did, but so far as Luscious was concerned he didn't have to.

Early on it was easy to dissuade Ginger from spending the night. She knew Timber was still something of a fish out of water; not to mention she was underage, so both the emotional and legal ramifications made it clear that they should take their time. Plus, there was me, a newborn baby, so having an overnight guest wouldn't be entirely optimal. And then, of course, there was the most obvious issue, which was Timber and Ginger weren't yet having sex—that wouldn't happen until nearly two years into their relationship, when Timber was seventeen and Ginger was twenty.

So the first two years were the easiest to keep Ginger away from the house in the middle of the night. But eventually she and Timber would start having sex, which meant that they would want their privacy. I was every bit as comfortable with Luscious as I was with Timber, which meant he could watch me overnight without much incident. So three or four times a month, Timber would spend the night in Ginger's apartment where they could do whatever they liked, fall asleep when they were done and wake up to each other in the morning.

It went like that, pretty seamlessly in fact, for the next two years. By then, I was four years old, Timber was nineteen and Ginger was twenty-two. It was during that last year—Timber's fifth year in the Outside—that their relationship began to grow tense. By then, Ginger was spending the majority of her time at Luscious' house, either working on the website or spending time with Timber and me. In a way, I had become something of a burden to Timber and Luscious' secret. Up to that point, Ginger had practically raised me with Timber and Luscious; yet, when the day was done, she was the only one of us who went to her own home at night. It was as if we had all built a family together, yet she was somehow excluded.

Luscious put off having Ginger spend the night for as long as he reasonably could, because he knew the moment he relented it would become a slippery slope of her staying one or two nights a week, then three or four, then a week and pretty soon she would be practically living there. But that couldn't happen, because he couldn't let it happen, which meant in order to stop it from happening he would have to have some sort of awkward and, potentially, confrontational discussion with Ginger. That discussion never happened and so, about six months before the five-year mark, Luscious gave Ginger his blessing to sleep overnight.

He made sure, of course, that it wasn't a night when Jared and Marcos would be making a delivery. Even still, he caught Ginger wandering in the backyard, investigating the perimeter of the Sustenance Dwelling. He walked out back to see what she was up to, inadvertently startling her with the sound of his footsteps crunching through the grass.

"Looking for something?"

"No," she said, "just curious."

"What about?"

"What do you think Goldstein keeps in here?"

"Your guess is as good as mine."

"I'm sure your guess is way better than mine," she said.

"Goldstein is a private man."

"Yeah, but why not build a secret shed—or whatever this is—in his own backyard?"

"This *is* his backyard."

"You know what I mean," she said. "You don't find it peculiar that seemingly overnight, without any warning, he just decided to build a big shed in your backyard without telling you why?"

"I'm sure he has his reasons."

Ginger stepped forward, pressing the flat of her hand to the door. Sliding it down, she stopped at the doorknob, gripping it in her fingers. She turned her head to Luscious and smiled.

"You ever try to open it?" she asked.

"No."

"What if it's not even locked," she said. "It could be a trick like the police officer who put Houdini into a jail cell, challenging him to break out. You know about that?"

Luscious shook his head, no.

"When Houdini finally gave up," she said, "the police officer told him it was never locked. All he had to do was walk out and he'd be free."

Luscious smiled.

"What if for all these years, you just assumed it was locked, when all along you just had to open the door?"

"And what?"

"And maybe you'd find a million dollars with your name on it."

"I doubt that's the case."

"You never know," she said.

With a mischievous smile, Ginger turned the knob and was disappointed to find that it was indeed locked. Luscious was sure that this wasn't the only time Ginger had snooped around, but it was the only time he had caught her doing it. It was all the more reason he was uncomfortable with having her spend the night, but after the first time it was hard to tell her she couldn't. Things didn't get bad until that fifth and most fateful year.

Ginger and Timber made plans for her to spend a Friday night at Luscious' house. We were all going to watch movies and eat pizza together and maybe go Cosmic Bowling or something. That morning, Goldstein called Luscious to tell him that something came up and he needed Timber to do a job. Jared and Marcos would be making a delivery that night and Goldstein needed it taken care of by morning. That was it—no further explanation was given. So Luscious told Timber who, in turn, had to tell Ginger that they had to cancel their Friday night plans. Ginger didn't take the news well, which led to her and Timber having their first fight.

It wasn't so much a fight, as it was Ginger yelling at Timber about not taking their relationship serious enough or not being committed enough. It could've been the chip Ginger carried on her shoulder about feeling like the odd one out, but she told Timber that she was tired of feeling like she was simply a convenience for her and that she could make and break plans without any concern for her feelings. Of course, none of these things were true, but Timber was smart enough to know that she couldn't tell Ginger anymore than she already had. So all she could do was watch Ginger storm out to her car and drive away, angry and crying. Timber cried, too. Luscious held her, assuring her she had done the right thing. Timber knew he was right, but it sure didn't feel like it.

Ginger stayed away for a few days, as she was too upset to be around any of us. Timber, of course, was upset too, but she didn't know what to do about it. Seeking forgiveness from your gay lover was never discussed on *Sesame Street*. When Luscious dropped us off for the second week of my bowling league, Timber was still upset. Luscious knew it too, but he'd found that, aside from hugging her and promising everything would be all right, he didn't really know what else to do.

What Timber needed—even if she didn't know it—was some good girl talk. And Rita was tailor-made for girl talk. But before they got into what was bothering Timber, they were content to watch Winston and me bowl. Matilda had taken a liking to me on account of my enthusiasm for her sport. And on account of my advanced level of intelligence—which she was always quick to compliment Timber on—Matilda enjoyed spending extra time with me, teaching me the details of bowling, such as the difference between plastic and resin balls or the importance of deducing how much oil was on the lanes.

"Most people think bowling is about power," Matilda said, "but it's not. Bowling is about *adjustments*. Identify the variables and make the adjustment. That's all there is to it."

Matilda always made it sound so easy when she explained it and when she bowled she made it look even easier. She was a big woman—hefty, though not obese—powerful and imposing; but when she bowled, she moved with the grace of a dancer, every step sharp and precise, placing the ball exactly where she wanted it, knowing exactly how it would strike the pins the moment it left her fingers.

There was no grace in my game, not yet anyway. Where Matilda swung the ball with the fluid consistency of a pendulum, I jerked the ball back hard, like I was trying to start a lawn mower—all muscle, no grace—clumsily whipping it onto the lane. Were it not for the bumpers, I would have thrown a high number of gutter balls.

Wintson, on the other hand, was like a young professional. He took his ball in both hands, working his fingers into the holes. Stepping up to the dots on the floor, he held the ball under his chin and stared down the lane, measuring it with his eyes. When he was set, he would take three measured steps, coordinating the swing of the ball with each stride, so that when he slid into his third step the ball swung past his leg and he gracefully released it down the lane. He couldn't yet make his ball hook the way Matilda did, but it was clearly just a matter of time before he would have the whole sport mastered.

Overhead, above the lanes, were two monitors that showed the score for each player and the team they were on. Between those monitors was a TV. Often times, the TV would be showing some sporting event, but being that Winston and I bowled in the late afternoon, there was nothing particularly interesting to watch other than the news. Rita had happened to look up at the TV and noticed that the newscast was reporting on the California Cannibal.

"Have you heard about this guy?"

"Who?" Timber asked, looking up.

"The California Cannibal."

"No, who is he?"

"He's a serial killer who eats his victims," she said "The police don't know much more than that, yet. They don't know how long he's been doing it, but recently bodies have been showing up."

Rita, on account of being married to a police officer, had an abundance of trivial information regarding serial killers. She told Timber about William Bonin, "The Freeway Killer," who, between 1979 and 1980, killed a number of young men, often finding his victims in roadside bars, sexually assaulting them and dumping their bodies along the freeway. Then she told her about Gary Leon Ridgway, "The Green River Killer," who, between 1980 and 1982, murdered 71 prostitutes and teenage runaways. Finally she told her about the Inland Empire's very own William Lester Suff, "The Riverside Prostitute Killer," who, with the help of his wife, beat their two-month old baby to death, before murdering a series of prostitutes in the Riverside and Lake Elsinore area. Suff, she told Timber, once integrated the breast of one his victims into his chili recipe, using it to win the Riverside County Employee Chili Cook-Off.

While Rita knew this information, she hadn't experienced any of it as a public bystander. She expressed this with a certain amount of disappointment, before acknowledging, for that very reason, she was unreasonably titillated with the idea of living through what could be a historic time, what with a brand new honest-to-goodness serial killer on the loose.

"You must think I'm just awful," Rita said.

"No, not at all."

"I guess maybe it just helps to distract me from my own problems," she said. "You want to hear something else?"

Timber nodded.

"Alright," she said, "but I'm not supposed to know this, so you can't say anything."

Rita told Timber that the California Cannibal's fifth and most recent victim was a twenty-seven-year-old elementary school teacher from Montclair, which was about a fifteen-minute drive from Rancho Cucamonga. The victim's roommate had last seen him the night before, when he left to pick up some groceries. He never came home and the next morning, after becoming aware of his absence, the roommate called the police. The victim's body was discovered in an alley just a few blocks from his apartment. This much the media had already reported on. But, thanks to Officer Kirkland, Rita knew some of the more gruesome details.

The victim, she told Timber, was found with large portions of his thighs, chest and biceps missing. And beside the victim's body was a pile of charred wood, which had been used to make a fire; presumably, Rita said, to cook the flesh. The victim's groceries were spilled out beside the wood, including a loaf of French bread, which had been mostly eaten; what remained of the bread was soaked in blood.

"I should be ashamed of myself," she said, "gossiping about other people's misfortunes. How're you and Ginger doing?"

Timber told her about their recent fight and how they hadn't really talked much since. Rita told her she and Officer Kirkland fought all the time, that it was normal in a relationship. When Rita asked what the fight was about, Timber told her she had to cancel plans at the last minute and Ginger wasn't happy about it.

"Well, I know how that goes," Rita said. "The way to make it better is to plan something else, but bigger and better than whatever it was you had to cancel."

"Really?" Timber asked. "That'll work?"

"Sure it will," she said. "Tell you what, you send Charlotte Luna over to my house this weekend for a sleepover, so you and Ginger can take the night for yourselves."

"You would do that?"

"Of course I would," she said. "Winston would love the company and, frankly, it would be nice to have another lady around."

chapter**thirty-one**

The Sleepover

Aﬅer Rita picked me up on Saturday aﬅernoon, Timber and Ginger headed to Beverly Hills to spend a few hours at Goldstein's most recent barbecue; Luscious was going too, but he drove separately, as Timber and Ginger had plans for later that night. Timber and Ginger were sitting at one of the many tables Goldstein set up in the backyard, chatting over their food. Timber, as usual, was eating the mystery meat, along with potato salad, baked beans and a square of corn bread. But she found that her enthusiasm for the mystery meat had all but disappeared.

In the Divinity, Timber's world was small. She was witness to countless Sustenance Sacrifices, which indirectly taught her how she was to view human life. Humans were meant to die, so there was nothing strange about eating their flesh; to simply let it rot away would have been the real tragedy. But during those last five years, as Timber assimilated into the Outside, she came to learn that the human shell was regarded as more than a source of sustenance; it was considered part and parcel to the person who inhabited it. To eat a person in the Outside was frowned upon not simply because it was eating human flesh, but because you were eating everything that person was—you were eating their love and their compassion, their imagination and their empathy, their hopes and their dreams.

The more Timber came to understand this, the more her connection to humanity evolved. She came to understand—really and truly—that humans were people. And while she continued to eat the mystery meat, she did so with conflicted emotions that grew gradually more pronounced over the last five years, until they unwittingly reached their climax during Goldstein's most recent barbecue. So it made sense that the meal Timber was eating that day in Goldstein's backyard would be the last time she would ever eat human flesh again—though, at the time, she wasn't aware of it. It wasn't a decision she would make, so much as a decision that would be made for her, in a roundabout way.

Not too far away from Timber and Ginger, Goldstein sat at his glass table beside the pool. Amongst the hundreds of guests he was entertaining that afternoon, there was only one man sitting with him. He was long and thin. His skin was pale, almost white in the literal sense, and he had short black hair, which was neatly parted to the side. When Luscious joined Timber and Ginger with a plate of food in hand, Ginger asked him about the long, pale man.

"I've never seen him before," Luscious said.

"Goldstein seems to know him well for someone you've never seen before."

"Goldstein's known me for fifteen years," Luscious said, "and I'm sure some people at this party are wondering who *I* am."

"How does he know so many people?" she asked.

"He probably hasn't met half of them."

"I suppose things aren't always as they appear."

Rita took Winston and me to the bowling alley for a couple hours of Cosmic Bowling, which Brunswick hosted on Saturday afternoons. While we waited for a lane, Rita took us to say hi to Matilda at The Little Lebowski. Ever the teacher, Matilda showed us the different bowling balls and explained how each one had a weight inside; she told us that each ball reacted differently on the lanes based on the shape and position of the weight. She then told me that my bowling was improving at such a rate that my mom should consider buying me my own ball, which sounded like the best idea I'd ever heard.

After hanging out with Matilda, Winston and I bowled, while Rita sat back and watched. Once the lights came back on and Cosmic Bowling was over for the afternoon, Rita asked what we wanted for lunch. Winston and I both agreed on pizza, so Rita took us to Round Table. While we waited for the pizza, she gave us each five dollars worth of quarters and let us wander about the small arcade, where we played every game two or three times. After lunch, Rita took us across the street to Dairy Queen, where we all got chocolate-dipped ice cream cones.

After a quick stop at Vons, where we picked up supplies both for dinner and dessert, we went back to their house. It was early in the evening and Officer Kirkland hadn't come home yet. Rita let Winston and I play video games in the living room, while she started dinner. She was making meatloaf, mashed potatoes, corn on the cob and buttered rolls. When it was time to make dessert—chocolate cupcakes with chocolate chips and a maraschino cherry center, topped with cherry frosting—she invited Winston and I to help.

Rita did the more involved steps, like cracking the eggs, while letting Winston and me do the simpler steps, such as pouring in the oil and water; she even let us mix it all together with the cake mix by spoon, before shoring up our work with an electric mixer. Winston and I set the cupcake paper into each slot of the cupcake pan, before Rita filled each one up with the chocolate batter. She then let Winston and me place two maraschino cherries into each cupcake, before she set them in the oven. However simple the whole process seems now in retrospect, for me at that time it was all so exotic.

As night came and Goldstein's barbecue transitioned into what-ever it was to become, Ginger and Timber slipped out to begin the rest of their night. From Beverly Hills, they got themselves onto Route 66 where they drove into Upland, eventually arriv-ing at Oasis, the Inland Empire's largest gay nightclub. Exit-ing Ginger's car, she and Timber held hands, interlacing their fingers as they walked to the club entrance. The bouncer, a tall woman with healthy proportions, asked to see their IDs, but, of course, Timber had no identification. Anybody else might have gotten turned away, but with a little seductive banter and a few bats of her lashes, Ginger convinced the bouncer to let Timber in.

The air inside Oasis was stale and warm, dimly lit by a series of tall palm tree lamps and strobe lights. The music pulsed loud and hard, echoing off the walls, a tornado of sounds. Men and women both packed Oasis, dancing and drinking, flirting and touching. There were two men tending bar, each of them shirtless, their muscles slick with sweat. Ginger ordered a couple of beers, before leading Timber through the heaving crowd on the dance floor, past the deejay, sit-ting down at a bamboo-style table.

Sitting there with their beers, drinking and laughing, Ginger reminisced about their first trip to Oasis together—which, for Tim-ber, was her first time ever. It was also the night Timber drank for the first time; after two or three beers she was feeling particularly relaxed and uninhibited, so when Ginger took her hand and asked her to dance, she didn't give it a second thought.

Timber was awkward on the dance floor, as she had never danced in an environment such as Oasis. Ginger, for her part, was right in her element. The deejay went from song to song, while Timber and Ginger worked up a sweat, their bodies touching more and more the longer they were on the floor. Twenty or thirty minutes passed and the music got faster and faster, the lights above flashing about, the heaving crowd pulsating like one giant heartbeat.

Timber couldn't remember the exact moment when it happened, but all at once she became aware of Ginger's hands on her hips, holding their bodies together and leaning in for what would be their first kiss. Timber wrapped her arms around Ginger's waist as they made out, taking to it like a natural, considering—not only was this her first kiss with Ginger—it was her first kiss ever.

On this night however, years removed from their first trip to Oasis, Timber and Ginger were content to sit back and enjoy their drinks, watching the giant heartbeat pulse on the dance floor without them for the time being. At various points during the night, they snuck off into dark corners, embracing in long make-out sessions, reminiscent of the first time they made love. At that time, as they made out in an inconspicuous corner of Oasis, Ginger guided Timber's hands under her shirt, placing them on her breasts, where she groped and squeezed with all the enthusiasm of a teenage boy whose fantasies of the flesh had finally been realized.

While Timber had had sex before in the Divinity, it was only ever something that happened *to* her. So the night she spent with Ginger, being the first sexual experience in which she was intimately and erotically engaged, beheld the sort of sacredness that loses its magic when talked about too much. Or, as Timber told me: "I've shared a great many stories with you, darling, offering you my life in the most vivid details I can recall. But, in the interest of modesty, I'm not sure how appropriate it would be to recount my first sexual relations with Ginger."

Even though I was sleeping over at Winston's, they chose to spend the night at Ginger's apartment, which was a decent size for a one-bedroom. All of Ginger's furniture was red, as was the clock and the various paintings that hung on the wall. Ginger had a big red bed where she and Timber had shared many intimate moments together. But on this night, fueled by the momentum of their heightened passion for each other, Timber and Ginger never made it to the bedroom.

Hours later, as they lay on the floor of Ginger's apartment, dewy and breathless, Timber lay awake while her new lover fell asleep. She ran her fingers through her ever-growing hair, the sweat of her love-making matting it to her temples. Laying on her side, her chin resting in her palm, Timber looked over at her sleeping lover, admiring her beautiful features—her fair skin, her freckled cheeks, her full lips and her auburn hair—and, as she did, her mind began to wander.

For just a few brief moments, Timber was back in the Divinity, sitting at the Learning Tree with Pepsi, wading through Marlow Stream with Jupiter, sitting at Charlotte's feet as she rocked in her chair, assisting Luna in the Sustenance Dwelling. Closing her eyes, Timber was back in the freezer, cornered by Daddy Marlow. She shuddered to think how, had he had his way, this moment with Ginger—and all of the joyous moments she had experienced those last five years—would not have been.

That night Timber fell asleep by the side of her lover, grateful that the worst was all behind her, unaware that Three Marlow's return was little more than a week away.

When Officer Kirkland came home, he went straight to Winston and lifted him up in the air, kissing his cheek; Winston giggled, wrapping his arms around his father's neck. Officer Kirkland smiled at me and said what a pleasure it was to have me over. We all sat at the dinner table together and Rita served us each a plate. Before we ate, Officer Kirkland asked us all to bow our heads, while he said grace. I'd never heard of this before, but it was very nice. After we ate, he told Rita what a marvelous job she had done with dinner, before leaning over and giving her a peck on the lips. Rita then retrieved the cupcakes we made, setting one in front of each of us. She told Officer Kirkland that Winston and I helped make them and, for his part, he feigned passing out at how delicious they were, which made Winston and I laugh.

After Rita put Winston and I to bed, she and Officer Kirkland sat on the couch together and watched television. I got up to use the bathroom, mostly because I wasn't sleepy yet, but also because I wanted to see what was on TV. I hid behind the corner of the hallway wall, giving myself a good view of the living room. Rita and Officer Kirkland were watching the news, which was reporting on a new victim of the California Cannibal. Unlike the other victims, this one, a young woman, had inexplicably survived the attack. Her survival didn't appear to be anything more than a medical miracle, one that she would probably, in time, come to resent. She was being treated at San Antonio Community Hospital where she was put into an induced coma, shielding her from the tremendous physical pain she would eventually have to deal with.

She was discovered unconscious and tied to a chair inside of the small house she rented in Montclair only after her landlady showed up to collect the rent. The victim, who usually paid her rent on time and without incident, hadn't sent the check out, nor was she returning any calls. The landlady said she wouldn't normally let herself in, but she just knew something had to be wrong. It was determined that the victim had been tied to the chair for three to five days before being discovered. That was all the news reported, however, which disappointed Rita.

"I've got some more details on this one," Officer Kirkland said.

"Do you now?"

"Oh yeah," he said. "There's a few interesting tidbits the department is trying very hard to keep away from the media."

"Oh, pray tell."

"Well it seems that large portions of the girl's thighs were missing," he said, "crudely carved away. And her right arm had been cut off beneath the elbow, with the open wound cauterized."

"What's that mean?"

"It means the wound was burned with something hot to keep her from bleeding to death."

"He didn't want her to die?"

"Not right away, at least."

"Oh my!"

"The severed arm," he continued, "was found on the floor, the flesh having been removed from the bone."

"Goodness," she said, "he ate that, too?"

"Believe it or not," Officer Kirkland said, "the department wouldn't get too bent out of shape if the gruesome details got out. It's the *strange* details they want to keep quiet."

"There're stranger details than that?"

"The department is already having to wade through a bunch of false confessions from freaks looking to get famous," he said. "So they want to keep the really weird stuff quiet in case the actual California Cannibal comes forward."

"Quit teasing me," she said, straddling Officer Kirkland's lap. "What do you know?"

"When they found the victim," he said, "she'd been shaved bald."

"Her head?" Rita asked, unbuttoning his shirt.

"*Everything*," Officer Kirkland said.

"Is she the first?" she said, kissing his neck.

"No," he said. "Turns out he's done this to all of his victims."

"He sounds like a bad, bad man," she said, unzipping Officer Kirkland's fly.

"Oh, he is," he said. "The worst."

"Looks like we're gonna need Superman to save the day," she said, dipping her head down where I could no longer see it.

"Don't worry, baby," he said, resting his head back, eyes closed, "Superman will be coming before you know it."

chapter**thirty-two**

All Good Things

Timber was sitting in the living room watching TV while she waited for Marcos and Jared to arrive. It was about two in the morning, so I had been put to bed hours before. Luscious stayed up for a little while to keep Timber company, but he too was now in bed. Timber was a night removed from her sleepover at Ginger's and was feeling particularly good about how things had gone. Ginger too seemed happy and, at the very least, satiated, as she didn't even ask to spend the night. Timber was glad for this, as it made it easier to do her work. Ginger would be at the house in the morning, anyhow, as she and Luscious also had work to do.

And so, there Timber sat, waiting, occasionally looking away from the TV into the backyard. It was dark out, nearly pitch black, but for the moonlight. She looked for any sort of stirring or movement in the darkness. Marcos and Jared were always punctual; they had to be, because that's what Goldstein asked of them. They always made their deliveries at two in the morning and it was just about that time.

Scarcely a minute past the two o'clock hour, Timber finally heard some rustling. She could just make out Marcos and Jared's silhouettes as they set down the body and unlocked the Sustenance Dwelling. They generally left the bodies in the freezer, unless they knew ahead of time that Timber would be doing her work immediately after they left. Such was the case on that night, so Timber knew the body would be waiting for her on the heavy wooden table.

She waited about five or ten minutes, even after she saw Marcos and Jared exit the Sustenance Dwelling. As a courtesy, she always made sure they had time to get to their car and drive away, before going into the backyard. It was a cool night and, as she headed towards the Sustenance Dwelling, she wondered if she should've worn a sweatshirt; she figured she'd be okay, as she would soon enough be breaking a sweat from the work that lay ahead.

As she reached the Sustenance Dwelling, Timber flipped through her keys. She could hardly see them for the darkness, but was able to make out the right key by feel. Slipping it into the lock, she opened the door and let herself in. She waited to turn the lights on until the door was completely closed, which meant there was always a brief moment when she was alone in the dark with the body. When she turned on the lights, Timber was immediately surprised by what she saw.

On her wooden table lay the long, pale man from Goldstein's barbecue. He was completely naked with dark bruises all about his ribs and face. His dark hair, which was so neatly parted the day before, was all messed up. His eyes were shut, like he was asleep. Timber had never met him nor had she ever spoken to him, yet she found herself feeling a pang of remorse for his death. Just a day earlier he had been smiling and laughing.

Timber pulled her rubber apron from the wall, putting it on. With her back to the long, pale man, she also removed Luna's cleaver from the wall. She rarely reflected on the work she did, but on this night, as if she somehow knew it was different, Timber found herself really thinking about her life and what it was all made of. And as she did, she heard a slight stirring—followed by a cough. She turned around with the cleaver in hand and saw the long, pale man had opened his eyes.

Timber wondered if maybe she was imaging things. Perhaps, she thought, his eyes were open all along and she was simply scaring herself. But when she stepped closer to him, there was no mistaking the shallow breaths that came from his mouth. The long, pale man who was supposed to be dead was alive on Timber's table. Even still, he was in a severely weakened state, practically dead. He managed to shift his head just enough to see Timber standing beside him and, when he did, the long, pale man tried to speak. She could barely make out his words, but he seemed to be asking for help.

The idea of this poor man lying all but dead on her table, asking Timber for help, broke her heart. She didn't know what to do. While she lost herself in the surreal humanity of the moment, the long, pale man saw the cleaver in her hand and began to panic. Since he was severely weakened—and, really, how was it that he *wasn't* dead?—he posed no real threat to her, however the adrenaline of fear must have been pumping through his body, because he managed to reach back and grab Timber's wrist in his long, bony fingers.

All at once, she snapped back to reality and began thinking about the possible repercussions of the situation if she didn't handle it just right. She wanted to go get Luscious and ask for his help in deciding what to do, but if the long, pale man found the energy to take her wrist in his hand, Timber worried he might also find the energy to get out of the Sustenance Dwelling in her absence. There was really only one solution and Timber knew what it was.

She had to kill him.

It was the only answer that made sense. She didn't know what would happen if she didn't—she couldn't even wrap her mind around the possible fallout—but she knew it wouldn't be good. Not good at all.

The long, pale man tried to scream, but he couldn't muster more than a strained breath that sounded like he was clearing his throat.

Timber had only ever killed three men in her life—Richard, City Marlow and Daddy Marlow. With each of them, their deaths were preceded by the dark seed in Timber's heart sprouting its charcoal branches. But there was no charcoal now. No hate, no rage. If Timber was going to kill this man, she would have to do so with a level head and a heavy heart.

She thought about me and Ginger and Luscious, about how all of our lives would be put in jeopardy, our safety compromised if she didn't kill him. She hoped that by seeing him as some sort of conduit for the potential destruction of her family—which, in a sense, he was—she might find the necessary rage to kill him. But it had been five years since she killed a man and since that night she hoped she would never have to again. And if she did have to kill a man, she always figured he would have it coming, she figured he would have earned it. But this man—this long, pale man—had not earned his death, at least not by Timber's hand. Nonetheless, Timber could imagine no other solution.

So she removed his bony fingers from her wrist, placing his hand down on the wooden table. With her left hand, she covered his eyes, both to steady his head and shield his view; if he had to die, Timber didn't want his last moments to involve the terror of seeing the cleaver come down. His breathing quickened as Timber lifted the cleaver over her head. The long, pale man let his hands lay limp on the table, as if resigned to his fate. Timber took a deep breath and, before doing what she knew had to be done, she whispered an apology.

With three powerful strokes of her cleaver, Timber killed the long, pale man, leaving him decapitated on the heavy wooden table. Dropping the cleaver to the concrete, Timber removed her rubber apron and sat down on the floor. Hugging her knees to her chest, she began to cry. This was not the first man she had killed, but it sure did feel like it. Instead of rage and hate coursing though her veins, Timber felt remorse and shame.

She didn't have it in her to do anymore work that night. She didn't even care about putting the long, pale man in the freezer.

She just wanted to get out of there and try as best she could to put it all behind her. Turning off the light, she exited the Sustenance Dwelling. So caught up in the weight of what she had done, Timber didn't realize she had forgotten to lock the door before heading back inside the house.

The next morning, when she stepped into the Sustenance Dwelling for her first and only time, Ginger's scream was muffled by the door as it shut behind her. Luscious was working in the office when Ginger arrived that day. Whatever he was doing, he needed to finish it, so he told Ginger to hang out for a bit. Ginger went into Timber's room, where she and I were asleep; she kissed us each on the forehead, before going downstairs. She hadn't planned on going in the backyard. She was just going to go to the kitchen to make some tea.

But the kitchen window had such a nice view of the backyard and, seeing the Sustenance Dwelling, Ginger couldn't help herself. It was a routine that had, over the last five years, become an exercise in futility. The door was never open. But *what if*, she often thought— what if today *it is*? She walked around its perimeter, dragging her fingers along the outside wall, eventually making her way back to the front. Without much ceremony at all, she took the doorknob in her hand and turned it, assuming it would be locked anyway—but, to her great astonishment, the knob turned.

Ginger pulled the door open slowly, skeptically, as if she still didn't believe it was unlocked. She paused for a moment, looking back to the house to see if anyone was near, before entering. Even with the door open, it was dark inside. With one hand holding the door, Ginger felt along the wall, looking for a light switch. When she found the switch, turning on the light, she instinctively let go of the door. It closed completely, just as Ginger saw the decapitated man on the table. That's when she screamed.

Ginger burst out of the Sustenance Dwelling as fast as she could, sprinting through the grass and the weeds, back into the house. She ran upstairs, nearly tripping, before reaching Luscious' office. Collapsing to her hands and knees, she tried to catch her breath, but it was a struggle. It was immediately clear to Luscious that something bad had happened, so he kneeled down beside her, trying to calm her down.

"What is it?"

Ginger pointed a quivering finger at the wall that faced the backyard.

"You saw something?"

"We have to call the police," she said.

"What's going on?"

"There's a dead body in the backyard."

"Are you sure?"

"Yes," she said. "There's a man in the shed with his head cut off."

Luscious put his face in his hands. He knew that this likely spelled the beginning of the end. Whatever else happened—no matter who was to blame—this situation was going to get rectified by Goldstein.

"How did you get in?"

"It was open."

"The door was *open*?"

"It was unlocked," she said. "We have to call the police."

"Not yet," he said. "Let me process this for a second."

"Process *what*?" she said. "There's a dead man in your backyard!"

"I need to talk to Goldstein first."

"He's probably the one who killed him," she said. "I knew there was something wrong with that shed."

"Listen," he said. "I want to make this situation right, just like you do. But the last thing I want is to invite a circus of police and reporters to my house before I know what's going on. I've known Goldstein a long time, Ginger, and the least I can do is tell him what you've seen."

"I can't imagine what his explanation will be."

"Whatever it is, I owe him that much," he said. "Will you let me do that first?"

Ginger took a deep breath, gathering herself, before conceding.

"Thank you," Luscious said.

"What about Timber?"

"She's already seen enough bad things in her life," Luscious said. "No need to tell her about this. Not right away, anyhow."

Ginger agreed.

After sending Ginger home, Luscious woke Timber and brought her into his office. He told her what happened with Ginger, how she freaked out when she saw a decapitated man in the Sustenance Dwelling. Before he could finish, Timber was already in tears. She told Luscious that the long, pale man was alive when she went inside to do her work. She told him that he asked for help and grabbed her wrist and she didn't know what to do.

"Everything's going to be all right," Luscious said.

He pulled Timber into his chest, wrapping his arms around her, wishing so badly he could shield her from whatever was to happen next.

After a brief meeting by his pool, where Luscious told him everything that happened, Goldstein said he needed a day or so to figure things out. By the end of the day, Luscious received a call that Goldstein needed to meet with both he and Timber the following afternoon. The meeting conflicted with my bowling league and, despite the chaos, Timber didn't want to disrupt my life. So she asked Rita if she wouldn't mind picking me up and taking me to the bowling alley.

"Sure," she said. "I don't mind at all. But Winston has a doctors appointment right after, so I won't be able to take her home."

"That shouldn't be a problem," Timber said. "I'll be able to pick her up before they're done."

On the day of the meeting, Luscious and Timber sat beside each other at the glass table, each of them facing Goldstein, who sipped from his gin and tonic.

"This is quite a situation we have on our hands," he said.

"Yes," Luscious agreed.

"You say the man was alive when you found him?" he asked Timber.

"Yes."

"How alive would you say he was?" Goldstein asked. "Was he aware of his surroundings? Was he active?"

"He looked at me," Timber said. "I think he asked for help. But he was very weak."

"You did the right thing," Goldstein said. "Marcos and Jared are the ones who messed up. You had to clean up their mess and I'm sorry about that."

Timber nodded.

"It probably goes without saying that they'll no longer be working for me."

"What will happen to them?" Luscious asked.

"Whatever needs to," Goldstein said. "Unfortunately, that's not the only problem in need of solving. You say Ginger saw the dead body?"

Luscious immediately regretted sharing that detail. Only now was he realizing that maybe—just *maybe*—he could've gotten away with telling Goldstein everything but that.

"Yes."

"And you say she got in by herself?"

"Yes."

"Are you sure?"

"I must have forgotten to lock up," Timber said.

"Of course," Goldstein said. "You were upset, not thinking straight. Anybody else in your situation might have made the same mistake. It's understandable."

Goldstein paused, sipping from his gin and tonic.

"The problem is she knows too much," he said, "and that puts me at risk. I can't have that."

"What has to happen?" Luscious asked.

"She has to disappear."

"No!" Timber cried.

"I don't understand," Luscious said. "Just let me talk to her."

"It's too late," Goldstein said. "It's bad enough you must do business with Officer Kirkland. I don't like having the law so close to my affairs, but that's hardly your fault. The problem now is I can't have Ginger and Officer Kirkland in the same circle. It's too risky. One of them has to disappear and Ginger makes the most sense."

"Why can't you make Officer Kirkland disappear?" Timber asked.

"Killing a cop is a tall order," he said, "and since Marcos and Jared will no longer be working for me, I don't have anybody in place that I trust for such a risky operation."

"But if you had someone to do it, then you would support the decision to kill Officer Kirkland?"

"Sure," Goldstein said, "but the only two people I trust to do it are you and Timber. I wouldn't even consider putting you two at risk in that way."

"You don't have to kill Ginger," Timber said. "Please, you can't."

"Even if you could convince Ginger not to go to the police," Goldstein said, "and, mind you, that's a big if, she would still be too close to Officer Kirkland."

"We can keep them apart," Luscious said.

"You also said you could keep her out of the Sustenance Dwelling," Goldstein said.

Luscious said nothing.

"My mind is made up," Goldstein said. "Unless you two want to kill Officer Kirkland, then I have to put in the order to make Ginger disappear. The sooner it's taken care of, the sooner we can move on."

"I'll kill him," Luscious said. "Let me do it."

"That doesn't work for me," Goldstein said. "With all due

respect, you're not a killer. I would insist on Timber helping."

"Why?"

"Well, apart from having more experience than you, she has the added advantage of being a ghost," Goldstein said. "Her fingerprints and DNA are untraceable. If Officer Kirkland's body were ever discovered, there would be no way of tracing his death back to me."

"Okay," Timber said.

"You don't have to do this," Luscious told her.

"Yes I do."

"I'll need to see the body, of course," Goldstein said. "I know that sounds gruesome, but I really can't leave anything to chance."

"How do we do that?"

"Upon killing him, get Officer Kirkland's body into the Sustenance Dwelling," Goldstein said. "Once I see the job has been done, I'll see to it that he is properly disposed of."

Timber nodded.

"This really is for the best," Goldstein said. "You have my word."

Winston and I ended up finishing our games early, as the team we were scheduled to bowl against didn't show up. Even still, Rita waited with me at the bowling alley for as long as she could. She even called up Timber via Luscious' cell phone, only to learn that they were stuck in traffic. Once Rita really couldn't wait any longer, she asked Matilda if she wouldn't mind looking after me until Timber showed up. Matilda said that was fine, so Rita called Timber again to let her know. Timber, for her part, was still processing the idea of having to kill Rita's husband, so she was pretty amenable to the concession.

Matilda set me up with a hamburger and fries from the snack bar, then sat with me for about ten or fifteen minutes. She checked her watch more or less the whole time, eventfully asking me very sweetly if I knew when my mom would be picking me up. When I told her

I didn't know, she excused herself for a minute and came back with one of the bowling alley attendants, a young man named Pete.

"Charlotte Luna," she said, "I've got to go, so Pete's going to make sure you're okay until your mom gets back, okay?"

I nodded, though I was mostly consumed with watching people bowl.

"If you need anything—more soda or anything—you just let Pete know and he'll take care of it."

Again, I nodded.

While I'm sure Pete had the best of intentions, I never saw him again after Matilda left. I sat alone for about five minutes, eating my food and watching people bowl, before being joined by a strange man whom I had never seen before. He was a big man, physically imposing, with broad shoulders and strong arms; his head was completely shaved and he didn't have any eyebrows. The right side of his head looked like melted wax; his ear was all but gone, a lump of shriveled skin with a small crater where the noise went in. His right eyelid drooped at the corner and beneath it the eye was fogged over, almost completely white.

"Hello there, youngling," he said, his voice deep and raspy. "Do you know who I am?"

I shook my head, no.

"My name is Three Marlow," he said. "I know your mother."

"You do?"

"My father raised her," he said. "His name was Daddy Marlow."

I said nothing, mesmerized by the scars on his face.

"Daddy Marlow is dead now," he said. "That makes me an orphan. Do you know how my father died?"

I shook my head, no.

"I do," he said.

Three Marlow spoke methodically, choosing every word—every beat—with hypnotic precision, lulling me into a false sense of safety. He told me about the Divinity, how it was this wonderful place in the mountains, surrounded by trees and rivers; how there were children everywhere and they played all day, without worry of class-rooms or homework. He told me about his two brothers and how, collectively, they were triplets. He told me that they were dead, that they perished in the Great Fire, which destroyed the Divinity, killing off more than half of its people. He told me that the other survivors wandered off, trying and failing to survive in an environment that they didn't understand.

"There's only three survivors left," he said. "Three people with any connection to the Divinity at all. You know who they are?"

I shook my head, no.

"Me, Timber and *you*" he said, pressing his index finger gently into my forehead. "We're the last living kin of Daddy Marlow. That makes us special."

This made me smile.

"I'm going to be visiting your mother very soon. But I want it to be a surprise," he said, holding his index finger to his lips. "Okay?"

I nodded, yes.

"I'll be seeing you."

Standing up from his seat, Three Marlow turned and walked away, pushing through the exit and disappearing into the bright glare of sunlight. I ran to the exit in time to see him get into his rusty orange pickup truck. He smiled as he backed up out of his parking spot and I watched him drive away for as long as I could, before he disappeared out of sight. Just a few minutes later, Timber and Lus-cious arrived to pick me up.

chapter**thirty-three**

Business As Usual

"Is this a suicide mission?" Timber asked.

"It seems it's our turn," Luscious said.

They were sitting at the kitchen table, each with a glass of tea steaming in front of them. It was the middle of the day and I was upstairs playing in my room. Ginger would be coming over soon, though not to work. She wanted to know what Goldstein had to say. Luscious didn't know what he would tell her. Officer Kirkland would be coming over as well to pick up Luscious' next payment.

"What happens now?" Timber asked.

"Letting Ginger die isn't an option."

Timber agreed.

"So I guess we *know* what has to happen."

"But, Goldstein wants us to fail?"

"Looks that way."

"Is it my fault?"

"No, it's not your fault, love."

"Then why?"

"I think maybe things got a little too messy for Goldstein," Luscious said. "He probably wants to get rid of *everybody* involved in the mess and move on. Either way, we don't have much choice in the matter."

"How do we do it?"

"I don't know," Luscious said. "He's a cop. If he were just a regular guy, then maybe we'd stand a chance. But he's got training in the art of not getting killed. Not to mention he's got a gun, which he probably carries with him at all times."

"Is there a chance he'll use it on us?"

"If we don't kill him quickly and efficiently," Luscious said, "you can count on it."

"If we die, what will happen to Charlotte Luna?"

"Well," Luscious said, "I would say Ginger can take care of her, but…"

He trailed off, unwilling to finish the thought.

"But what?"

"Whether we succeed or fail," he said, "I don't really expect Goldstein to let Ginger live."

"Why couldn't I have just locked the door?"

Before Luscious could say anything to comfort her, there was a knock at the door. It was Ginger. After letting her in, Luscious went upstairs to his office. He opened the safe in the wall and looked at the piles of cash inside, nearly half a million dollars in all, most of it earned by Timber with the work she did in the Sustenance Dwelling. Retrieving an unmarked envelope, he slipped a small stack of bills inside, before closing the safe.

Lately, since Timber told him that Officer Kirkland's son was sick and they were struggling financially, Luscious had begun wondering if he was ever really collecting money on behalf of District Attorney Michaels. It made sense to him that Officer Kirkland could be bluffing the whole thing, figuring Luscious would go along with it, which he had been. He supposed it wouldn't be so bad if Officer

Kirkland were using the money to care for his family—frankly, Luscious would've preferred it if that were the case.

When Luscious went downstairs with the unmarked envelope, Timber and Ginger were sitting at the kitchen table. He sat down with them, placing the envelope in the empty chair beside him. All things considered, Ginger looked good, but Luscious knew she was still shaken up. Of course, she wanted to know what Goldstein had to say.

"He has no idea what happened in there," Luscious lied.

"And you believe him?"

"He swore he would get to the bottom of it," he said. "He only asks that we keep it quiet."

"I hate to say you sound gullible," Ginger said. "But you do."

"I trust him."

"I know you do," she said. "And it's really sweet, but I don't think you should. I just worry if you keep trusting him like you do, you're going to end up hurt. Or worse."

"Give him a few days," Timber said. "Luscious will figure things out."

"I don't know why *you're* not more freaked out," Ginger told Timber. "You live here, too, which means somebody killed a man in *your* backyard as well."

"I know."

"Some animal cut his fucking head off," she said, her voice rising. "That could've been you, it could've been Luscious. What if Charlotte Luna had gone back there when it was happening? There's no telling if she'd still be alive."

Timber dropped her head and began to cry.

"I'm sorry," Ginger said, stroking Timber's hair. "I'm just so fucking scared."

"Me too."

"Is he still back there?"

"Not sure," Luscious lied. "The door is locked up, though. So there's no way to find out."

"May he rest in peace," Ginger said. "Whoever he was."

Mercifully, the three of them fell into some semblance of small talk. It was comforting to finally be talking about things that didn't matter so much, issues that didn't have life or death consequences. Mainly, they talked about my new bowling ball. It was actually Ginger's idea that I should have one; it hadn't occurred to Timber or Luscious before she mentioned it. They had all taken me to The Little Lebowski a few days prior and let me pick out a ball and I was thrilled beyond thrilled when I saw that Matilda had a pink Minnie Mouse bowling ball on her shelf. Matilda measured my fingers for the holes and said she would need a few days to drill, as she was backed up with a lot of other orders. She had actually called the day Ginger discovered the decapitated body of the long, pale man to tell us the ball was ready; for all the obvious reasons, they hadn't taken me to pick it up yet.

They might have gone on talking like this for days and days if Officer Kirkland hadn't shown up. His visits had evolved over the last few months into something less than upsetting. Maybe it was that Luscious wasn't really losing anything he cared to keep, or maybe it was because Officer Kirkland was possibly trying to help his family. Or maybe it was because, in his own way, Officer Kirkland was sort of pleasant to have around, as we didn't ever get company at the house. It would be a stretch to say that Luscious looked forward to the visits, but he certainly didn't dread them.

And since Timber and Rita and Winston and me had all become close, Officer Kirkland just sort of felt like an extension of that closeness. Of course, it didn't stop him from collecting Luscious' money. But even that didn't matter so much, not anymore, because while Officer Kirkland and Ginger sat at the kitchen table, Timber and Luscious knew that one of them had to die.

Timber was sitting beside Officer Kirkland and she couldn't help but look at the gun attached to his hip. It was always there, every time he came over—and probably even when he wasn't in uniform, such as the night they met at Cosmic Bowling—but she never noticed it before. Funny how that works. There were no guns in the Divinity, at least, none that Timber knew of. There was plenty of violence and more than enough death, but Timber didn't see her first gun until she entered the Outside; and it was during a movie, at that. She knew what they did, because she'd seen their violence dramatized hundreds of times over the last five years. But until that afternoon, she had never actually seen a gun in real life. She wondered what role it would play before it was all said and done.

Officer Kirkland thanked Luscious, picked up the blank envelope and went on his way. Ginger also left, but before she did, she gave Timber a kiss and told Luscious she would need a few days before getting back to work. He told her to take as much time as she needed. It wasn't until she was gone, that Luscious told Timber he had an idea.

chapterthirty-four

The Almost-Assassination of Officer Kirkland

"It's not perfect," he said, "but it might work. We do it here."

"Officer Kirkland?"

"Yes, but not here in the house," he said. "It would be too messy, one way or the other."

"Where, then?"

"The Sustenance Dwelling," he said. "We just need to get him in there."

"And then what?"

Luscious looked at Timber, but said nothing.

"Will it just be me and him?"

"I think maybe it has to be," he said. "If something goes wrong and he gets out, I'll have a chance to get him."

"How am I supposed to do it?" she asked. "I mean he's bigger than me, and stronger. Being isolated won't give me an advantage."

"You'll have the element of surprise on your side," he said. "It's not much, but it's something."

"I suppose," she said. "Why would he come over, anyway? He already collected his money for the month."

"I'll get in touch with him," he said, "and tell him I'd like to make an extra payment. We'll schedule it during Charlotte Luna's bowling league so nobody else is here."

Timber nodded.

"Do you have any ideas how you'll do it?" he asked.

"Not really."

"It has to be fast," he said. "You'll want to avoid any struggle with him."

"Maybe if I can put my cleaver in his back, it will stun him long enough to slit his throat," she said. "I'll have to have the cleaver positioned near the door. When he walks in, I'll follow behind him and pick it up."

Luscious nodded.

"If I stick it between his shoulder blades, he'll drop to his knees," she said, "if I'm lucky. That'll give me a pretty clear shot at his throat."

"You think maybe you should go straight for his neck," Luscious asked, "as soon as you walk in?"

"He's too tall," Timber said.

"Maybe his leg, then," he said. "That would almost definitely bring him down."

"When he reaches for the injured leg," she said, "his hand might instinctively find the gun. If I hit his shoulder blades, his hands will reach up and away."

"It could work. I'll wait outside with a baseball bat or something, in case..." Luscious paused, taking a deep breath through his nose. "In case the first part doesn't work."

The whole conversation was surreal and neither one of them could believe what they were talking about. They didn't know the probability for success, but it didn't feel very good. And even if they did succeed, poor Rita and Winston would be left alone. But if they failed, Charlotte Luna would be left alone and Ginger would probably be killed anyway. No matter how many ways they looked at it, there just didn't seem to be a solution that didn't involve bloodshed.

The following Tuesday, Timber asked Ginger if she would take me to my bowling league; she told her that Luscious was going to talk to Goldstein again and wanted her to go along. Ginger agreed without making a fuss. I imagine she was satisfied to know—or at least to think—that Luscious was still trying to get to the bottom of why there was a dead man in his backyard. As for Officer Kirkland, he had agreed to come to the house to collect the extra payment Luscious offered. He didn't even ask any questions, which Luscious found interesting; he just seemed happy that there was more money.

While they waited, Timber and Luscious went over the plan again. Officer Kirkland would sit down and they would all drink tea and chat. Luscious would leave the chair where he normally put the unmarked envelope empty. He would wait for Officer Kirkland to mention it. If he didn't, Luscious would simply point it out and immediately apologize. He would then ask Timber to show Officer Kirkland to the Sustenance Dwelling—or the "shed," as they would call it in front of him—as that's where they keep the money. They talked about the possibility that Officer Kirkland might resist going out back, but were banking on the hope that he would think nothing of it. If he opted not to go out back with Timber, then the whole plan would be for naught.

Assuming he went out back with Timber, she would lead him to the Sustenance Dwelling, open the door and invite him to go in first. Timber would step in behind him, take hold of her cleaver and immediately swing it between Officer Kirkland's shoulder blades. If he didn't immediately drop down, Timber would kick the back of his knees and hope that would put him down. From there she would remove her cleaver and swing it full force into the front of his neck.

At that point, she would make sure Officer Kirkland died as quickly as possible; she didn't imagine she would be able to spare him much pain, but she would do her best. Luscious would wait outside the Sustenance Dwelling with a baseball bat, so if Officer Kirkland came out, then he would know Timber had failed and he would immediately try to knock him out. If, however, Timber came out first, then he would know she succeeded.

Luscious told her that if she wanted to back out at any point, she could. Timber acknowledged she wasn't comfortable with the idea of killing Officer Kirkland, but Ginger was more important and she would do anything to keep her safe. Nonetheless, Luscious told her, if she changed her mind at any point, she didn't have to go through with it.

"If you do change your mind," Luscious said, "then when Officer Kirkland asks about the money and I tell you to take him to the shed, you simply have to tell me that you lost the key."

"Okay," she said.

"If you say that, I'll understand you want to back out."

"What then?" she asked.

"Then I guess I'll have to take him back there myself."

"You think you'd be able to do it?"

"I have no idea."

"What if we both decide we can't go through with it?" Timber asked.

"We can't let that be an option," he said.

Officer Kirkland arrived soon after the final run-through of the plan. He sat down at the kitchen table, beside the empty chair. Luscious served them all tea, as was their routine. As they drank the tea and made small talk, Timber noticed Officer Kirkland subtly eyeing the empty chair, no doubt wondering where the unmarked envelope was. As they finished their tea, Luscious collected the glasses and told Officer Kirkland what a pleasure it was to have him over, as usual; he said it in such a way as to imply that the meeting was done and Officer Kirkland should be on his way. He took his cue, as if he were following the script right along with them.

"I don't mean to be a bother," he said, "but the chair is emptier than usual."

"Really?" Luscious said, before making a show of looking at the empty chair. "I'm so sorry about that." Then, looking at Timber, he said, "I must have left it in the shed. Would you mind taking Officer Kirkland out back to the shed?"

Timber stayed put for a moment.

"Did you lose your key?" he asked.

After a brief hesitation, Timber said, "No, I have it."

"Thank goodness," Luscious said.

Timber stood up and headed for the sliding door, opening it up and stepping outside. Again, as if he were trying to make their work as easy as possible, Officer Kirkland followed Timber into the backyard to the Sustenance Dwelling. Unlocking the door, she let him in first. As he stepped inside, she followed behind, turning on the light. She knew as soon as the door closed, Luscious would run out with his baseball bat and wait beside the door. Officer Kirkland looked around, fascinated by the inside. Stepping forward to the heavy wooden table, he ran his hands over the smooth surface, possibly wondering why it was stained with red.

"Is this some sort of a workroom?" he asked.

"Yes."

"It's pretty big in here," he said. "What's in there?"

"That's a freezer."

He walked over and opened the door, looking inside.

"It's empty," he said. "Looks like you guys need to go to the supermarket."

"Yes," Timber said, "we probably should."

All the while, he kept his back to her, as if he knew what was supposed to happen next and was resigned to it. The reality was, Timber had ample opportunity to kill Officer Kirkland. There was more than enough time to retrieve the cleaver, step behind him and stick it between his shoulder blades. He had been so cooperative with everything else, Officer Kirkland probably would have gladly fallen to his knees to give her the best possible angle to chop his throat. Timber knew all along what she was waiting for. She wanted the dark seed to sprout one last time, to grip her heart in its charcoal branches. She wanted to feel some sort of rage or anger—any emotion that would draw her hand to the cleaver and let her do what needed to be done.

But the seed stayed dormant, her heart remained unclenched. She was not filled with anger, at least not for Officer Kirkland. Even before he turned around, she knew that she would not kill him. She walked around the Sustenance Dwelling for a few moments, making a show of looking for the money that she knew wasn't there.

"What's this for?" Officer Kirkland asked.

Timber turned and saw he was holding the cleaver.

"For cutting," she said.

"Of course it is," Officer Kirkland laughed. "I just meant what do you cut with it?"

"Meat."

"You cut it there?" he asked, pointing the cleaver at the heavy wooden table.

"Yes."

"Must be some big pieces of meat, huh?"

Timber nodded.

"Is the money here?"

"I can't find it."

Officer Kirkland set the cleaver down on the table.

"I'm sure Mr. Jones will find it," he said, heading for the door. Before he opened it, Officer Kirkland stopped and turned back to Timber. "You know, it's really none of my business, but something has been weighing on my mind."

"Really?"

"Before we met, I did a background check on Mr. Jones," he said. "It made sense I should know as much about him as possible ahead of time."

Timber nodded.

"Later, I did a background check on you and Ginger."

Timber said nothing.

"The part that bothers me is there was no record of you."

"Really?"

"Yeah," he said, "like you don't even exist. The same turned out to be true for Charlotte Luna."

"That's strange," Timber said.

"I thought so, too," he said. "I guess I was hoping you might have an explanation."

Timber shrugged, shaking her head, no.

"Like I said, it's none of my business," he said. "Rita sure does like you, though. Charlotte Luna, too. You've got yourself a real nice family."

"Thank you," she said.

Officer Kirkland smiled, then turned for the door. Before he opened it, Timber remembered Luscious would be outside waiting with his baseball bat, so she yelled for him to wait.

"What's the matter?" he asked.

Timber was already hustling for the door.

"Nothing," she said. "I just wanted to get the door."

Before Officer Kirkland could say anything else, Timber opened the door and stepped outside. She saw Luscious poised with his baseball bat, like he was waiting for a fastball.

"Oh hey, Luscious," she said loudly, "I couldn't find the money. Should I look somewhere else for Officer Kirkland?"

Luscious looked confused, until he saw Officer Kirkland step out of the Sustenance Dwelling. Luscious quickly tossed the bat, before he could see it.

"I was just about to check on you two," he said.

"Timber couldn't find it," Officer Kirkland said.

"I can keep looking, if you have time," Luscious said.

"I really should be going," he said. "It's not a big deal."

"You sure?"

"Yeah," he said, already heading for the house. "A cup of tea and the pleasure of your company was good enough for me."

Timber and Luscious followed Officer Kirkland into the house, walking him to the front door, standing on the porch as he drove away.

chapter**thirty-five**

The Reckoning

Luscious was relieved that Timber didn't kill Officer Kirkland and he told her so as soon as he was gone. They went back into the house and collapsed on the couch, each of them physically and emotionally drained by what had nearly happened. Luscious didn't bring it up right away, because he knew they both needed at least a brief reprieve, but he eventually told Timber that they needed to figure out what to tell Goldstein. Luscious feared that none of us would be safe when Goldstein found out he and Timber hadn't gone through with the plan.

"We could lie to him," Timber said.

"Yes, but he'll want to see the body."

"Right."

"So I'll show him the body."

"But it won't be there."

"It doesn't matter," he said. "All I have to do is get him into the Sustenance Dwelling. I'll lock him inside and we can make a getaway."

"Will he die in there?"

"No," Luscious said. "He'll have his cell phone with him, I'm sure. He can call his driver. I can even tell him that Goldstein wants to see him inside the house. By the time he figures it out, we'll have a pretty nice head start."

"A head start to where?"

"Someplace far. Far enough away that Goldstein won't care to look for us."

"We're going to disappear?"

"You got it, love."

"What do we tell Ginger?"

"The truth," he said. "We'll tell her that we're leaving and her safety depends on coming with us."

"What will we do for money?"

"I've got some money put away from all the work you've done for Goldstein. We can live off that for at least a couple of years, until we figure out something permanent."

It all made perfectly good sense and, more than that, it sounded like something that might actually work. Timber laid her head on Luscious' shoulder and smiled, feeling for the first time in a long time that maybe—just maybe—everything was going to be okay.

Luscious called Goldstein the following morning to tell him Officer Kirkland was dead. As he expected, Goldstein wanted to see the body—but what he wasn't quite expecting was that Goldstein would want to see the body immediately.

"My driver will have me to your home in about an hour," he said.

This short notice didn't change the plan, but merely accelerated it. An important part of the plan was that Timber and Charlotte Luna couldn't be there when Goldstein showed up. It just wouldn't be safe. Because Timber didn't drive, Luscious told her to walk Charlotte Luna to Beryl Park, which was about ten to fifteen minutes away.

"Give me at least an hour to come pick you up," he said. "From there we head out, hopefully with Ginger. If you don't see me in an hour, you and Charlotte Luna head straight to Rita's and wait there until Officer Kirkland gets home. There's a good chance that I may be dead, so you go ahead and tell him everything. Whatever happens from there will be out of our hands."

"Do you think that might happen?" Timber asked.

"Not really," he said, "but we need to be prepared for the possibility. Promise me that if I'm not there in an hour, you'll go straight to Rita's."

"I promise," she said. "But what about Ginger?"

"I'll get in touch with her," he said. "I don't want you to worry about that."

Timber sat on a bench near the sandbox of Beryl Park, watching me play on the jungle gym. She thought about the night before, which she spent with Ginger, Luscious and me. We watched *Sleeping Beauty*, which, collectively, was out favorite Disney film. It was a simple night, which was why Timber enjoyed it so much. She and Ginger sat beside each other on the couch; I sat on the floor between Timber's legs, my arms hanging over her knees like a scarecrow. Luscious was in the kitchen, making popcorn and preparing root beer floats. When the movie was over, Timber put me to bed, kissing my forehead and telling me over and over how much she loved me. Ginger came in the room to say goodnight as well, kissing my cheeks; she told me she loved me the most, more than any Disney movie ever made.

"More than *The Lion King*?" I asked.

"More than *The Lion King*," she assured me.

"More than *Dumbo*?"

"More than *Dumbo*, *Snow White* and *Cinderella* combined," she said.

Timber and Ginger stayed up for a few more hours, cuddled on the couch and watching TV, before Ginger went back to her apartment. They didn't talk much, but they didn't have to. They were completely comfortable in their loving silence, content to be together.

It was this memory—not even a day old—that consumed Timber, as she sat on the bench at Beryl Park, watching me play. She wanted the rest of her life to be like that, watching Disney cartoons with me, Ginger and Luscious, cuddling on the couch, drinking root beer floats. No more butchering, no more Sustenance Dwelling, no more bloodshed. Just a simple life lived in peace with the people she loved.

Timber didn't wear a watch, but by her estimation we'd been at the park for about thirty minutes. She called me over to her on the bench, deciding it was time to fill me in on how our lives were about to change. She told me that soon Luscious would pick us up with Ginger and we were going to drive far away.

"Where to?"

"I don't know."

"Will we come back?"

"No, I don't think so."

"What about Winston?"

"Winston will stay here with his parents."

"Will I see him again?"

"I don't think so, sweetie," she said, stroking my hair.

I was quiet then, feeling the sadness of leaving my first and only friend.

"What about my bowling ball?"

I had only just gotten my pink Minnie Mouse ball from The Little Lebowski a few days earlier. Rita had taken me to pick it up, at Timber's request; she let Winston and me bowl a few games, mostly so I could use it. It was while we were gone that Luscious and Timber devised their now-defunct plan to kill Officer Kirkland. I only got to use my Minnie Mouse ball the one time, as I forgot it in Rita's car. Timber had assured me I would get it back the next time, but that was before she knew that we would be going away.

"We're not going to be able to get your ball before we leave, sweetie."

This was when I started crying. Timber held me in her arms, rocking back and forth, trying to comfort me, promising that everything would be fine and that she would get me another ball as soon as possible. As much sadness as I felt for the loss of my pink Minnie Mouse bowling ball, I think I was also crying because I wouldn't see Winston again. When I finally calmed down and my tears fell a little more silently, Timber took me back into the sandbox, where she sat me on the swing, gently pushing me forward.

When the hour passed and Luscious hadn't shown up, Timber began to worry. She wasn't yet ready to panic and decided to wait a little while longer before leaving the park; but she could only stand to wait about five minutes, before gathering me up.

"Where're we going?"

"We're going home."

"Aren't we supposed to wait for Luscious and Ginger?"

"I'm sure they'll find us."

Timber knew all along that she wouldn't go to Rita's. Even when she promised Luscious, she knew. She imagined he had to know as well, which was why he was so adamant about making her promise. Neither one of them figured it would come down to this, but now here they were.

Timber's heart was pounding when we got home and she saw that the front gate had been knocked off its hinges. She picked me up then and walked through, onto the long driveway that led to the house. Goldstein's black car was parked in front beside Ginger's car. And next to them, parked crookedly in front of the house, was the rusty orange pickup truck that Timber assumed she'd never see again.

"That's Three Marlow's car," I said.

Timber's arms tensed around me.

"Charlotte Luna, sweetie," she said, "how do you know that?"

"I met him at the bowling alley," I said. "He told me it was a surprise and that I wasn't supposed to tell you."

She quickly walked me over to one of the large trees in the front yard and told me to stay behind the trunk. She told me it was very important that I hide until she came out of the house. She made me promise that I wouldn't move. Then she began heading for the front door, stopping when she noticed the driver's side window of Goldstein's car had been shattered; the driver was dead, slumped over the steering wheel. Timber ran to the porch, stopping at the front door, which was ajar. Taking a deep breath, she entered the house.

There were fresh bloodstains on the wall and the wooden stair banister was knocked crooked. Progressing forward, through the short hallway, over the broken glass of fallen picture frames, Timber broached the living room, where she saw Luscious bound to a chair, his arms tied behind his back and duct tape covering his mouth. His nose was bleeding and he had shaving cream on his head. Three Marlow stood behind him, gripping Luscious' jaw in his hand as he shaved his head. He was halfway done when he saw Timber standing in the hallway. This made him smile.

"Join us," Three Marlow said.

Stepping into the living room, Timber first saw Goldstein bound to a chair, not far from Luscious. His slumped-over head was completely shaved. She watched his torso, looking in vain for the rise and fall of his ribcage. Goldstein was dead. Timber next saw Ginger lying sideways on the floor, also bound to a chair. Her face was bruised, one eye swollen shut. Her head, which had also been shaved bald, hung awkwardly against her shoulder. Her beautiful red hair was spread across the floor. Timber ran to her, kneeling at her side side, laying her hands on Ginger's face. Her skin was cold, her body still.

Leaving Luscious in his chair, Three Marlow moved to Timber, standing over her.

"I killed them both," he said. "I'm going to kill *him*, too."

Timber looked to Luscious, who was struggling to free himself from his bindings.

"It hurts, doesn't it?" Three Marlow said. "Finding the ones you love dead? I experienced it myself some time ago, but you already know that."

Timber kneeled beside Ginger's body, caressing her dead lover's cheeks, too much in shock to cry just yet. Three Marlow laughed to himself, pleased with how things were turning out.

Placing the bottom of his boot on her chest, Three Marlow pushed Timber onto her back. "I've been dreaming about this day for a long, long time," he said.

About five years, as it were.

He stood over Timber, looking down on her with his partially deformed face, a straight razor in his hand. Neither Ginger nor Goldstein appeared to have been killed with the straight razor; it seemed that they had simply had their necks broken. Timber wondered if Three Marlow planned to kill her the same way. Or did he have something else in mind, something worse. Laying beside her dead lover and looking up at the man who killed her, Timber thought she might be able to snatch the straight razor from Three Marlow's hand. It would be risky, she knew—she might not be able to keep all her fingers in the effort—but what other choice did she have?

"Is that little girl of yours here, too?" Three Marlow asked.

With that, Timber jumped up to charge Three Marlow, but he struck her down before she could rise all the way, kicking her beneath the chin with his heavy boot, sending a shock of pain through her skull, leaving her half-conscious. She was just awake enough to know there was nothing she could do. Her fate had been settled. For five years, Timber had successfully run away from her past and now, as she lay waiting to die, she thought herself a fool for ever believing she had escaped the Divinity's inevitable reckoning.

All at once, without warning, the living room was filled with the sound of a loud bang, followed immediately by Three Marlow's forehead exploding, his brains spraying out onto Timber. As he collapsed to the floor, razor still in hand, Timber saw Officer Kirkland standing behind him, his smoking gun pointed in the direction of where Three Marlow's head had been. After taking a few moments to survey the macabre scene, Officer Kirkland freed Luscious from his bindings. Luscious went straight to Timber, holding her in his arms and crying.

chapter**thirty-six**

Semblance of Peace

It seemed there were two things that saved Timber Marlow's life that day. One was the fact that she hadn't killed Officer Kirkland. The other was my pink Minnie Mouse bowling ball. Rita had come across it in her car and had given it to Officer Kirkland to drop off while he was out patrolling. It would be a while before Timber or Luscious could appreciate the precarious circumstances that ultimately spared their lives, partly because not every life was spared that morning. Goldstein, it might be argued, got what he deserved—and quite poetically, at that. But Ginger had done nothing to deserve her fate; for many years to follow, Luscious would shoulder the blame for Ginger's death, beating himself up for ever bringing her into his tainted world.

There would be more than enough time for reflection, but in the mean time Officer Kirkland wanted to sort things out.

"That's the California Cannibal!" he said.

Officer Kirkland was about to call for backup, when Luscious stopped him.

279

"Please," he said, "let us go first."

"Everything here needs to be accounted for."

"We need to go," Luscious said. "Timber, Charlotte Luna and me."

"Where's Charlotte Luna?" Timber asked, suddenly realizing I was unaccounted for.

"She's outside, waiting for me on the porch," Officer Kirkland said. "She ran to me as soon as she saw her bowling ball."

Luscious stood up and walked to the couch, picking up a black duffle bag that Timber had never seen before. Placing the bag at Officer Kirkland's feet, he unzipped it, displaying the nearly half-million dollars he had planned to use to support us all.

"It's yours," Luscious said. "Please take it. Just let us go."

"I don't understand."

"I don't want you to understand," he said. "I just want you to take this money and pretend that this all happened without us."

"Did you have something to do with these deaths, Mr. Jones?"

"No," he said. "I just want to take my family as far away from here as I can and never look back."

It was at this point that I walked into the living room with my Minnie Mouse bowling ball and saw the terrible, bloody scene that would be burned in my imagination for the rest of my life. There was my mother, sitting with Ginger's shaved head in her lap, quietly crying as she caressed the scalp. There was Goldstein, slumped over in the chair, bald and dead. There was Three Marlow, the strange man with the ghostly eye, laying dead on the floor, his blood fanning out into a crimson puddle. And then there was Luscious and Officer Kirkland standing face-to-face, talking as if neither of them were aware of the carnage around them.

"Mommy."

Everybody looked back towards me, each of them struck by the same instinct of not wanting me to see what I had already seen. Officer Kirkland reacted first, quickly lifting me into his powerful arms and taking me back outside to the porch. I scarcely had time to protest or cry for Timber, as she followed right behind us. Officer

Kirkland put me into my mother's arms and watched as she cried into my neck. Luscious came out last, moving slowly onto the porch, putting his arms around Timber and me.

Perhaps it was in that moment that Officer Kirkland knew what he would do. It's possible he already knew that the home Luscious, Timber and I lived in was actually in Goldstein's name, making it plausible to argue that we never lived there at all. Officer Kirkland probably didn't know yet who Goldstein was, but he would find out soon enough. I'm certain Officer Kirkland knew that the man who killed the California Cannibal would be celebrated in such grand fashion that nobody of consequence—not District Attorney Robert Michaels or anybody else—would care to risk the reputation of their hero by asking any potentially incriminating questions. And I'm confident Officer Kirkland decided he could use the nearly half-million dollars Luscious laid at his feet.

"Go on," Officer Kirkland said. "Before I change my mind."

Luscious looked at him, almost in disbelief.

"You can't come back," he said. "There's only so much I can do to fix this up."

"Thank you," Luscious said.

With me in Timber's arms, we made our way to the garage, having to once more—and for the final time—see all the death that lay on the living room floor. Timber paused for just a moment to say goodbye to Ginger, who looked to me like she was asleep. As we piled into the yellow Cadillac, I would ask both Timber and Luscious why we weren't waking her up to come with us. Neither one of them knew what to say yet, so they instead said nothing. As we pulled out of the garage, reversing onto the long driveway, Officer Kirkland ran to the car with my pink Minnie Mouse bowling ball.

"You almost forgot this," he said, smiling at me.

"Tell Winston hi," I said.

"I surely will, sweetheart."

And with that, Luscious pulled out, past the rusty orange pickup truck and onto the street, where we would head out onto that historic Route 66 and drive it for as far as it would take us. As we drove, sunshine pouring in through the windshield, Timber wondered what would become of her life now. She hoped that the final hurdle of rectitude had been cleared, that she might finally be able to live her life in some semblance of peace. She hoped that she suffered the grief of tragedy for the last time. And she hoped against hope that she could give me a life free of all the brutal and bloody experiences that shaped her own, a life filled with love and laughter, peace and serenity, Disney films and pink bowling bowls.

Acknowledgements

I'd like to thank my brother, Greg, who set the bar of excellence unreasonably high for me the moment he learned I wanted to be a writer and found a way to convince me that I would someday surpass it. I'd like to thank my brother, Aaron, whose insatiable love of horror movies surpasses my own and who never tired of finding new ways to scare the shit out of me. I'd like to thank my sister, Reina, whose love and support I've always been able to count on. I'd like to thank my father, Larry, who, aside from being an endless well of love and a constant source of protection, quietly provided for me the model of hard work that would carry me through so many late nights when I was convinced this book would never get done. I'd like to thank my mother, Kathy, who could teach a master class on how to love and who, when I was in junior high school and exhibited the first seedlings of my future love affair with writing, took me to Sears and bought me my first (and last) electric typewriter, even though we couldn't afford it (don't worry, I still haven't told Daddy!). I'd like to thank my best friend and favorite person in the whole goddamned world, Chanel, for always being my biggest fan, for always convincing me that I'm more talented than I really am, and who, when I wanted to quit writing for good, asked me to at least write stories for her, even if I thought they were terrible. And, finally, I would like to thank *you*, gentle reader, for without you this book would otherwise not exist.

CPSIA information can be obtained at www.ICGtesting.com
Printed in the USA
LVOW041806270911

247820LV00005B/4/P